## DEDICATION

I would like to express my love and thanks to Joe Elvis, Isaiah and Emmanuel, as well the entire clan of Born Bad/Married Bads of which I'm proud to be a Born Bad, and who have provided me with a vast treasure trove of insanely hilarious material to write. I love you all so much. Also, to my friends, who make me laugh, provide me with an ear, and help keep me on track through the gauntlet of life. Thank you.

A very special debt of gratitude to the book clubs who graciously invited me to meet with them when HONEYMOON WITH HARRY was released. If it weren't for these wonderful women, there would be no SECOND HONEYMOON. It was at these book clubs, meeting these insightful readers, where the seeds were planted for this sequel. They saw something I didn't not and it started an idea rooting which blossomed into the reconnection between Todd and Harry, two characters with whom I love sharing head-space. Thank you to the book clubs not only your joy of reading but also your support (and the wine, let's not leave out the wine.) I've benefitted each and every time I speak with readers. And this book wouldn't exist without them. Thank you.

My life is blessed because I get to write. I hope A SECOND HONEYMOON offer you laughs, allows you to shed some tears and brings you joy. (And you recommend it to friends.)

Thank you

Bart

## A Little Love For A SECOND HONEYMOON

"While reading "A SECOND HONEYMOON…" it irked me when I had to stop reading and focus on the mundane, like eating and sleeping. Seriously. This book will take hold of you and not let you go, even weeks after you've finished it." **Dan Duffy** (activist/author of THE HALF BOOK: HE'S TAKING HIS BALL AND GOING HOME and HUFFINGTON POST contributor)

"Wow. If you liked "HONEYMOON WITH HARRY", you're going to LOVE this second outing with the love/hate cocktail that is Todd and Harry. Author Bart Baker takes these two men and you the reader on a mixology of emotional adventure. I was glued to every word of this novel from page one, anticipating how all the twists and turns were going to play out. I laughed so hard I cried, I cried so hard I laughed. Wow!" **Jason Lassen** (award winning author of HOLLYWOOD CLOWN)

"The long awaited sequel to one of Hollywood's most storied novel makes for a wildly fun second romp." **Michael Loynd** (best-selling author of ALL THINGS IRISH)

"Few authors I know can write dialogue as vibrantly, emotionally, aggressively and funny, as Bart Baker. It's just a pleasure having Todd and Harry back. And a joy to not only see them go at each other with affectionate disdain, but also deal movingly with their own, very real and adventurous issues." **Robert J. Elisberg** (author of THE WILD ROSES and A CHRISTMAS CAROL 2: THE RETURN OF SCROOGE)

# A SECOND HONEYMOON WITH HARRY

© Bart Baker
Big Muddy Books 2016

# LEDGES

How did I end up here again?

Perched on the precarious side of a balcony rail, six stories up, bare-assed, my calloused heels the only thing holding me onto the narrow ledge, gripping the thin balcony railing with one hand, my clothes gathered to my chest with the other, debating whether I can jump around an unfortunately intrusive wall separating me from the neighboring balcony without plummeting to my death, is not the time to get reflective. But I'm a champ at armchair-quarterbacking my choices. Usually after those choices have led to my life circling the drain. I can't help but question how a guy who has learned everything the hard way — that'd be me — with an embarrassing litany of bad decisions piled up like crushed autos at a demolition yard, can disregard every scintilla of common sense and end up yet again on the wrong side of the railing peering down at potential death.

Like a boulder falling on Wile E Coyote's head, it suddenly strikes me what my problem is. Each positive change I've struggled to make in my life ends up being devoured by the parasitic idiocy inside me. A couple years shy of forty and I finally realize my heart is a coliseum where all life lessons I've learned are fed to the lions. They die excruciating deaths, leaving me not only unchanged but pitifully more of myself.

My moment of self-examination is gratefully shattered when a Lynyrd Skynyrd guitar riff blares from the cell phone buried in my shorts pocket. The loud argument raging between Angry Guy and Hot Wife inside the hotel room I hastily exited minutes before falls silent as my thick, knobby fingers fumble for the silencer on my phone through the madras shorts I'm holding. Finding it, the phone goes silent; I take a thankful breath as the battle inside resumes at full volume.

I admit to having had a wild night of crazy-ass debauchery with Hot Wife. Angry Guy I am assuming is her husband—who I knew nothing about until he made his entrance in the hotel room just after sun-up this morning, by splintering the door with a fire extinguisher as I raced to collect my clothes and disappear out the balcony door to what is proving to be anything but an easy escape. As accustomed to not-so-fine moments as I am, this one is particularly humiliating. Each ledge I end up on seems narrower than the last.

"Damn me!" I mutter, sending up a silent Hail Mary that Angry Guy and Hot Wife stay entangled in their battle long enough for me to figure a way out of this predicament that doesn't include dying.

Not to brag but I do seem to be catnip for women who either want to get back at their husbands, are pissed-off at their boyfriends, or simply hate men. I am their go-to guy because they can use me for a little loving and hate me at the same time. Women are funny like that. They're capable of two disparate feelings about a guy simultaneously. Guys are incapable of such depth. When we're getting laid, there's seldom an ulterior motive outside of the sex itself.

We might tell ourselves there is, but nope, we are singularly about the physical pleasure. The rest is a distraction and we hate distractions during sex. Women can moan wildly, screaming in ecstasy as their body's shudder as they come and still remain pissed off. They are capable of complexity. Orgasms born of rage.

Hot Wife, whose warm bed I unceremoniously fled and whose name either eludes me or introductions were ignored, was physically stunning. Most of the time, I've had too much to drink and I'm not really sure if they're beautiful until the next morning. This one I knew immediately as she sat at the bar with her equally hot sister. Playing the odds that my patter would work on at least one of them, I went in for the kill. And even though she was not wearing a ring, had my better sense not been closed for repairs I would have known she was married.

General observation from years of gaming women into bed: the hotter they are, the more psychotic the guys in their lives tend to be. Again, no charge for the insight. Hot Wife was not only beautiful, she was abnormally inventive in the sack, which should have been my second clue since most women who are trying to piss off their husbands or boyfriends will go to great lengths to feel they've sated their revenge. Experience should have warned me that this particular brand of beautiful/crazy is guaranteed to come with a notorious deranged male attached.

"My husband. He'll kill you!" are not words you want to wake up to as the door to the hotel room is being bashed in.

In all fairness, if I hadn't thrown back about a half-dozen scotches and she hadn't exhausted me with the carnally crazy shit she was into, I would have made my exit from her room post-sex. I'm not big on sleepovers with relative strangers. But the bed was a California King and my tired body sunk into it like it wanted to hug me. Even better, she wasn't a cuddler. Sex is perfectly acceptable with someone I don't really know but cuddling, strangely, is a little too intimate for my liking.

Reaching my foot as far as I can toward the balcony around the wall, I'm a full stride short of bridging the gap between balconies because of the architecture of the hotel. If this goddamn wall wasn't jutting out at such an acute angle to give each balcony its privacy—or I were ten years younger and more limber—I could make the hurdle. But no, the building has to cock-block me from leaping to safety. Thus, my balls dangle in the warm, salty air as I continue to try and stretch my big ass over to the refuge of the next balcony while below the hotel pool shimmers in the morning sunlight, while two people leisurely swim laps, the staff preparing for another day of sunbathers.

Jumping into the pool below is an option. Except I'm not entirely sure a person could live if they hit water from this height. I'd have to Google that but unfortunately my phone is in my shorts which are in my arm, and I'm not dexterous enough to dig it out and do a search singlehandedly while gripping the railing with the other. Again, contemplating my possible death is cut short by another blast of Lynyrd Skynyrd from my phone. Goddamn, doesn't this person know I'm having a dilemma here? I almost slip as I hurriedly silence the phone again. Who the hell wants to talk to me this bad?

This time when my phone riffs loudly, the argument inside goes chillingly silent. Fuck! He's heard. Whomever Angry Husband is, the look in his beautiful wife's eyes as he was smashing in the door and she announced he would kill me, communicated clearly that she wasn't kidding. And as much as I am accustomed to confronting bad-asses, anyone who does—even on a semi-consistent basis—can sense when his luck is running low.

"Who's out there?!" he bellows, stomping toward the balcony door, pushing over furniture as he does.

Heaving everything in my arms around the corner to the neighboring balcony, my lucky blue underwear catches a trade wind and opens like a parachute, descending mesmerizingly toward the pool deck below. As the door to the balcony swings open, I let go of the railing behind me and dive *Matrix*-style around the sharp corner to the neighboring balcony. My arms and legs flail in the air as I spring across, my penis flopping in the breeze, my mouth open in a silent scream that if it were audible would be an octave higher than a seven-year-old girl getting a flu shot. I smash into the balcony railing with my chest, my breath rupturing from my lungs, my hand tenuously clamping around the metal. If I wasn't in so much pain, I'd be proud of myself. As I hear the balcony door slammed open violently around the corner, I muscle my big ass up and flip over the railing, landing with a bruising thud on the concrete deck of this balcony.

Angry Husband stomps around on his balcony, irately cursing in a muddy Greek accent. After a moment, his head appears from around the angled wall, glaring lethally.

He freezes. His glare disintegrates. His eyes widen.

I am splayed on a deck chair, my legs wide, my junk in plain view, cell phone up to my ear, feigning I'm on a call.

"Uh-huh, uh-huh, you bet man, I'm with you," I prattle, giving a breezy performance into my phone even though my entire body throbs and I still haven't caught a full breath. I open my eyes, pretending I've spied Angry Husband peeping at me from around the corner. With mock indignation, something I perfected when I was in sales, I fumble for my shirt and cover my junk, then jump to my feet.

"Goddamn man, what the hell is the matter with you!?!" I bark out with faux-fury.

Chagrinned, Angry Husband swiftly slips back around the corner as I grit my teeth and suck in an aching breath. Thankfully he didn't look long enough to see the bruises on my chest from slamming into the balcony railing.

Just to make sure, Angry Guy takes a second peek around the wall only to find me giving him a view of my big ass as I pull on my shorts, returning to my fake phone call.

"Yeah, I'm still here. There's a pervert next door staring at my junk while I'm trying to catch some sun. Of course I'm naked! This is Malta for Christsake and I'm six floors up! You should be able to do that here without some asshole peeking at you from around the corner," I snap loud enough for Angry Husband to get an earful.

"I'm sorry, I thought my wife was…I'm sorry," he mumbles in his heavy accent, never reappearing around the wall.

"Yeah, yeah," I respond. "Tell it to security, pal. 'Cause that's my next call."

I hear his balcony door slam shut and lock.

Finally able to compose myself, I toss my phone to the chaise and wince as I massage my shoulder and chest. Shamed by my inability to recognize patterns that have been with me since the dawn of puberty, I hang my head, giving a quick shout-out to heaven for pulling my ass out of another boneheaded mess before achingly tugging my shirt on over my head.

The stink of booze and sweat mixes with the lingering aroma of Angry Woman's perfume, swamping my nostrils with last night's folly. Didn't I promise the woman I loved I would change? Didn't she make me better? Why have I let whatever goodness she bestowed on me decay over the last five years since her death? I loved her. Harder and more completely than I ever thought I was capable of. But after she was killed and I almost succeeded at getting myself killed, I swore with my whole heart to protect the better man she made me. My intentions pure, my belief strong, my tenacity unflinching.

And I failed.

I dishonored Tami's memory so thoroughly that it only serves as a blanket of guilt. She was the lightning that struck me and caused me to change. Prior to meeting her I was the guy on the balcony. She pulled me off that ledge, loved me for me, and because of that I wanted to change for her. Certainly no easy task for a man who had steadily built an impenetrable casing around my heart and owned a bad attitude just as rock solid. But she got through that, leaching away my armor, teaching me not only to love but to be comfortable being loved. I'd never experienced that before. And I fell so deeply in love with this woman; I wanted her to love me so achingly that all the efforts I put into my selfish, often horrible, behavior I transferred to her.

I wanted to be the man she saw in me. And I did. I became that man. Happily. Willingly. For her.

Once she had herself wrapped around my heart, she was ripped from me. Taking my soul with her.

Being a man who needs a constant jolt of love, a daily electroshock of acceptance to stay the course, once I lost Tami I reverted back to the person I can be with the least amount of effort. The new 'old me' once again took up residence in Casa Todd, enlarging the back deck and adding a hot tub overlooking the River of Past Sins that leads into the Ocean of Sins Yet To Come. See, it's not hard to go to hell. And it's not like it happened all of a sudden. It was a slow, meandering progression returning to my old self. I wish there was an instance I could point to that I could say, "That's it! That's what caused me to regress!" But there isn't. It doesn't happen like that. It's water torture. Drip by painful drip. You find your heart scabbing over. You find ways to rationalize your awful choices. And you keep making them. Because they allow you to hide inside a feeling of soullessness. And feeling that is way better than the agony of loss.

Tapping on the sliding glass door rouses no response inside the hotel room, which either means the occupant is sleeping off last night's party or left early on a sea excursion around the archipelago. Jamming my shoulder into the door, I try muscling it open but it doesn't budge. I debate using a chaise to smash it but not having the money to replace it means spending a year in the Corradino Correctional Facility and that isn't on my list of vacation stops here in Malta. Leaping back to the balcony I escaped from isn't an option, which leaves me with only one choice: climb over the rail of this balcony and take another leap to the next one; then hope that someone there will take pity on me and allow me to exit through their hotel room.

Unfortunately, whatever floppy, Labradorian magnetism I once possessed in my six-foot-five frame has oxidized with age. And while my bad attitude is manufactured in hopes of keeping idiots at bay, I've been practicing it for so long I can't shake it. While I like to believe I'm dexterously charming, especially when sitting next to a pretty girl in a bar at the end of the night, in the harsh light of day most people only see that I am barrel-chested, broad-shouldered with a heavy brow and creases in my forehead that make me look more pissed-off than I usually am.

So even if I can muster up a genuine smile and a soft tone, no sane person would allow Magilla Gorilla to tip-toe through their hotel room. I pray I find an open balcony door allowing the morning trade winds to waft through the room. I can wrap my shirt around my face so as not to be recognized, and bolt through so quickly the unsuspecting souls inside won't have time to realize they should be screaming.

Having already had a practice jump and now dressed in everything I came in other than my lucky blue underwear, which hangs in one of the trees that shades the pool, this leap is easier. I know how to maneuver around the wall and grab the railing. And being clothed gives me the illusion that I am less conspicuous than when I was dangling my nutsack six floors from the ground. Climbing over the railing, my lucky underwear once again catches my eye. Although considering some of the places I've woken up and with whom, in retrospect maybe they really haven't been that lucky. More like karmic. Those blue underwear always seem to get me exactly who—and what—I deserve.

Pecking at this sliding glass door like a hungry bird brings a pair of eyes from behind the closed curtains. I smile with placidity, raising my hand in a docile 'I come in peace' semi-wave.

"Sorry to bother you. I locked myself out of my room next door," I say, pointing to the neighboring balcony. "Could you let me in or call down to the front desk and have them come and open that room and let me in?

"How'd you get on this balcony?" the person whose eyes were the only part of them I could see asks in another thick Greek accent.

"I jumped," I answer, pointing to the neighboring balcony. "You have a much better view of the bay from your room," I continue, hoping to win some sympathy with the dopey, passive grin still planted on my face.

"We are six floors up. Are you a crazy person?"

"I realize that and yes, yes I am. Please, let me in, I promise to walk straight to the door and leave," I offer up just as my phone blasts Lynyrd Skynyrd again.

Mental note: change my ring tone before I crush this goddamn phone with my bare hands.

The curtain falls back into place, the eyes disappearing. Silencing my phone, I tap on the balcony door again, calling, "Hello?! Hey in there!"

Nothing. Nada. Are the eyes going to abandon me out here, leaving me to make a leap to the next balcony? At this rate I'll be back at the room I started at before lunch.

Catching a glimpse of the azure Mediterranean from this scenic perch at the Hotel Ducares in St. Julian's, a moment of tranquility falsely eases my agitation. Why does so much shit go down in such beautiful places? I make peace with the fact that I have two options: either jump to the next balcony and continue my search, or wrap my shirt around my fist and punch in this balcony door, smack the crap out of the person whose left me stranded on their balcony, and then make a hasty exit.

B…I think I'll go with Plan B.

Just as I yank off my shirt, slurring curse words through the door, the curtains flings open, flooding the hotel suite with morning sunlight. A slim man with a full mane of white hair that almost shimmers in the stark light and wearing a bathrobe equally as white, stands on the inside of the glass door. Seizing the moment, my snarl reverts back to a dopey smile.

Until I notice the gun in his hand.

This never happened to me when I was wearing my lucky underwear.

"Sorry. I'll go back to my balcony. I just needed some help but you don't look like you're offering…" I sputter as I pull my shirt back on, surmising it might have been smarter to battle it out with Angry Guy instead of White-Haired Guy With Gun.

Clearly the sixth floor is where they put every guest they assume to be unhinged.

The man quickly yanks open the balcony door wide enough to shove the gun through. Waving me inside, he opens the door wider to offer me entrance. Am I being robbed? This old fart will blow my head off when he discovers there is nothing in my wallet but a couple Euros and a few fading phone numbers.

Shuffling into the room, my eyes never leaving the pitch-black hallowed end of the gun barrel, I chatter like a coke-addled magpie. "Look, man, I didn't mean to bother you. Seriously. But I really appreciate you letting me in. I'm going to walk across the room now. I'm not going to touch anything; I'm not even going to look at your face. I'll thank you for your hospitality in advance."

Taking my first step, all the while waiting for the explosion of white-hot light from the gun barrel, I hear nothing so I continue ginger-stepping across the room's plush carpet like a dancing monkey on a hot pavement. My nervous smile which I was hoping to use to defuse any trouble, twitches on my lips, betraying how freaked-out I am.

That's when I hear "You!", causing me to turn and discover a woman lying in the bed. She's much younger than White-Haired Guy With Gun. And damn if she doesn't look familiar. But before my befuddled pea-brain can put a location with the face, she crows, "You're the guy that fucked my sister last night!"

Oh crap!

"Sister?" I ask, confusion dripping from the single word.

"Twin sister," she responds, her nose in the air like she smells something foul.

Finally getting a real look at her, she doesn't just resemble the woman I had sex with two balconies over, she's her spitting image, which causes my heart to pound even more. Then I remember. There were two of them! Maybe it was the scotch but they didn't look as identical last night as they do this morning. This morning this one looks exactly like the sister whose bed I fled. I vaguely recall at one point the previous night mentioning how great it would be if I could get both in the sack, but this sister gave me bitch-face while I was at my most charming before turning to talk to the guy on the other side of her as if she were allergic to me.

My eyes dart between the Twin Hottie and White-Haired Guy With Gun, as I mull over the best way to handle this conundrum, opting for my over-used fallback. Plead ignorance.

"You must be mistaken. I don't know you or your sister. I'm staying in the next room," I lie. "But I appreciate you letting me cross through your room. Sorry for the inconvenience. I don't know how my balcony door locked," I articulate almost as a single word, stepping closer and closer to the door leading to the hallway.

"You think I am a fool?" she snarls. "You had sex with my sister and her husband comes back this morning and finds you," she pronounces snidely. "She is always having sex with other men when she hates her husband."

"That could be anybody's relationship," I chuckle uncomfortably, reminding myself it would be best to shut the hell up and get to the door. But no, I can't even heed my own advice. Turning to White-Haired Guy With Gun I joke, "I mean, am I right or am I right?"

He says nothing, his dark eyes holding a mixture of bewilderment and contempt.

"You're exactly the type she drags back to her bedroom when she's furious with Theo," she says with a derisive laugh. "A big man with handsome dumbness on his face and a shallowness in his soul."

I think she's nailed me dead-to-center until she adds, "No woman could ever love you."

I can't get a handle on exactly why this statement pisses me off past the point of self-preservation but it does. My nostrils flare like a gored bull; my eyes go dead as they stare through her.

"There *was* a woman who loved me!" I spit out contemptuously.

"She must have been very stupid!" she slams back, not bothering to notice how incensed I am.

As a sneer washes across my face, my body recoils. There's a spark in her eyes that tells me she finally grasps she's pissed off the wrong guy.

"Maybe she was," I snap. "But she was also the most amazing woman in the world, a woman that someone like you can only gossip about behind her back because you're so inadequate and out-classed by comparison that the best you can do is wallow in your petty insecurities to your equally inferior friends. Maybe she didn't have the best taste in men, because I am exactly who the fuck you think I am, but she loved me. And I loved her. And as much as I am nothing more than a dick to most women, figuratively and literally, I was a man who would have given my life for hers. In fact, I did. I gave up my life for her. To be worthy of her. Only to have her die.

So, bitch, I'm back to being me! With a vengeance. I tried not to be, I tried being the man she saw in me, but without her, I can't. I'm not strong enough. Which should be every woman's fucking nightmare because I'm genuinely not a nice guy by nature. I like to get drunk and I like to fuck. The order of that doesn't matter to me, as long as both get done. There's only been one woman in my thirty-eight years who has been able to make me give that up. The rest of you…I'm Mr.-Right-For-The-Night. Have Condom Will Travel. I pick off the weakest of the herd, have my fun and disappear. And every once in a while, I get really lucky and meet a woman like your sister who I don't even have to bother seducing to get into bed. Do you think I give a shit that she's fucking me to get back at her husband? I applaud her for it. It's why guys like me exist. Use me! Use me twice! Be mad at the man you married, I mean really mad because the sex will only get crazier," I sniff with arrogance and defiance. "We all have problems. Mine are apparent. Yours will come if you ever speak about the woman I love again. You're going to find out just how big a prick I can be."

Her eyes stare at me without blinking. "Why are you telling me this? I don't care about you."

"That's exactly why I'm telling you!" I snarl.

With high-handed snootiness, she flips the comforter off her body, standing and posing with total calculation so I can see every curve of her naked body. I never got a great look at her sister naked, we were twisted around each other in the darkness most of the night, but if she has anything close to the body of this sister, I should high-five myself. Even tangled amid the sheets and intoxicated, I knew the sister was pretty impressive but this one standing across the room from me, her nudity should be applauded in public.

Twin Hottie makes sure I get an eyeful before she pads over to White-Haired Guy With Gun. He watches me closely as I ogle her, as if any straight man and at least ninety-five percent of gay men could actually turn away from her spectacular body even under penalty of death. She whispers into White-Haired Guy With Gun's ear, her eyes darting toward me a couple times. He neither nods nor shakes his head, his dark eyes glowering without blinking.

I'm done. I've exceeded my quotient of crazy people today and it isn't even breakfast. I need a nap. And I need to swear off having sex with strangers. But as my eyes wash over every curve of this woman's amazing body, I know I won't. On the other hand, a bullet lodged near my spine would certainly make me think twice about ever fucking someone else's wife again.

As she and White-Haired Guy With Gun continue whispering back and forth, I spin toward the hotel room door and grasp for the handle.

"Do not leave!" Twin Hottie barks out, shifting her weight to her other foot, her tight body almost undulating as she does.

As my eyes slither in her direction again, she smiles with a cool malignance.

"He has agreed to let me have sex with you," she states with confidence.

Come again?

Already enraged at this crazy bitch for picking at my personal sore spot, she now pulls a u-turn, confusing the hell out of me. I don't function well in either state but both together is enough to make my head explode. I should just take a lunge at White-Haired Guy With Gun, smack the weapon out of his sun-wrinkled hand, shove this Twin Hottie down on the bed and congratulate her for being the most gorgeous woman I ever turned down a romp in the sheets with—because she's too crazy, even for me.

Yet there's this other part of me, the part whose terrible advice I often heed, that wants me to stay to see how this colorful insanity plays out.

Succumbing to the bad part of myself and wanting to mess with her head a little longer, I snarl in her face, "I fucked your sister all night, why would I want to bang a cheap replica?"

Furious, she nudges White-Haired Guy With Gun, causing him to raise the gun at my head.

"Put the gun down before I shove it up your ass!"

"He will shoot you if I ask him to. If you don't have sex with me, I will have him do it."

"And what's he going to do, watch?"

"Yes."

"Yes?"

"Yes," White-Haired Guy With Gun answers, nodding with resignation.

I've been caught having sex enough times that maybe I'm a little blasé about having someone watch and I've certainly never been ashamed about it but this is a personal first, someone actually willing to watch me have sex with their wife. Getting specific, their ridiculously beautiful wife. At gunpoint.

"Your husband is into you doing guys while he watches?" I ask incredulously, which is rare for me.

Laughing perversely, she says, "He's not my husband, he's my father. My husband would have killed you by now."

And with that revelation, this situation circles the drain.

"You are smoking hot," I butter her up, knowing I have to escape this asylum before I'm lured into yet another episode of personal damnation, or worse, having the old man shoot me in the ass for refusing to have sex with his voluptuous daughter, as ironically karmic as that might be, "…but you are the most in-fucking-sane bitch I've ever met. And if you knew me and knew the women I've known in my life, that's saying something. And while I'm not a guy who usually…well…ever until now, turns down a beautiful woman, especially when she is the one offering it up, I'm not going to perform with a proverbial gun to my head. Your whole family is fucking loony tunes. I'm out of here!"

"No!" she declares sharply, "My sister had her fun. It is my turn!"

Traveling Europe these last five years after leaving St. Carlos where I spread the ashes of the only person I ever loved, I have pretty much encountered about everything I imagined was out in the big, bad world. Many I hope to forget. Today is already inching up that list. I participated in as many as I could stomach, even the ones I thought were a little nuts or took me out of my sizable comfort zone. I drank it, I ate it, I slept with it. I experienced as much as one human body could tolerate, convincing myself I was living not only for myself but for Tami who never got the chance.

But as the months went on, my tenuous hold on Tami's memory winnowed through my fingers, dissipating into chronic heartache. Spreading her ashes was the single hardest thing I have ever had to do, slamming me like a gargantuan tsunami, crushing me under the debris of sorrow. I couldn't breathe, I couldn't see, I couldn't hear, all I could do was thrash around violently, striking out at anything I came in contact with. And while I was eventually able to reach a level of toleration and understanding with her father, Harry, I buried the true depth of my anguish so I could survive. I didn't even know how deep that pain was. And I toiled overtime to trick myself into believing I was doing all this freaky, crazy shit for her.

At first I did it to blot out the gnawing heartache, then the isolating numbness that festered. I didn't just morph back into the self-absorbed, destructive, foolish asshole I was before I met Tami; I hulked out, becoming more of everything awful I had ever been. Maybe loving Tami as much as I did sent me into a stratosphere I could have never maintained even if she had lived. Maybe I would have crashed back to earth and destroyed her in the process. Because once she was gone, that long, slow spiral back to reality — dropping out of the rarified air that pleasantly consumed me when I was with her and back to the dirty, polluted crap I stink up the world with — made me so angry.

I was no longer sure whether I had just been living a cruel lie when I was with her, and she was only saved from the inevitability of me trouncing her happiness by some pathetic piece-of-shit drunk driver.

Twin Naked Hottie steps toward me, her arms crossing as if negotiating a business deal *au naturel*. "If you leave, I call my sister's room and speak to her husband. He is there; you can hear them through the walls."

She's right. Being preoccupied with other stimuli, I hadn't noticed but you can hear them screaming two rooms away.

As I open my mouth to respond, she strolls over, making sure her every asset is on display and picks her cell phone off the desk, holding it up in an effort to intimidate me. I smile. Here's where me being a dick-in-general comes in handy because bullshit like this only serves to piss me off more. While the concept of being blackmailed into having sex with a beautiful woman is on its face kind of hot, her snarky attitude and the whole dad-with-gun thing has soured me. Plus, I've had more than enough experience with insane women to know that if you give in and do what they want, it's not over. It's more impetus to keep screwing you around.

As I'm readying to launch into this chick with some extra savory insults, my cell phone blasts Lynyrd again.

Imitating her, I pull out my phone and strike a pose similar to hers. "Mine's bigger," I smirk, hoping to piss her off even more as I signal her to wait a moment before turning away to answer the call.

"Hello."

"Todd?"

The voice is familiar like a malt scotch but I can't put a face or name to it.

"Yeah, it's Todd. Who's this?" I ask.

"Kat. Kat Brennan. From St. Carlos."

"Holy shit! Kat! Great to hear from you!" I chirp excitedly as I make the connection, turning to Twin Hottie with a Cheshire Cat grin on my lips. "Long time, no speak," I add, my eyes darting between the crazies as I continue to talk into the phone, "What's going on?"

"Is this a bad time?" Kat asks.

"Couldn't be worse. But that's my cross to bear," I chuckle warmly, signaling Twin Hottie not to do anything hasty causing her to sour further. She steps toward me, reaches for my phone and demands, "Hang up!"

Hearing this, Kat laughs awkwardly. "I can hear you're…busy. Call me when you're free," she says quickly and then hangs up, the misdirection I had at my disposal abruptly disappearing.

I can no longer buy myself time to put together a vanishing act. Especially not if the crazies figure out I'm off the call. So I keep talking into the phone, my mind grinding on a plan to make my escape from this loony bin as I stroll back across the room, moving like a meandering, lazy river toward the balcony door, jabbering incessantly, hoping to put some distance between the crazies and me.

"Where are you going?! I said hang up!" Twin Hottie screams.

"This is important," I snap, covering my phone with my hand. "You want to fuck, fine, we'll fuck. And your geezer father can watch me bone you, sick as that is. Happy? Now shut the fuck up, crawl back into bed and I'll be there in a goddamn minute!"

I go back to my nonexistent phone call. "No, I'm here…just dealing with the most batshit crazy father-daughter duo ever. Total psychos. Oh, she's hotter than a pistol but wacked out of her mind. Uh-huh, uh-huh…" I add, stepping back through the sliding glass door, shutting it behind me.

As I do, I grab hold of a balcony chair and jam it under the sliding door handle, kicking it in snugly to prevent the door from opening. Seeing this, Twin Hottie runs to the door and tries to open it, banging on it, screaming at me.

I smile, giving her the finger. "There, I just fucked ya!"

I peer over the railing at the pool below. Still no. I'd be like a sack of potatoes thrown in front of a train. It's over to the next balcony for me, praying the occupant isn't another relative of these two loons.

The sound of the gunshot explodes in my ear as the glass from the balcony door spits at me like fire from a dragon's mouth. Holy fuck, White Haired Guy With Gun blew out the balcony door and the diabolical screams of Twin Hottie pour out through the shattered glass as she orders her father to kill me.

White-Haired Guy With Gun maneuvers his bony body through the jagged opening. I'm left with no time to leap to the neighboring balcony as he raises the gun to my crotch.

"Shoot him! Shoot him in the penis!" Twin Hottie screams.

While I'm not a hundred percent sure that having my penis shot off is the worst idea I've heard all day—after all it was my penis that got me into this mess, and the mess before that and the mess before that—regardless of which body part is to blame, I prefer to keep all the original pieces that came with my game.

Without hesitation, I pitch my body over the railing, my cell phone still clenched in my right hand.

Salty air jets up my nostrils as I plummet wildly, doing everything I physically can to control my body as it descends like an errant missile. Random thoughts crowd my head, wrestling over each other like puppies, one finally staying on top of the pile long enough to take action. I manage to cup my junk with my left hand and straighten out my body just as I slam into the water as if it were a cinder block wall. Hitting water from six stories up doesn't just hurt; it is like stepping out onto the track at the Indy 500 and bending over so you can take a car up the ass. The air explodes from my lungs as I curl up my legs, crashing ass-first into the bottom of the deep end. My ass, my back, my legs feel like they've caught fire.

It would have been less painful to fuck her and then have him shoot me.

But I'm alive. I emerge from the water with a scream that echoes off of buildings blocks away, as hotel staff race to the edge and scoop me from the pool.

"FUCKITY, FUCK, FUCK, FUCK!!!!" I yowl at the top of my lungs, squeezing my eyes shut, unable to feel any sensation in my legs other than pain.

The sting engulfs my entire body like it's been tattooed into my soul. Four men hold me up because I'm unable to stand on my own until I actually see that my toes move and I'm not paralyzed. I take an anguishing step, tears coming to my eyes, futilely attempting to fully inhale but it feels as if I knocked my intestines up into my lungs. Hitting the water with that kind of velocity shot a chlorine enema up into my colon, kidneys and liver; I'll be crapping hotel pool water for days. Though on the bright side, I've proven an idiot can survive a six-story fall into a pool.

Forcing the tears from my eyes, I look up and spot White-Haired Guy With Gun and Twin Hottie peering down at me. Raising my hand I give them the finger again as I growl toward the sky, "Fuck both you nutbags!"

I leave a snail trail of water as I limp across the pool deck and into the hotel. Everyone in the lobby stares in my direction. But no one dares say a word as my walk of shame continues through the lobby, my wet feet squeaking across the cool marble floor, and I shuffle out the front entrance to the waiting valets and taxis.

"Jesus H. Christ. How can I be so stupid?" I mumble, limping down the steps, one at a time, past the line of cabs, finally dropping myself into the first one with an open door.

The young driver glares at me as I scream in pain when I sit, dripping all over his cab.

"The beach, please," I say, still unable to suck in a full breath.

"It's across the street, sir."

"If I thought I could walk that far, I'd do it. Drop me as close to the sand as possible."

The sand offers a therapeutic warmth to my glutes which have journeyed past their initial agony and settled into stabbing throbs of pain. I'm sure I knocked my back out of alignment. And I hope when I take my next dump I'm only shitting pool water, not blood. But it wouldn't surprise me, I probably damaged something internally. Sipping from a beer that I had some kid sneak from his parents' cooler by bribing him with my water-logged watch, my hand digs into the warm sand where I buried my phone in a ripped towel I lifted from the trash as I staggered closer to the sea. The phone didn't work when I first tried it, no surprise there, but I'm hoping against hope that if it dries, it'll once again turn on.

Sadly after falling six floors into a swimming pool, I couldn't think of a single person on Malta who I could call for help. Not one. I decidedly made no friends in the last five years and cut myself off from anyone that could possibly care about me. I didn't want them to know what I was doing, who I'd become. Again. Worse. There was no one on this continent I could call and I was too ashamed to call anyone on another. There's something staggeringly wrong about that.

Pulling the towel from the sand, I unroll it, letting the phone fall out. It's hot and dry, buoying my hopes that I won't have to buy a new one with money I don't have. My curiosity as to why Kat called me after all this time is the only thing keeping me from focusing on the pain. Snapping it open, I recite a quick Hail Mary and hold the on button. Nothing. I keep holding. Nothing. Now instead of praying, I'm cursing at the phone.

The screen stays black but a buzz whimpers inside. Then suddenly, it lights up.

"Halle-fucking-lujah!" I say, checking to see whether my call diary still works. There it is, Kat's number. Calculating what time it is in St. Carlos, I push redial.

"Hello…" a hazy voice says.

"Hey, Kat, it's Todd."

"Thanks for calling me back. Sorry I bothered you earlier."

"You didn't bother me. It was just…a bad time that got worse and then my phone fell into the pool and I had to wait till it dried before I could — anyway, long story. It's good to hear your voice."

Kat laughs that throaty laugh of hers, one of the things that attracted me to her when I met her almost fourteen years ago. "Been a while," she says.

"Yeah. I meant to keep you in the loop of my whereabouts but life got a little crazy and I got a little crazier. Nothing really good to tell. How's Earl?"

"Suffice it to say Earl is a teenager."

"Little Earl?" I laugh.

"He's not little anymore. The last couple years he shot up and filled out. He's big. Defiant and disrespectful. Most of the time I want to kick him in the ass, but I'm his mother, so I guess that's pretty normal."

Our conversation goes silent for a moment as the elephant in the room plops itself down.

"So…something tells me you didn't just call to catch up…"

She laughs again. Sweetly but tinged with melancholy. "Harry asked me to find you."

"Harry?"

"He's here."

"On St. Carlos?" I ask, my mind clicking back through the days, making sure it isn't the anniversary of the day we spread Tami's ashes.

I begrudgingly traveled to St. Carlos with Tami's father, Harry, to spread the ashes of the woman I loved at a place she loved. That wasn't my intention of going to the island; my intention after her death was to lay waste to every moral fiber of my being, even if it meant dying. Something I almost succeeded at doing. But being there with Harry, who I hated from beyond the depths of my soul, helped me understand something. I wasn't alone. We shared the same anguish. Not much pleasure in that but for Harry and I, strangely and spitefully, it bonded us. Almost son-in-law to almost father-in-law, in a way I still haven't come to fully comprehend.

"Yeah," she responds, never really putting a period on the sentence. "With a woman."

"That old dog! Good to hear that he didn't go back to Chicago and lock himself away with cases of canned tuna and toilet paper."

"They're getting married."

For the first time since my big ass hit the pool, I sucked in a huge breath. "Holy Mother of All That Is Good, what did you say?!"

She laughs. "He's getting married. He asked me to see if I could find you. He told me he lost track of you a few years ago. He'd love for you to be here."

"I can't b-b-b-believe it," I stammer. "Harry getting married. Wow! That's one I didn't see coming. What's she like?"

"Southern I think. Petite, pretty in that loads of make-up and big hair way some women gravitate toward as they get older. Not that she's old-old...she's younger than Harry. By a lot. I've only said hello to her. Seems to prefer the room to the bar or the beach."

I attempt to wrap my mind around the image of old, saggy Harry with some nubile, hot chick twenty years younger but even my vivid imagination can't conjure up a mental image of Harry with anything youthful. It's not that he's that old, it's that I imagined he'd fossilized himself to the point of immobility. The concept of him with a young, vivacious woman is too foreign, too incongruous to imagine.

"Can you get here, Todd?"

I don't say anything as I stare out at the sea, trying to conjure up some solid reason to decline. The sunlight bounces off the waves in a shimmering whiteness as if some magical riposte is about to appear before my eyes. But I'm left with momentary blindness and no answers.

"That's a pretty tall order right now," I respond under my breath, not wanting her to hear the fear in my voice. "I don't know…I…don't know."

"Is it money? Harry said that—"

Cutting her off, I stammer, "There's a lot of memories on St. Carlos I don't want to revisit."

"Oh. Okay," she responds with disappointment. "What do you want me to tell him?" she queries after a long silence.

"Tell him you didn't find me. No harm, no foul."

"He's not getting married until next weekend," Kat replies. And then to punctuate the point, she adds, "I think it would make him happy if you were here."

That knocks the air out of my lungs almost as hard as hitting water from six stories up.

"Look, uhm, lemme…lemme think about it, okay?"

"Well, I did what I told Harry I would do. I found you," she tosses off with such indifference I can almost feel her shrugging. Then she hangs up.

I should have let my phone drown.

Being a person who doesn't bank on happiness, whose cumulative life experience has been watching the foundation of joy crumble in an instant and wash away on the current of calamity and errors, I cannot for the life of me fathom how Harry got himself together enough after Tami's death and everything he and I experienced together, to give love another shot. Sex, sure. Last time on the island he proved he could still climb up in the saddle. But love? It boggles the mind. And not that it is any of my business but if this chick is as Kat describes and Harry is, well, Harry, this chick's working an angle.

And it probably shows on Harry's Visa statement.

And while intrigued at the notion of meeting this woman in person and unmasking her motives, I do not want to return to St. Carlos. Even with my ass and legs stinging, the hot sand of Malta feels safer. As stupid as my life has turned out here, there are many more difficult, complicated memories on that island in the Caribbean.

"Not my monkey, not my circus," I say to no one.

But truth is, Harry *is* my circus. Which makes me his monkey. The circus wants its monkey back. Only this monkey bites people and slings feces.

What the hell is Harry doing? And why, goddamn it, is he doing it on the island where we said goodbye to Tami? I'm racked with enough guilt over not being able to sustain the change I promised her. I do not want to go back to the place where I committed some of my most egregious sins. I shouldn't feel obligated to Harry. It's been years. I made some sort of pretzeled peace with him. Returning to the island for his wedding. Why the hell would he even want me there? It's over, whatever it was we had. I let it go. I don't need to do this. You can almost smell what a rotten idea this is. No guilt. It's wrong. It would be wrong to go.

With a pitiable chuckle, my eyes travel back to the Hotel Ducares, traveling up to the balcony I threw myself over. Weighed down by memories and failures, my head shakes involuntarily and my eyes fill with tears. I begin to sob, laugh and curse simultaneously. I'd like to believe I'm capable of emotional multitasking but this is more of a confused, slobbering mishmash of butt-hurt feelings that lead me to a single, scary thought. No matter how bad it hurts, I have to throw myself over the rail again and plunge back into dangerous waters.

On St. Carlos.

## WING WALKERS

If there is anyone who loathes flying more than me, next time you spot my snarling mug hunkered down in a seat at an airport lounge, introduce yourself. It would be like meeting an Aborigine or spotting a white lion. I know they exist but I've never seen one up close.

From the moment I walk through the doors of an airport, my jaw clenches. My teeth grind together as I'm rushing to put everything I have into a bin to go through X-ray. My ass puckers as I stand in line to step into a booth and place my arms over my head, only to then have my nuts contract as I'm inevitably pulled out of line to have some guy feel me up from my armpits down to my crotch. My entire face prunes up into a giant grimace as I jam my ever-widening ass into a seat designed for a short-legged, anorexic twelve-year-old girl. It's as if commercial airplanes were designed by some snaggle-toothed East German who designs equipment for their secret torture prisons.

And God forbid I'm seated next to another adult male who has shoulders or is twenty-five pounds overweight. The two of us are practically related by the time the flight ends. Who designs something that doesn't allow you to even shift in your seat, with a damn vent above your head that toots out warm, recycled air with about as much force as a baby's fart? I abhor leaving a warm stool inside a modestly comfortable terminal bar to stand in line with a bunch of other pissed-off people girding their loins for the discomfort they know they are about to endure.

I used to flop sweat and bear it, white-knuckling it to my destination. Not anymore. I'm over being nice about it. I've been on flights where having a couple air marshals beat the shit out of me and drag me off in handcuffs sounds way more appealing than being stuffed into a middle seat. I no longer have any hesitation to announce my distaste for flying to anyone who works for an airline, hoping that if I whine like a pathetic, little bitch, someone with wings on their lapel will either take pity on me — or be fed up enough to upgrade me to first class.

So far that hasn't happened. But not for lack of trying.

Flying from Malta to St. Carlos requires a choreography of airports and airlines. Flying from Malta to St. Carlos on very little money requires not only that but an outrageous amount of pre-planning which I don't have time to accomplish. Perched in front of a hotel computer last night, working until early this morning, a scotch neat by my side, I finagled the cheapest flights for each leg of this journey: Malta to Rome and then — because I find a start-up airline running a special to drum up business — Rome to Madrid. Then from Madrid to New York, New York to Miami, Miami to St. Carlos. All in just under two days.

I will smell like Gouda cheese left out at a July picnic by the time I arrive, but it's the best I can make happen on short notice and shorter funds.

Making the best of a bad situation, I apportion a hefty chunk of my airline money for liquor. The more I can salve my discomfort the safer for all involved, I explain to the flight attendant who refuses to serve me my sixth scotch on the flight from Madrid to New York. "Here's how it works," I spout, pointing to myself. "Not drunk, a colossal pain in your ass; drunk, cuddly like a stuffed animal you won at a carnival. Your choice."

She scowls. Then brings me a double.

Liquored up, I ooze into my seat better. It's like I'm okay with performing some Cirque du Soleil contortion to get my ass into my assigned seat, which makes the person plugged in the seat next to me much happier that I'm not leaning up against them, my sweat seeping through their clothing where we are crushed up against each other. Being not-so-secretly terrified of flying, I perspire. Profusely. It's not pretty. Not that I care but when you look like you're suffering from cholera, other passengers tend to give you stink-eye.

Coherent but buzzed, I stagger through Miami International, my shirt still stuck to my back from sweat, my legs wobbly not only from the booze but from the large black and blue bruises that cover my hamstrings up to my lower back. I have a couple hours to kill while I wait for my flight to St. Carlos. And I intend to do it on a bar stool. I'm bad enough on large commercial airliners but unless something's changed since the last time I flew there, the flights to St. Carlos tend to be on a dinky, tin, multi-seat coffin designed to compound my claustrophobic agitation. I've survived this far, I'm not about to lose it now and have them throw me off the flight because I panicked before take-off.

If I don't get on this flight, I know I'll never get on another to St. Carlos.

Shuffling up to the counter of Seabird Airlines, I pull out my reservation information and shove it across the counter to the beautiful black woman. "I'm guessing there's no first-class seats on this flight," I say with my best hammered smile, hoping she's been sheltered enough to think I'm charming or handicapped. I don't care which.

She smiles back courteously, shaking her head.

"I'm kind of a big guy, is there any seat that has a little more room than the others?"

"The seats are all the same."

"Okay, okay," I mutter. "How crowded is the flight?"

"Full."

"Shit!" I mutter. "Front or back row?"

"Taken."

"Aisle?"

"I have one left, mid-plane," she states in an accommodating voice.

Taking a second to ponder whether or not I could swim to St. Carlos from Miami, I sigh. I'm going to have to be extra-drunk for the last leg of my trip.

"Whatever…" I snort, unhappy and bound to get unhappier.

She punches something in on her computer, her eyes once again rising to my face.

"We owe you a refund," she states.

"Excuse me?" I ask, unaccustomed to hearing good news lately. Finally something to celebrate after being cooped up on airplanes and wandering airports in the middle of the night, trying to find an open bar before the next leg of this suck-ass trip.

"There is a credit here for your flight to St. Carlos, Mr. Cartwright. And you also paid. You can either keep the credit for a future flight or we can refund your purchase to your credit card."

"I'll take cash."

It takes some wrangling with her supervisor to convince them to give me the money in dollars. I understand that the airline normally doesn't deal in cash. But I really get that the goddamn money is mine and I want it.

Flipping through twenty-dollar bills like a high roller at a penny-slot casino, I whisper blessings to Harry who I am sure sprang for the ticket, probably hedging his bets that if I didn't use the ticket, the smart, little devil would get his money refunded.

At the gift shop, I lay down some cash for a new shirt, mouthwash and baby wipes. Commandeering a sink in the men's room, I pull off my shirt and take a whore's bath, using the baby wipes to clean the liquor stink off my body before ripping off the tags and pulling on the fresh shirt. After running a comb though my hair, I almost look like a new man. The whiskers are in need of a shave and my eyes are bloodshot, but I can actually endure the reflection in the mirror.

After two drinks at the sports bar, coupled with everything else I've imbibed over the last couple days on the ground and in the air, I feel his presence next to me. Dr. Buzz, my imaginary partner in crime, occupying the stool to my right, bubbling over with scintillating conversation. And while I know that whenever Dr. Buzz visits, trouble magically appears, I am pleased as punch to put my arm around my old pal. I warn him that I cannot get arrested in Miami and not make it down to St. Carlos, pleading with him not to lead me astray.

Well, unless he thinks St. Carlos is a mistake. Then he should lead me as far astray as possible. I leave that up to him, like shaking a Magic 8 Ball.

As we catch up, two old pals reminiscing about good times, Dr. Buzz points out an exceptionally sexy woman sitting at a table solo, her fingertip absently spinning the cocktail straw in her drink as she stares across the room. Dressed casually yet put together, there is an intensity to this woman that quickens the pulse. Checking her watch, her dark eyes rove the room as if she's been stood up and can't believe any guy would have the balls.

Unluckily for her, I'm trashed enough to pull myself from my bar stool especially with Dr. Buzz cheering me on. No harm throwing a little Todd Cartwright charm her way; guaranteed to brighten anyone's day.

Wincing from sitting on an unforgiving bar stool after being stuffed into an airplane seat for a day and a half, I make my approach. Her eyes bore through me like she's hoping I spontaneously combust mid-step. Having survived Harry's death-stares throughout my relationship with Tami, this woman does not know that nasty looks bounce off me like rubber bullets. And with Dr. Buzz now standing atop the bar doing high kicks and chanting my name, I'm in this to win this.

As I give her a nod, she turns her attention past me. She's not making this easy but I've been participating in this game for almost thirty years. I'm a professional, used to being rejected only to end up sneaking out of some woman's apartment the next morning without waking her. For some women it's about making a guy jump through hoops until he's exhausted and out of options. Then and only then do they pounce, feeling like they have the upper-hand. What women fail to note is that a guy doesn't care if he's being led around by the nose as long as he gets laid. If I added it up, I would speculate I've been laid by more women who initially put a hand in my face than ones who offered me a seat after the initial hellos.

For most folks being loaded fogs the mirror. I am an anomaly. Drinking clears my head. My Spidey-senses tingle. Being sober, I'm self-conscious, self-reflective and critical. Drinking alleviates that and I evaluate the world from a confident vantage point.

Usually.

Every once in a while the demon rum fails me and things go haywire. And damn if I don't feel my head go wonky as I stand on the other side of the table from this woman, who has gotten better-looking with every step. A weird panic sets in. My jaw flaps. Sweat beads. I can't think of a single thing to say and with Dr. Buzz busy with his bar-top Rockettes routine, I'm left without my wingman whispering heart-melting one-liners into my ear.

"Are you drinking that?" I bleat, pointing to her drink, a lopsided smile on my mug.

Her eyes stay fixed on whatever's behind me as she replies with dripping sarcasm, "You want my drink?"

Chuckling with self-deprecation, I respond, "No, no…I was hoping to buy you a drink."

"Go away!" she announces flatly, almost before I can finish my sentence.

Now if I were sober there's a chance I'd slink away. Slim chance but a chance. Lucky for me—which makes it unlucky for her—I'm nowhere near sober. Hopefully obnoxiousness is the key to her heart. It's worked for me in the past.

"Well, fuck you very much. I was being a gentleman. But apparently those are in low demand," I snort the air like an angry bull. "You know, my friend Dr. Buzz specializes in stickectomies. He'll pull out that stick you have stuck up your ass. Why don't you join us at the bar and we'll set you up with an appointment?"

"Move away from me before I call security," she answers, her eyes never leaving what she's focused on across the room.

"Call them," I snicker. "Maybe they'll let me buy them a drink. You may be the most beautiful woman in this place but let me tell you something: real beauty comes from the inside---."

"Sit! Sit down!" she cuts me off as she yanks me into a chair by my shirt.

"Who are you watching?" I quiz. "Ex-husband? Boyfriend? The woman your husband is cheating on you with? Wait, it's not someone famous, is it?"

She doesn't respond, her eyes never leaving her prey as she tenses acutely. "Move! Now, move!" she orders loudly to whom I don't know, jumping up before I can comprehend what's going on.

Running toward the bar's entrance, she pulls out a sleek, black handgun that was hidden behind her. Damn it, Dr. Buzz, you should have done some recon on this chick before sending me into the line of fire.

The guy she's apparently after spots her and grabs a small suitcase, jumping to his feet. Panic electrifies the bar, some patrons screaming, everyone ducking at the sight of handguns.

As Beautiful Lady Cop closes in, one of the two perps rounds two tables to avoid her before leaping over a half-wall, suitcase in hand, darting for an exit leading into the terminal. Two other men, which I surmise are plain-clothed policemen, step into the opening, blocking his escape.

All of this is so cool I don't notice the other guy who was at the table surreptitiously standing and swiftly stepping toward the kitchen behind me.

He'd have made it too…if the idiot hadn't decided to dash right in front of me.

Diving toward him, muscling my shoulder into his midsection, I jack him in the chin with my elbow, driving him backward. Staggering back a few steps, he collapses to the floor as I drop back onto the seat of the chair, my heroics sending a shockwave of pain throughout my entire body as I scream, "Motherfucker!"

As he tries to roll over, I lift my leg and kick him right in the face, dropping him to the floor again. "Don't," I warn through clenched teeth, "If I gotta get out of this chair again, I'm gonna grind your head into the carpet!"

Scooting the chair a few feet closer, I put my foot on his head as a precaution.

The guy with the suitcase gets tackled to the floor by the two policeman as Beautiful Lady Cop dives at him, her knee landing in the middle of his back, her gun going to his head. Another cop wrestles the bag from the guy's hand and the cops pile on, handcuffing him.

Looking back at me with my foot on the head of this other guy, Beautiful Lady Cop climbs off Suitcase Guy and charges in my direction, planting her foot on this guy's back, the barrel of her gun aimed at the back of his noggin. Quickly, she's joined by airport police and a couple plain-clothed officers.

"Take your foot off his head!" Beautiful Lady Cop demands.

"Oh, sorry," I respond, pulling my foot off and scooting my chair back, my ass never leaving the seat.

As the other cops cuff the guy and pull him to his feet, the arrestee glares at me, grumbling more at the cops than me, "Is he a cop?"

"Just a concerned citizen," I reply with a smirk.

"I want him arrested for assault!" he barks out as the two officers yank him to his feet before his eyes lock on mine, "I'll sue you, you son-of-a-bitch!"

"Call me when you get out of whatever swampy-ass prison they drop you in. We'll have drinks."

"Are you always a smartass?" Beautiful Lady Cop asks.

My eyes slide back to her. Her hair, which was neatly pulled back, now falls around her face, messy, allowing me to guess what she looks like in the morning. Yep, I'd be happy waking up next to that.

"It's a gift," I answer, unsuccessfully trying to stand.

"You hurt?" she asks.

"Not from this. Couple days ago."

I hope for a little sympathy but her expression announces she's not surprised, as both perps are moved out of the bar and things return to relative calm.

"Thank you," she says. "You didn't have to knock him down. But it made my day a lot easier that you did."

"That's the kind of guy I am. Todd Cartwright," I say sticking out my hand to her, which she dubiously shakes. "You might need my name in case there's a reward or something."

"There's not. Deb Prowess, DEA," she answers, finally getting her hand back from me.

"What did these guys do?"

"I can't say but you can pretty much guess what's in the suitcase by what organization I work for," she responds, before asking, "Where are you heading?"

"St. Carlos."

"Beautiful place. Vacation?"

"Wedding. At least I think so. I'll see when I get there," I answer, stretching my arms out in front of me.

"I hope not yours."

"No, no," I laugh, adding, "Damn. Seems all this excitement has sobered me up. And I don't fly well sober. I think you owe me a drink."

"Mine's still on the table. Tonic with a piece of lime. You asked for it before, have at it." She smiles, before pulling out a business card and handing it to me.

"Thanks," I say with a grin, holding her card.

"Consider it a 'get-out-of-jail-free' card. You seem like a guy who might need it. Have fun in St. Carlos. Don't talk everyone's ear off. You're not as charming as you believe."

Without giving me another look, she walks away, joining some of the other officers talking near the entrance to the bar.

Dr. Buzz has left the building. Police, as a rule, scare him.

Parked on a stool at the bar again, I laud anyone who will listen with my tale of taking down a major Miami drug kingpin, or whatever the hell that skinny whiner was, scoring a few drinks from folks who are as generous as they are hammered. A couple women hover, chatting me up. Yes, there are women who respond to this kind of nonsense. Those are the women I'm partial to. Women who love a guy who is full of shit.

As I finish the third drink, Dr. Buzz sidles up next to me again and takes a seat.

"Where did you run off to?"

He tells me he was afraid of being killed in the crossfire so he made a hasty exit when guns were drawn, adding that if I weren't so big and in so much pain, he would have helped me out of the bar as well. But him being a self-preservationist and me being damaged goods, I was on my own.

"I lived," I say out loud, realizing no one else at the bar can see my imaginary drinking buddy.

Everyone raises a glass to me. Since I have nothing more to drink, the bartender pours me one on the house. We all raise our glasses and drink. Even Dr. Buzz.

I need to be drunk before I crawl into that teeny plane. My inebriation must last not only through the plane ride but my first few acclimating hours on St. Carlos. Even through all the excitement and the liquor I can already feel memories sneaking up on me. Memories ready to take me down so they can feed on my soul.

## CRASH HAPPY LANDINGS

Stepping into the tiny plane, I pull in a deep, unnerving breath like a junkie sucking on a crack pipe. My last breath of real air. Even loaded, I can't handle being in this itty-bitty plane with only eight rows of seats, two seat on either side of a main aisle. I have an aisle seat in row five, but I have to walk sideways to make it down the aisle and still my big ass bumps the people I pass.

I fall into my seat next to a dapper gentleman in his fifties, his skin tanned, wearing off-white madras pants and a colorful shirt. Obviously a recent ex-pat. The new ones think this is the official uniform of the Caribbean. As I fall into the seat, he greets me with a chipper smile, obviously wanting to chat. But getting an eyeful of the sweat trickling down my forehead and my glassy, blood-shot eyes, he heeds the warning signs and pivots toward the window.

Smart.

Closing my eyes tight, I strain to block out all sounds, focusing on my breathing. Since there is no liquor service on this forty-minute flight, which is something they need to rethink—considering most people are going to the island on vacation and alcohol is a staple of most vacations—I have no need to open my eyes at all during this flight. Even if I feel the engines fail, my eyes will stay tightly shut. I don't want to see what we hit, I don't want to scream, I don't want to see flames or smoke or body parts. Especially if they belong to me.

I don't even peek until the wheels of the plane bounce against the St. Carlos runway. The pilot welcomes us to the island causing the tourists surrounding me to cheer, though I'm not sure if they are happy to be on St. Carlos or happy he didn't crash into the ocean. I close my eyes again and wait for the sound of the plane door opening, bringing with it that warm, moist island air which rushes into the plane, letting everyone know they've arrived. I pinball my carry-on, packed tight with every piece of clothing I own, most of it dirty, up the aisle and out onto the rolling stairway that leads to the tarmac.

With each step I descend, I entertain the idea of turning around and returning to Miami. No one would know. Harry might since he bought the ticket, but by then I would be safely somewhere else.

I'm not sure I can do this.

But when my aching legs wobble and I lose my suitcase, sending it tumbling down the steps to the tarmac, I take that as a sign that regardless of my trepidation, I'm here. I have to deal with both the past and the present on this island.

Sitting out front of the airport, three cab drivers ask if they can take me somewhere. Yeah, sure…I just don't know where. It's after midnight and so far the only thing that being back on this island has done is notch up my hankering for more scotch. I debate calling Kat. She doesn't know I'm here and I could pretend I decided to surprise Harry. But she's either working or asleep. I imagine that Harry is at the Resort Club, he and his bride-to-be tucked into bed as well. I should jump in a cab and ask the driver to take me to the nearest liquor store. Seems like the safest place.

Suddenly, I find my face buried into a shirt as two arms wrap around me tightly. I can tell it's a he, and he's squeezing my face into his chest too tightly for a man who has fallen six floors a few days before. But as he pulls back, allowing me to see his face, I can't help but smile.

"Mr. Todd!" Tomas says, his thick accent making it sound like three syllables instead of two.

"Tomas! Holy shit! How are you, my friend?"

"You are back! Mr. Harry is back on the island as well, with a young woman he intends to marry," he says, nudging me playfully with his elbow.

"Yeah, I got wind of this wedding," I respond with a raise of my brow.

Five years hasn't touched Tomas' smiling face. This is one of those guys who will never age. Lucky bastard.

"Are you staying at the Resort Club?"

"I'm…not sure where I'm staying. Honestly, Tomas, I'm not sure why I am even here. I didn't want to come. But I did. So maybe I did want to come, I'm just not clear why."

"Where can I take you?"

"The jungle that leads to that beach. Remember?"

Tomas nods. "It's no longer a jungle. They are building on that side of the island. It's not a quiet place anymore."

The world didn't stop because I've been gone.

"I want to go to that beach."

"In the dark?"

"Yes. Now."

Tomas nods, his eyes relaying what a bad idea this is. But what the hell, if I didn't have bad ideas, I wouldn't have any ideas at all.

I reach up to Tomas to have him help me off the bench.

"Are you hurt, Mr. Todd?" he asks.

"A little."

"Did someone beat you up again?"

This makes me smile.

"Semi-self-inflicted," I say as Tomas grabs my bag, pointing to his cab.

"We are all our own worst enemies," he states assuredly.

"True enough," I respond, walking along with him. "Can we stop so I can get a little something to drink before we get there? I'm going to need some liquid encouragement."

The construction is changing the complexion of this side of the island from a sleepy cove of ex-pats with its bungalows and thick greenery to being the next concrete and stucco faux-Caribbean getaway. Even in the dark of night these changes are ugly. Progress…if progress is defined as altering natural beauty and tranquility into a quagmire money-grab.

Tomas gets out first and helps me out of the cab. I make sure I don't leave the bottle of Jack that he bought me at a funky gas station.

"They've cleared some of the jungle but there is still a lot there," Tomas warns as he leads me along a chain-link fence surrounding a construction site. "Especially in the dark, Mr. Todd."

"I want to get to the beach. Can you help me?"

Tomas nods, smiling. He digs under the seats and pulls out a flashlight, flipping it on. Keeping the beam a step ahead of us, we slowly traverse the thick brush. I'm in no shape to do this but my need to be on that beach is fiercer than the pain. I'm saddened that Tami's beach will become a condo village's private playground. There is something enchanted about that beach that tourists in timeshares will never appreciate.

Our secret is out. Crass and commercialized.

Crossing through the last line of trees, the sound of the ocean offers me a refreshing moment of hope. I am here. The place I left my love. Tomas leads me through the last of the trees and flips off the flashlight, allowing me to see the surf lit only by the moonlight.

I turn to him and shake his hand. "Thank you. I can make it from here," I say.

"You want me to wait in the cab?" he asks.

"No. Go. Make some money," I say, touching his shoulder warmly, "Come back in the morning and find me. Tonight, I need to be alone."

I can see understanding in his eyes. My history on this island is a modest legend.

The beam of Tomas' flashlight disappears into the jungle as I maneuver my way through the soft sand, down to the ocean's edge. It's low tide and the water curls off in small waves about twenty yards away, which allows me to walk further out without fear of getting bowled over in the surf. Tossing my shoes and socks into the soft sand, I let water rush over my feet in a warm invitation to take off the rest of my clothes and swim out. Getting my shirt over my head takes a deep swig from the bottle of Jack, which I slide into my pants pocket so I can get my arms high enough over my head to wriggle the shirt off. The pants are easy as they drop into the sand and I step out of them. Wadding everything into a ball, I toss my clothes in the direction I heaved my shoes before padding out into the ocean, letting the sea move up my body until the weak waves wash over my stomach.

In the moonlight, the scars I received my last visit to the island shadow deeply, like ravines crossing my chest. Touching them, I remember my deserved ass-whipping. I'm glad Tami wasn't around to see me then. Bad enough Harry was. But these scars are part of my vacation souvenirs. Roadmaps of my life.

My eyes search the horizon for Tami. What I want more than anything is for her to tell me whether returning to the island is a wise decision. Because right now every molecule in my brain screams for me to go, escape to the mainland as soon as I can. But as I survey the dark waters, I see nothing but the waves' crests aglow in the moonlight.

Crawling back to the sand still holding some of the heat from the sunny day, I lay back and stare up at a sky filled with stars. I don't even know I've fallen asleep until I sense her near me. "Welcome back, Todd," I hear her say before I am able to open my eyes and sit up.

I spot her. Out in the water. The gentle waves float around her, not touching her. In the moonlight, her eyes glow, radiating from within, almost daring me to come toward her.

"I'm not doing well, Tami."

As she laughs, it sounds like wind chimes on a breezy day.

"No, Todd, you're not."

"I tried being the man you saw in me, but I can't. I don't have the wherewithal to be that man if you're not with me."

"I've never expected you to be anybody but who you are. That was good enough for me. But I don't think it is good enough for you. You need to find yourself again."

Diving back under, she swims out to open water. I rush in, wanting to stop her, needing to hold her, kiss her. But she disappears under the inky, rippling water and I can't find her even in the moonlight. I dive in and out of the surf, searching for her, my hands combing the water hoping to feel her, to grab hold of her and bring her to me. I continue until my body sears with pain and I'm forced to drag myself back onto the sand, fighting the sour fear caused by Tami's words, until I collapse.

"Mr. Todd…"

One eye opening, I see Tomas smile as he stands over me. The sun is shining, there is construction going on behind him at the condo site. "Better put something on, Mr. Todd, before they send for a Constable and arrest you. There are indecency laws on the island."

My eyes adjusting to the harsh morning sunlight, I sit up. "My clothes…what'd I do with them?" I ask.

"I believe those might be them," Tomas says, pointing about 20 yards down the beach.

A seagull nests in them.

"Great," I sigh, staggering to my feet while Tomas chases the bird away and retrieves my clothes.

As I'm sliding into my pants, Tomas asks, "What happened to you?" as he stares at the purple and blue bruises that cover the back of my legs, ass and back.

"Another bad decision," I respond, wiping bird guano off my shirt before pulling it on. I was smart enough to leave my bag with Tomas, so I know dry clothes await but I cannot find my shoes or my bottle of JD which I assume are halfway to Florida by now.

This is why I don't have nice things.

Tip-toeing back through the jungle barefoot and considering the condition of the rest of my body, this hike proves excruciating. And deserved.

I cannot get what Tami said to me out of my head. She is past saving me. She expects me to do it. She knows so much about me yet seems oblivious to the extent of my cluelessness as to how to do that. Especially if she wants me to just be me. That's never good. And if she's saying be the best possible me, well, it's a proven fact that's impossible for any length of time. Was she being intentionally vague or did I not hear her right? I work much better if someone tells me exactly what to do rather than relying on my figuring it out. That always goes into the crapper, usually sooner rather than later.

After changing into dry clothes and sliding a pair of flip-flops onto my now-chewed-up feet, I toss my bag back into Tomas's cab and climb in. He slides into the driver's seat and turns to me, smiling widely, his entire face glowing with some innate joy. God, I love this guy because he actually seems bemused with everything that happens in life.

"Where to, Mr. Todd?"

"That is still a really good question," I answer, lying back and closing my eyes.

"Do you want me to take you to the Resort Club?"

I don't answer for a moment and Tomas leans over the backseat to see if I'm awake or conscious. "Mr. Todd...?"

"No, no," I quickly answer, "don't take me there. Uhm, let me..."

I don't finish the sentence. Instead I take out my phone and redial a number.

"Hello..." I hear a very sleepy voice purr.

"Kat...I'm here."

"Todd? You're on the island?" she asks before falling into silence for a moment. "You did the right thing. For Harry."

"We'll see how right it is. But I'm here and I need a favor..."

There's a pause, almost as if she knows what I'm going to ask.

"Would you like a houseguest?"

I hear absolutely nothing on the other end of the line but breathing.

I have that effect on a lot of women.

## THERE ARE REASONS I DRINK

Tomas's cab pulls up in front of Kat's place. I knew she wasn't living in one of those oceanfront villas that now plague the island in ever-growing numbers, but driving down the narrow road consisting of more dirt than pavement, past tiny bungalows all painted notoriously Caribbean colors, I am somewhat surprised when Tomas stops in front of a bright blue house with sunshine yellow shutters. A metal sculpture of the sun, rusting but sturdy, hangs between two front windows, and there's a pick-up truck parked next to the house.

Checking the paper he wrote the address on when I recited it as Kat told it to me, Tomas says, "This is it, Mr. Todd, this is the address."

Actually wishing I could live in Tomas' cab for however long my stay is on the island, I dig into my pocket, pull out the remaining cash from the plane ticket refund and shove it into Tomas's hand.

"You are one of the good guys, Tomas."

Tomas smiles again. "You are a good guy too, Mr. Todd. You just don't know it."

As the cab pulls away, Tomas waving all the way down the street, I don't move from where I stand. Kat didn't even try to cover her hesitance at letting me crash at her place. But beggars don't get to choose how they're treated. It's either sleep here or sleep on the beach. On the bright side, I don't intend to be on St. Carlos very long. Once I sniff out what Harry's fiancée's deal is and scare her off, demolishing Harry's world only to have him despise me again, my job will be done and I can jet off this spit in the ocean.

Knocking on Kat's front door, I hear the heavy plodding of feet on creaky floors getting closer before the door swings open. I'm wearing my best smile as a lumbering giant of a kid stares at me through the screen door, his face still cherub round with a small blonde tuft of whiskers, curling like sleeping grub on his chin, a mop of sun-bleached hair shadowing his distrustful eyes.

"I know you. You're my monster," he states with more of a smirk than a smile.

"Damn, Earl…you did get big," I announce, surprised as I greet him with a nod.

"Stitches heal?" he asks.

"Back to normal. Well, normal is relative and not something I'm often accused of but yeah, I've healed."

Earl pushes open the paint-chipped screen door and lurches a step back, allowing me to enter. His eyes follow me closely from under the hair, I'm sure hoping to see the scars that run across my head, but my own hair is too gangly and untrimmed for him to see old wounds. He doesn't speak, just stares, his eyes narrowing and widening as he bounces the weight of his big body from foot to foot, giving me the once-over.

"What grade are you in now?" I ask, testing to see if I can get him to say anything else.

"Freshman. Sucks."

The living room is comfortable, with that shabby chic look favored by people with a modicum of taste but less money. There's a large TV against one wall, with a ton of electronic equipment that does God knows what. I'm sure Earl is the master of all those boxes and wires. There are sofas on either side of a coffee table and various non-matching chairs dotting the festive green walls of the room.

"Where's your Mom?"

"Shower," Earl answers in another single-word sentence as if putting a noun and a verb together has become passé. At least he bothers to point toward the back of the house.

"She's out of the shower," Kat's voice drifts into the living room before she makes her entrance a moment later, wearing shorts and a t-shirt. "Earl, you could have invited him to sit down. Sit, Todd."

"Nice place," I answer, causing her to laugh.

"You must have been living in a youth hostel if you think this is nice but thank you, we like it," she responds, still chuckling as she moves over and plops down on one of the well-worn sofas.

I slowly inch myself down on the other sofa. It soaks me in, comfortable enough so that my ass doesn't ache but deep enough that returning to a standing position is going to be a bitch. Earl plants himself nearby, staring. My eyes keep staggering back in his direction uneasy, his intent gaze making me squirm.

"I can't wait for you to see Harry," Kat says. "He's changed."

"How?"

Kat shakes her head. "You have to see for it to make sense."

"Please tell me he didn't get hair plugs."

She laughs, flipping her damp hair off her face. "Suffice it to say, he's different."

"Tell me more about the fiancée."

Kat shrugs. "Only met her once. She seems nice. Nothing like I would expect Harry to be with but I never really expected him to be with anybody."

"What's she drink?" I ask. "That'll tell me everything."

Kat grimaces. "She asked for a Bacardi and Tab…"

"Tab?"

"Yeah. Do they even make that stuff anymore? I gave her a Bacardi and Coke, it was the best I could do. I don't think she took but a sip before she shook my hand and told me it was nice to meet me, kissed Harry on the cheek and disappeared. When I asked Harry about her, how they met, how long they've been together, he kept steering me to another topic so I figure he doesn't want to talk about it."

"I'm intrigued," I assure her. "And I appreciate you letting me crash here. I don't have the money for a hotel room."

I have a moment to take Kat in. I'd forgotten how casually beautiful she is. Probably why she makes a decent living slinging drinks. There's nothing studied about her, she seems quite at peace in her own skin, something I wish I could say about myself. She has a light tan that comes from simply living on an island even when you work indoors. Her hair is the color of a wheat field, browns and yellows that tumble over each other naturally. Even the lines on her face crease with a sense of balance.

She looks like a woman should.

Her eyes drift back to Earl, still standing over me. "Might be good for him to have someone new to talk to. I'm the enemy now."

I glance back at Earl who scowls at his mother, causing her to giggle.

"Teenagers. I thought he'd connect with Roger, but that never happened either," she adds.

"Roger?"

"That'd be me," I hear someone say from the hallway. He's tall, though not taller than me, his tanned skin broadcasts that he works outside. I imagine he's a few years older than me though not as well-worn. Blue eyes, warm smile, couple days' growth on his jaw, giving him a rugged, yet laidback, island vibe.

Awkwardly, I slowly stand as he shoves his hand into mine, giving me a very firm handshake.

"Roger Goford."

"Todd Cartwright."

"Yeah. Kat's told me about you. Welcome back to St. Carlos."

"Thanks…" I respond, my voice trailing off, not having anything else to say to a complete stranger I never heard anything about until this moment.

Roger slides over to Kat and kisses her, saying, "I'll see you when you get off tonight."

He smiles at me, his hand shoving into mine again and giving it a hyper-masculine shake as he says, "See you tonight too, I guess."

"Yeah, yeah…" I mumble like Brando, only with more confusion.

Roger grabs a pair of gloves off the kitchen counter and exits out the back door, allowing the screen door to slam.

"When'd you get in?" Kat asks, as the sound of the pickup truck starting shakes the small house.

"Last night."

"Where'd you sleep?"

"The beach."

Breaking up laughing, the lines around her eyes dancing with delight, Kat shakes her head. "You are my favorite hot mess, Todd," she says, still chortling.

"Hot mess? You have no idea," I respond with a shake of my head that matches hers. "But back to you…" I add, pointing out front as we hear the pickup truck rumbling down the short driveway and roaring away.

"Roger?" she asks, surprised I am bringing it up. "He's a landscape architect. He was doing some work at the resort. Does a lot of resort and condo communities on the island."

Earl rolls his eyes as he tromps toward the front door.

"You got school?" I ask.

"Yeah. Blows," he responds, grabbing a book bag from the corner near the door and flipping it over his shoulder.

"Have a good day. Learn something," I announce with a half-parental chuckle that I think is sort of charming, but I'm sure to him sounds sarcastic and lame.

His response is letting the front screen door slam.

He's not the cute, little bullied boy I remember. He's morphed into an oversized teenager with a dubious glower and a wariness locked in his eyes that hints at his boredom of, and disdain for, most people. Including me. I imagine he believes anyone over thirty is an asshole put on this planet to ruin his life. While probably correct, I was kind of hoping he would greet me like a returning war hero, someone who saved his life, and gush with eternal gratitude. Standing up for Earl is one of the proudest moments of my life. I was hopeful he'd remember it as gloriously as I do and it would bond us like a sensei to his grasshopper. But obviously he's over it.

Kat lets out a long breath once Earl is gone.

"He hates Roger."

"Why?"

She stands, shrugging one shoulder.

"Roger tries too hard. Wants Earl to be, I don't know...normal."

"What's normal for a kid that age?"

"Roger loves the outdoors. He wants Earl to go kayaking and paddle boarding with him. You know, guy stuff. Earl's...not that kind of kid."

"You in love?" I blurt out, wishing I hadn't.

Kat bellows out a laugh. "You got your own problems," she answers with a non-answer before changing the subject all together. "I got some errands to run before work. There's a small room behind the kitchen. There's a bed. I'm sure you'll find the bathroom, there's only one. You need anything while I'm out?"

"Forgiveness of my sins."

"Good luck with that!" Kat responds, moving to the kitchen table and grabbing her car keys and shoulder bag. "When I see Harry, do you want me to tell him you're here?"

"I guess. I should find out what's the what," I sigh, letting Kat know I'm still not completely on board with being back on the island.

Pausing, she fires me a look. Pity? Exasperation? The gross realization that letting me stay in her home is potentially a titanic mistake? Whatever it is, it's not good. But she laughs mostly to herself and waves, kicking open the screen door and walking out.

I wander her small home, checking out the two bedrooms. Not hard to tell whose is whose; the cluttered, messy, dark hole where Earl caves, as opposed to the soft linens and light feel of his mother's. There aren't enough 'man touches' in Kat's room to lead me to believe Roger does more than sleep over periodically. Not that it's my business but it does give me the answer to the question I asked her earlier about being in love. She's not quite there yet. Though there are three toothbrushes hanging around a cup holder in the bathroom.

Padding my way to the kitchen, I check the coffee pot but it's dry. She must not need that morning kick that I do. Sticking my head into the small room behind the kitchen, I spy a single bed jammed into one end that doesn't look big enough for my body, a small table next to that and nothing else. I don't even think I could turn around in the room without clobbering myself against a wall. At least there is a bank of slatted windows to keep my claustrophobia at bay.

Showering after my continental travels and a night on the beach, I wash off the sand that stuck to my clammy, stinking body which must have halted the breath of anyone downwind of me these last two days. Knowing I will soon come face to face with Harry and his fiancée, I shave to at least appear like I got my shit together. Changing into the last clean clothes in my bag, I search Kat's home inside and out for a washer/dryer but my hunt is a bust. I hate doing laundry. I'd rather throw clothes away than find some place to wash them, but I don't have anything clean left in my bag and I'm far from flush so I won't be buying myself a new wardrobe anytime soon. I'm a bit of a slob but not enough to start pulling from the bottom of the pile to re-wear a shirt I had on a week ago.

Chucking everything back in my small suitcase, I haul it out of the house and lug it down the narrow road toward the little town we drove through on the way to Kat's home. I'm not sure there is a Laundromat, but either I find one or I search for a stream and beat my clothes with a rock.

The village on this end of the island is nothing more than a strip of small wood structures parallel from one another across a paved two-lane. With all the development happening on the island this area is bound to enter the twenty-first century eventually, but at present it still possesses a rural but rough quaintness. This is the side of the island where working-class islanders employed at the opulent resorts reside. Sooner rather than later, some corporation will start buying up this side of the island as well, piece by piece, and the old-world, bucolic atmosphere will be bulldozed and reconstructed into another stucco condo development surrounding a golf course, and the locals will be shoved into an even smaller corner of the island.

Strolling down the wooden boardwalk in front of the buildings, I pass a small market, a few touristy shops and local businesses, and clapboard restaurants where the aroma of brazed meats wafts out into the street making my stomach growl. Near the north end of the boardwalk, I find the laundromat, a narrow storefront with five washers on one side and five dryers on the other with an aptly named folding table in between them. The machines are all well-used, with rust crusting the edges. I open my bag and dump everything onto the table, the odor of week-old clothes stuck in a bag falling out with it. There are few whites and nothing is new enough to bleed so I have no need to separate the colors from the whites.

Dumping them into a washing machine, I shuffle past the one other person in the place, a heavy-set black woman who watches me out of the corner of her eyes, and slip a few coins into a machine mounted onto the wall to get some detergent. As I shove in my seventy-five cents, I spy a muscly guy in a tight shirt drag a young girl out of one of the storefronts across the street, and backhand her to the ground in the roadside parking area.

I freeze. When you see this sort of violence, no matter how inured you think you are to it, it stops you in your tracks as if it can't be real. It's not that I am shocked. I lived through enough shit like this for it to have that effect on me. But I am immobilized for a moment. My father took great pleasure in tormenting my mother as well as me and my brother physically. Ass-wipe that he was. But because I often pulled my mother away from getting her ass kicked by my father, I took the beatings instead. Until I was big enough to grind that pathetic son-of-a-bitch's face into the kitchen floor. But like many people who have seen battle, I have visceral flashbacks when witnessing a woman get hit. Blind fury electrifies me, shutting down any good sense of self-preservation.

This is for you, Dad.

Barreling toward them before I even know I'm out the door, the guy doesn't see me until I'm a few feet away, plowing full bore, my shoulder dropped so I can mow his sorry-ass over. His hand raised to strike the young woman again, he's off balance and oblivious to my rage. Even in as much pain as I'm in, I lope over the top of the girl without breaking stride and come up quickly with a shoulder to his chest, knocking the big guy back before he can strike her again. He wobbles back but doesn't go down. As he rears back I get a solid look at him. Steroidally muscled, mid-twenties, a wild mane of dark brown hair that frames his tanned, model-handsome face. If I hadn't just smashed into his body, I'd think he was a cartoon.

His nostrils flare wide like a bull's after it's been skewered by a matador. His forearms are tattooed with all sorts of shit that if I were sitting next to him in a bar, I'd ask him to explain. But in this case, I'd just like to rip one from the socket and beat him bloody with it.

"What the fuck!?" he snarls, his blue eyes boring through me with venomous ferocity. "Mind your business, tourista, or I'll be using pieces of you to bait hooks."

Death threats aren't exactly new to me, but something in the ease at which he spits out the words makes me think he believes he can actually do it. But if I've learned anything from years of dealing with dangerous assholes, if you back down they will immediately destroy you. So I continue toward him but with each step, he sizes me up. I surmise he might have the upper-hand on me physically, but judging from the time and effort with the body, the hair, the face and the clothes, his youth and strength are no match for my well-ripened insanity. He's cautious, not only apt to pick his battles but how they're fought.

"You ever touch this girl again, you candy-ass prick," I growl, picking her up by the arm, "that pretty face of yours will look like it was put back together by Picasso!"

Hey, if you're going to talk shit, go big or go home.

"This is my business, bro, not yours."

"My business is what I make my business. Bro. No fucking man hits a woman!"

"You're a dead man," he states with absolute certainty, adding a little smile that's meant to be intimidating but only serves to piss me off more.

"You don't know who you're messing with, tourista," the girl says defiantly with an accent that sounds more New England than Caribbean, as she wrests her arm from my grip. She has to still be in her teens, quite striking with pouty lips and a voluptuous body that a woman this young comes by naturally.

Firing her a harsh look, I can't figure out whether she's one of those women who enjoys being whacked around, if he's got her believing she deserves it, or if she's terrified it will get worse now that I've interceded.

"I don't care who he is. Men don't hit women!"

She looks right at me, her blue eyes pleading. "Be smart. Get off the island," she says backing away, before turning and running.

"We're not done," the asshole calls after her as she dashes for the storefront he pulled her out of and disappears inside.

This leaves me and the big guy standing within arms' reach. He grins with enough malevolence to bristle the hairs on the back of my neck. I haven't a clue who this clown is but I am smart enough to know if I hear a rattle it's not a baby's toy, it's a snake.

"You don't seem smart enough to take her advice," he says.

"I'd take too much pleasure putting your ass down," I respond, hating this guy more every second he stands in front of me.

"Attempting that would be a thousand times more stupid than what you've already done. What would be best is for you to apologize for shoving your nose into my business, scamper back to whichever hotel you're staying in to make a reservation on the first plane off MY island and pray to Jesus I never see you again."

"You might be able to trash-talk little girls you outweigh by a hundred pounds but me, it makes me want to smash your face in," I grouse, glaring into his eyes without blinking, which I've been told is a huge selling feature when I'm about to come to blows with another asshole.

He smiles again trying to sell me on his mettle. Unfortunately for him, he's too studied. Too self-absorbed to take this to the end of the line. My guess, he's only a badass in photos and leaves the real dirty work to someone else.

"I got business to take care of," he snorts. "But I'm going to find you, tourista. I'm going to find you and make sure this vacation is one you won't forget."

"Other people already beat you to that, bitch. Move along. Your whining is making my ears bleed and I want nothing more right now than to wreck that pretty smile of yours."

He swaggers toward a cherried-out blue Camaro, a blue that matches his eyes, making me hate him just that much more. Getting in, he revs the engine, throws it in reverse and in a total teenage dick move, spits gravel at me as he peels out.

I debate whether or not I should go after the girl he knocked to the pavement. A thank you would have been nice, especially in light of the lecture she gave me. But more than that, I'd like to know what species of animal I've tangled with.

Moseying back to the laundromat, I conclude I probably did something incredibly stupid. But what's done is done. I notice a few people eyeballing me from the neighboring buildings but no one says a word of thanks or warning, all of them going on about their business, leading me to believe this kind of thing isn't as rare an occurrence around here as I'd like to believe.

Either that or they are as scared of this guy as I should be.

Back in the laundromat, I dig in my pocket, pull out a crumpled bill and force it into the rusty coin changer. As I do, I notice the heavy-set black lady perched near the back of the narrow room, rock her body off a chair and stand. She moves to my washer and puts in four quarters, shoving them in and starting my wash.

"'Bout time someone knocked that boy down a peg or two!" she says in an island accent, before waddling back to her chair, her clothes circling the dryer next to her.

"Who is he?" I ask, hoping for some clarity to judge whether my actions were noble or crazy.

Surprise dances in her eyes. That's all it takes for me to know her response isn't going to be something I wanted to hear. If there is a life lesson I would like to pass on to those with the same proclivities as me, it's that naïveté goes a long way when wanting to punch someone in the face. Sometimes it's better not to ask.

"That particular piece of garbage is Michlean. That was one of his working girls he slapped. Likes to do it in public. Like a warning. I wanted to tell you you were brave stopping him but since you didn't know who he was, maybe not as brave as I thought."

Gee, thanks, there seems to be a consensus building.

"I get pissed off easy over abuse like that," I answer. "You know all this about him which means the authorities here on the island have to know all about him. They don't do anything?"

She smiles again. "He is very generous with those who look the other way."

Of course he is.

My own seedy history on this island corroborates that explanation. I bribed the island Constable, Gabriel, to get me a hooker for Harry with money wrapped around those single-serve bottles of booze. I wonder whether Regina worked for Michlean. It would really chap my hide if some of the money I funneled to the Constable to procure Regina for Harry ended up in the pocket of the douchebag I want to punch in the face.

"Hello…" I say, answering the beckoning of Lynyrd Skynyrd while folding my clothes back into my suitcase.

"It's me," Kat says, assuming by now I would recognize her voice. "In case you're thinking about running away, Harry already knows you're on the island."

"I figured that's who paid for my ticket from Miami."

"He's excited to see you. You want to come here?"

"Yeah…yeah. Sure. I'll be over in a bit. You still working the same bar?"

"Same bar."

"I might need some liquid courage before this reunion."

"Not too much. I need a sober evaluation," Kat adds.

"Let me see if I can get hold of Tomas and hitch a ride in your direction," I answer with as much excitement as I can muster.

"Take one of the mopeds. They're on the side of the house. Johnny Walker neat?"

"It's day time…on ice," I respond, wishing I had it in my hand right now.

## MEETING OF THE MEETING OF THE MINDS

My first drink disappears in less time than it takes to pour another.

Slapping the empty glass onto the bar, I smile at Kat who is dealing with a gaggle of inebriated, sunburnt tourists across the circular bar. She cocks her head and fires me a look that screams, 'enough', but undaunted, I wag the glass in the air like an asshole and beg, "One more. Please!"

She sighs, quickly refilling my glass. "I need you coherent, and you don't seem capable of that even when you're sober."

"Liquor is like steel wool for the senses," I relay, not being entirely untruthful. "It scrubs it clean and allows me to focus."

"Which explains the empty-headed things you do," she responds without a smile. "Down that and suck on a mint. I am calling his room."

Less than ten minutes later I spot him ambling confidently in the direction of the bar. Where's that hunched shuffle, that tight-ass waddle that transports Harry from place to place? On top of it, he's tanned and what's left of his hair is razored close to his head, giving him the salt-and-peppered look of a man who actually gives a shit about himself. I'm perplexed by the sureness of his appearance, the poise that was never even hinted at while Tami was alive.

Goddamn him!

Now I'm anxious, as if I'm entering Martin Howell Elementary after my Mom dropped me off out front and drove off when I was in first grade. While the other first graders' parents escorted them in, wiping tears and giving hugs, taking pictures of their little darlings' first day in big school, I stood against the wall, watching. Feeling, well, like I do now, clammy and unsure of how to act. As a first grader it would have been inappropriate to ask the teacher for scotch, but thankfully I've aged out of that. Calculating just how quickly Harry will make it over to me I am sure I can down one more before he gets close enough to see, but the stingy bartender is not about to let that happen. I fight the overwhelming urge to jump over the bar and crack open a bottle of Johnny Walker, letting the contents pour down my throat to the tune of "Rocky." But Harry couldn't miss my fat ass clambering over the bar. Not that he would be surprised, but still it certainly would put a bad spin on the reunion.

Why am I so stressed about seeing Harry? True, my life hasn't gone exactly as I foresaw five years ago, but he's witnessed me at my out-and-out worst. Though at this moment, it's not about me. It's about him. It's almost like he's floating toward me. I've never seen him so alive, so self-assured.

And me…not so much.

Glancing back at Kat, my eyes on their little retinal hands and knees, imploring her for another drink. But she shakes her head and goes back to work, busy enough to legitimately ignore me.

Harry smiles widely at me with the confident wave of a born salesman. He's not just tanned, it's a professional job. Sprayed on. Nobody gets that color, especially a short bastard who turns red like he's been holding his breath at the first exposure to sunlight.

Damn him. Damn him, damn him, damn him!

Never the most demonstrative person, I'm stymied when he bear-hugs me, attempting to lift me off the ground as I stiffen with astonishment. "You made it!" he says with a grin, finally giving up on his attempt to lift me off the ground. Did this little fucker have his teeth done? I never thought I'd be as physically close to him again as the night we danced together, but here I am being cub-hugged by a Hobbit with a make-over.

"I didn't know whether Kat would find you, but she did!" he exclaims, placing his hands together and bowing to her. "Thank you, thank you…" he chants, before turning back to me, announcing, "I'm so glad you're here. Where are you staying?"

"Kat's place," I mutter, trying hard to relax but feeling like a weasel trapped in a cage.

"Oh," Harry smirks as if I'm letting him in on some gossip.

"No 'oh', Harry. She's letting me crash in her spare room. Where else am I supposed to stay? Here? I'd never cheat on you like that."

"Still the irascible asshole," Harry replies, only unlike our last rendezvous on the island where everything had some dour connotation, he's cackling like a parrot.

"Just a run-of-the-mill asshole but thanks for the adjective," I shoot back.

Why does it piss me off that he's not a mess? Harry is the last person I ever thought would get his shit together. I believed he'd be miserable forever. As miserable as I've gotten over the last few years. Maybe even more so. But Harry's smiled more in the last couple minutes than I saw him smile the entire time Tami and I were together.

"So…" I say, leading him in.

"You want to meet her, don't you?" Harry asks, his mouth curling into a wider smile as he rubs his hands together like he's about to collect on a fat racetrack bet.

"If you're marrying her, I want to meet her," I answer, again glancing in Kat's direction only to be ignored.

"You're going to love her. Tami certainly would have."

"Tami wanted you to be happy, Harry. So if this woman makes you happy, yes, Tami would have loved her."

Again he smiles, but I register a hint of the old snarl. I chalk it up to old habits because I mentioned Tami as if I knew her better than him. Which I do and always will, but that'll always be a jagged wedge between us.

"Carolina has made me happier than I've ever been. I mean look at me," he chortles proudly, spreading his arms like a game show host, "You ever seen me like this?"

"You're not the same man I left on this island."

"Damn right I'm not!" he bellows.

Even before meeting the woman who changed Harry's life, he's working this happiness extravaganza a little hard. Probably to impress me but I imagine also because bliss is an unnatural state of being for him. He has no instinctive conception of joy so he has to mimic how he thinks someone else would act if they were happy, his behavior choreographed.

Harry and I have always had one common denominator. Apparently until now. We never let ourselves believe in happiness. It's a mirage. When you grab hold, contentment mockingly vaporizes, leaving you with nothing but a faint scent of what could have been. When I hear people talk about being happy, I always assume they are desperate to convince themselves of something they will never possess, something that at best is transitory, an illusion of a feeling they believe they should have.

"It takes her time to get dolled up. You know how women are," Harry says with a wink. "I'll go up and see if she's ready. You got some time to kill?"

"More than I'd like, Harry," I answer, and then adding loud enough for Kat to hear, "I'll order myself a drink and be right here at the bar."

They're on me," he exclaims, giving me a thumbs up before scampering off.

On him? Holy shit. I would wager that until this moment, Harry has never willingly bought a drink for anyone other than maybe his wife or Tami, in his life. I don't know what voodoo this woman has cast on him but she's turned Pinocchio into a real boy.

Kat turns to me, her eyebrows rising as if to ask, 'What do you think?'

"Time to stop watering down the drinks," I answer, "I need my keen sense of observation firing on all cylinders."

She pours me a double.

Ecstatic to feel the glass in my hand, I shake my head at Kat with a dazed chuckle. "Who was that man and what the hell did he do with Harry? Drinks are on him? Hell, in that case there's no reason to ever stop pouring!"

I savor the drink knowing he might never offer again. The shock of seeing Harry Everett vibrant, spit-shined and tanned — like a man who actually gives a rat's ass for the first time in his life — has me against the ropes. Of course, there's a woman involved. Without women, men wouldn't change their underwear, if we'd wear underwear at all. We'd grow hair out of our ears, scratch our balls continually, and only communicate with semi-audible grunts. Any guy who tells you different is lying. We're apes. All of us. Some cute spider monkeys, some shit-throwing chimpanzees, some chest-beating gorillas, but we all share the simian gene.

It's only women—more accurately, the hope of having sex with them—that forces us to step into a shower, shave, and learn rudimentary manners. But in spite of the number of women I've gotten naked, I don't know much about them. If you correlate the number of times I've had sex with women to my knowledge about them, my insight has diminished with each release of my swimmers, as if they are what actually holds my understanding of the opposite sex.

Spying a massive parade of platinum-blonde curliness bouncing across the lobby with Harry by its side, I attempt to get a peek at the woman that changed Harry's life, but it's as if the hair is a shield that protects Carolina from anyone actually getting a look at her, camouflaging her face and dwarfing her tiny frame. They chat intimately, Carolina whispering in Harry's ear, making him smile. Her body appears thin but her breasts are surprisingly ample for a body so small. I'll give Harry credit, I don't know how he did it, but he attracted this.

I should ask if perhaps he also recently won a lottery.

As a drunk husband and his pissed-off, sunburnt bride stumble past, I get my first solid look at her. The first thing I recognize is that I don't recognize her. I'm overtaken by a zen-coated calm because it crossed my mind that if she's from Chicago, I might possibly have slept with her somewhere in my unflinching past. But I'd never forget a woman with early nineties Dallas-housewife hair. Or large, heavily made-up eyes, with cheekbones pronounced from dieting, most likely to fit into her wedding dress a size too small. I imagine that if you take away the hair and heavy make-up she'd still be considered a beauty, which makes all the dramatics a peculiar choice. But to each their own. Not something I'm much attracted to sober and even less so drunk.

Harry grins like his dick grew ten inches as he parades into the bar with Carolina on his arm. That fucker's actually gloating and strangely, I've never been so proud of him. Punching me at Tami's wake comes a close second, but I think this tops that. He beams with a boyish charm which he probably never even had when he was a boy.

Harry almost pushes her at me, her hand thrusting into mine harder than she probably wants. "Carolina, this is Todd. Todd, this is Carolina Starren."

Her hair seems to undulate around her face as she shakes my hand with genuine warmth. "It's high time I met you after hearing so much about you," she greets, her accent matching her name.

"I don't want to know what Harry said about me," I joke, partly to put her at ease, partly because I really don't want to know.

She giggles. And as she does, I stifle a harsh gasp. I know that sweet, unfiltered laugh. It's the same damn giggle as Tami's.

"You know Harry, he leaves nothing to the imagination," she says, smiling. "But he says wonderful things about how you loved his daughter. That's the measure of a man. How you treat the women in your life," she adds again with a reminiscent giggle and a glint in her eye as if she's honestly excited to meet me.

"If Harry told you everything and you're still shaking my hand, you're a better person than me," I respond, my free hand reaching back to the bar to grab the glass that sits nearby.

"Well, some of the stories he told me were pretty unbelievable, if you don't mind me saying. But Harry's got a poetic way of putting things."

Poetic? Harry? Get this woman some alcohol; we need to dilute the Kool-Aid Harry's poured down her throat.

"Harry and I have a colorful history."

She leans over and hugs me with another Tami-giggle that paralyzes me for a second as Harry chimes in, "Best of friends, worst of enemies." Way to go putting a positive spin on something that only has spin.

"Usually worst of enemies. But I love Harry for what he did for me. And I loved his daughter. Still do."

Carolina smiles with a soft sense of understanding and pity. I know that look. Tami used to give it to me. For a split second I feel comforted, then comes the cold realization that it's not Tami offering me understanding but a woman I barely know. A woman engaged to Tami's father.

Suddenly and sufficiently creeped out, I want to grab Harry by the shoulders and shake him, barking, "Do you know who she acts and sounds like, you psycho bastard?! Your daughter! And it's wrong, way wrong, wronger than wrong!"

Carolina reaches out and touches my chest with her hand, holding it there as she chokes up, announcing, "I can sense your true, sweet nature."

Okay, this woman is nuts. Tami loved me and even she would have never accused me of having a sweet nature.

"Don't read too much into him, Carolina," Harry warns. "He's not that deep. Or sweet."

Kat arrives with diversionary drinks. Like a top-notch bartender, she remembers what Harry and Carolina drink and delivers without asking. It allows me to grab my glass off the bar and gulp down a mouthful. Popeye needs his spinach.

"You remembered," Carolina reacts, her drawl oozing gratefulness.

Kat nods. "I always remember."

Harry gives Kat a wink as if they are in on something together which I know they're not. It's part of the new Harry, pretending he's in on the joke.

We take our drinks and move to a nearby table. Harry pulls out Carolina's chair, his chivalry earning him a warm stroke on the cheek. I sort of feel like an ass for not thinking of it first but I'm out of practice.

"So," I start, my mouth dry even after the drink, "How'd you two meet?"

"Oh, that's sort of funny," Carolina jumps in, placing her hand on Harry's and giving it a squeeze. "I'll let Harry tell it. He tells it better than me."

I'm sorry…did she just say that Harry tells a story better than her? Forget the Kool-Aid, this must be true love. Harry and Carolina trade warm looks before Harry stammers into what feels like a well-rehearsed story of going home to Chicago and trying to resume his life after leaving St. Carlos. Trying to pick up where he left off and how difficult he found it. Which led him to attending singles functions, concerts, symphonies, restaurants "because that's what Tami would have wanted."

Suddenly, Carolina reaches across the table and grabs my hand as well as Harry's, interrupting his story.

"Why don't I let you boys catch up? I have some wedding arrangements that need to be taken care of. Would you mind very much if I went back upstairs and made some calls?"

Was it something I said? I thought I was being cordial but damn, that was quick! Maybe Harry warned her about my small window of charm and she felt it collapsing with each gulp from my drink.

Carolina says her good-byes, leaning over and giving me a hug, her mane mopping across my face with the aroma of lavender and vanilla. Walking out of the bar, she stops and gives Harry a coy wave.

"What a gal!" Harry beams like the high school quarterback who landed the head cheerleader, and both have been named king and queen of the prom.

"You both seem very happy," I respond with cagey, innocuous grace.

"I can only answer for myself, Todd. But her agreeing to marry me says a little about how she's feeling too."

As I force a smile, Kat arrives at the table with another for me.

"Everything okay with Carolina?" she asks.

"She wanted to give Todd and me time to catch up. The wedding plans have her a little overwhelmed," Harry answers.

As Kat reaches to take Carolina's nearly untouched drink, I abruptly grab her hand. "Leave it," I snap way too quickly, then cover with an apologetic smile, "No need to waste it."

Kat tosses off a patronizing glare but leaves the glass, beating a quick retreat back to the safety of the bar.

"I see some things haven't changed," Harry smirks coolly.

"This isn't easy for me, Harry."

"What? Seeing me?"

"Seeing you happy."

My words cause a seismically weird shift in Harry's demeanor. His sunny bravado dims and he shifts in his seat as if he wants to tell me the truth, only to plaster a rehearsed smile on his lips. Glancing at his watch he shifts again. How could my doubting happiness bother him so much?

"Hey, sorry..." I respond to his discomfort.

"No, no..." Harry waves my concern away. "I just feel bad for you, Todd. Happiness...it's, well, I want it for you. You could at least be happy for me."

"I am," I assure him. "Part of it is that Carolina reminds me—"

Harry gulps down half his drink and stands brusquely. "Carolina. She shouldn't be doing everything herself. It's not fair. And you know how women are when there's a wedding..." He wipes his hands on his pants like a kid who is getting in trouble. "I got a favor to ask."

"Sure..."

His nose curls up toward his eyebrows, either summoning courage or questioning his sanity. "I'd like you to be my best man at the wedding. You came all this way and well, Tami would really like that."

I'm not as stunned as I probably look. Considering our history, he could have easily not asked and I wouldn't have batted an eye. And he's right, Tami would have wanted it, most especially after everything we went through on this island after her death.

"Sure, Harry. I'd be honored," I answer, though there is some trepidation electrifying this entire conversation.

Harry nods, reaches over and shakes my hand. His white smile reappears.

"Perfect," he says. "I'll tell Carolina. It's why she wanted to leave us alone, so I'd ask. She'll be so happy. One more thing is off the list. I'll see you later. I want to hear all about where you've been, what you've been up to and why you've been so hard to get hold of."

As Harry ambles in the direction of the elevators, I get this vision of him standing in a booth in some storefront tanning salon as some gum-smacking girl in her twenties absently sprays his wrinkled body with a brown dye, while Carolina watches with a delighted smile on her face. Picking up Carolina's Bacardi and Coke, I take a swill, trying to exorcise that image from my head. Not that I haven't seen Harry in his underwear, but this is so out of context for the Harry I remember; his new look, the fiancée reminiscent of his deceased daughter, the island wedding, the whole thing feels like I'm being punked. I'm acutely sensitive to the aroma of bullshit and it wafts over this wedding thing like the odor of a public bathroom.

I wonder what Tami would have thought about all this. I'd like to believe she'd be ecstatic for her father, but in truth, if she hadn't died, Harry wouldn't be getting married. He'd be too busy trying to drag our marriage behind his Honda Civic until it was bloody and broken. He would look like the old Harry not the new Harry. He certainly wouldn't ask me to be the best man if he even allowed me at his wedding at all. I would be spending half my marriage deflecting his hands away from my neck, and the other half apologizing to my wife for hating her father so much.

Finding a seat at the end of the bar, away from the groups of partying tourists and grabby newlyweds, I wave Kat in my direction.

"She kinda reminds me of Tami," I say to Kat as she carries a bucket of ice and dumps it over a cooler full of beers to be taken outside to a group hanging out poolside.

She returns quickly. "What?" she asks, disbelief rocking her voice, "Like in a creepy doppelganger sort of way?"

"No, no. It's her laugh, it's a vibe, you know. I wonder if Harry even realizes it. Maybe it's subconscious for him, he's not the most dialed-in guy," I opine, taking a drink. "And does this new Harry seem manufactured to you? Like he's playing pretend because he doesn't know how people in love are supposed to act? I hate to get all B. F. Skinner on him but sooner or later the old Harry will return. I know. I changed for a while and voilà, I've returned to my old subpar self. We are who we are. Sucky as that might be for some of us."

"You're being too hard on him. It's certainly not what I expected from Harry, but dammit, if he's happy, accept that and be happy for him."

"I don't know. I don't know what to think. I mean why would anyone want to be reminded daily of their dead daughter? That's some bad juju."

"I'm sure he doesn't see it."

"He will when I point it out."

"Then don't," Kat states sternly, slamming the door on this conversation.

Maybe I should just leave it alone. Hang out a few days, drink, see what trouble I can bring my way, stand next to Harry as he pledges his love and devotion to his bride and then disappear into the night. Certainly would be easier.

But I don't do 'easy' very well.

As I pound back another, feeling woozy from my intake of booze and lack of food, I take a breath and hold it as if that will somehow clear things up. I'm already itching to get off this island, sensing the rest of this trip is certain to suck shit.

## THE SLOW TEASE

After lazing away the afternoon poolside, gandering at the surprising roster of hot, young female bodies oiled up and broiling in the sun in next to nothing, I see his shadow before I spy him. The puffed-up, tousled-hair, woman-punching Ken Doll I squared off with earlier in the day. Now I hate that I'm loaded. If he spots me, this could be the perfect setting for him to ram my head through a plate glass window. I'm meaner when I'm this drunk but I'm also slower and slightly off my game when it comes to tangling with someone. Not that I won't. But I've been warned that this guy is someone, at minimum, to be wary of, and at most be petrified of.

As he crosses the pool deck, he falls into a chair between two ridiculously beautiful women clad in next-to-nothing bikinis. Now it makes sense who all this taut, tanned flesh belongs to. These are the douchebag's harem. After pulling off his shirt in that way guys who spend an inordinate amount of time at the gym like to do, his hands fall onto both their asses simultaneously. Neither woman jumps. They arch up and chat with him, the sun glinting off their oiled bodies as he surreptitiously hands each something, nonplussed by all the eyes on him. One girl slips the small envelope of what I can only surmise to be coke into her bag, the other slides it beneath the tiny patch of material on her bikini top which barely covers her nipple.

One would think that this resort being a mecca for newlyweds, the recent brides would give management a ration of shit about barely clad working girls soaking up space around the pool, as their new husbands do everything within their testosterone-addled power not to let their new wives see them peeking. The men battle unsuccessfully against their base urges, reminding each and every new bride just what kind of bitter hell married life is sure to bring.

The alpha-douche chats with his girls a few more minutes, his hands resting on each of their asses, enjoying the attention he gets from the resort guests wondering just who he is to be surrounded by such delicious women. When he gets up to leave, I amble back into the bar and signal Kat, making sure there are enough people between him and me so the douche doesn't spot me.

Kat slides over with a sigh. "Are you going to hang out here and drink all day?"

"I'm your best customer."

"You're not paying, Todd."

"Oh right," I answer with a smile, holding up my glass, signaling for another.

King Asshole stops and gives a bro's handshake to some guy across the room, speaking with him closely before continuing through the bar toward the lobby.

"You know that guy?"

"Michlean? Stays in one of the penthouse suites. Good tipper."

"Could it be he has girls working the resort and brings party favors to the island?"

Kat's eyes widen as she pivots toward me, asking "How do you know that?"

"I got in a shoving match with the asshat this morning after I saw him knock around one of his girls. Thinks he's a badass."

"He IS a badass," Kat cautions. "Not somebody you want to mess with, Todd. He's a pirate. If you want something black market, you almost always have to go through him."

"Like a kidney?"

Kat shrugs, suggesting that might be possible before continuing furtively, "The authorities here have his back. His father is some Greek zillionaire or something. He was born with a silver spoon in his mouth and apparently he must have liked it because he likes the finer things, if you know what I mean. Showed up on the island a couple years ago, with his posse of beautiful women and access to a lot of drugs. Pushed the local dealers out of business. Hard to compete with a guy who employs women who look like that, can get anything your heart desires if you pay him enough, and has his own security to protect him," she pauses, watching him leave before turning back to me. "You're a magnet for trouble, Todd. But this kind of trouble is out of your league. He's a bad human being, his friends are bad human beings and the authorities here are his friends. You're not going to be on St. Carlos that long. Be smart."

"No one's ever accused me of that."

"Not funny. Seriously, be smart," she warns, moving across the bar to take orders.

I've been warned three times now. Isn't that the charm? And it makes karmic sense that my brand-new enemy resides here. This is just one more piece of mangled serendipity to keep my streak alive. I'm going to be around here because Harry's here. And Kat's here. And free drinks are here. It only stands to reason that this guy who threatened to kill me would be staying here as well, with the local authorities wiping his ass every time he gets done shitting on someone.

I don't realize I've been sitting at the bar most of the afternoon mulling over my old mortal enemy and my younger, shinier, new one until I spy Kat's beau, Roger, leaning across the bar and giving her a quick peck. Kat points down to me as she talks closely with him a moment longer before they both move in my direction. Great. Just what I don't want. Before Roger and I even have a chance for 'hellos' Kat settles a longneck down in front of him and tosses me a glower.

"Play nice," she says more to me than him, and walks away.

Turning to Roger, to make sure he can see just how bloodshot my eyes are, I smile.

"Now why does she say things like that? What does she think I'm going to do?"

"She said you've been drinking most of the afternoon."

"Like most of the people in this place."

Avoiding eye contact as he takes a long slug from his beer, he asks, "How long are you staying?"

"Until the wedding."

"Then you're gone?"

I turn to him with a half-grin, eyeing his profile.

"Whatchu asking, man?"

Roger turns to me, his pale blue eyes locking on mine.

"Not trying to be a dick but there are better places to stay than Kat's."

"Not when you're broke," I answer, not wanting to make this easy on him.

"I'll front you a couple nights someplace else," he answers, "I'm looking out for her and Earl."

"Earl doesn't like you. And I didn't know you and Kat were all that tight either. I didn't even know you existed until this morning."

"And I didn't know you existed until Harry Everett showed up and demanded Kat find you."

"I come in peace. Think of me as the long-lost friend in for the wedding of another friend. Okay, yeah, we did have sex but that was like fourteen years ago. Nothing to be afraid of, man, I'm outta here as soon as the 'I dos' are spoken."

He drinks again, leaving me in silence as he formulates an answer.

"You and Kat have a past. I'm trying to have a present. I don't need you in the middle of that. Seriously, I don't think having a drunk hanging out at the house, around Earl, or hanging around Kat all day here, is good for either of them. I mean, would you want someone like you hanging around your girlfriend and her son?"

Ouch. Fuck! Can't argue the logic behind that.

I hang my head and stare at the multiple rings my glass has left on the glossy wood bar. Some stand alone, some intersect, some have grown thick each time I picked up my glass and set it down. My life. If I'm not fucking someone else's woman, I'm drinking someone else's liquor.

"Sure," is all I can muster.

Roger turns toward me, surprise in his narrow glance. He doesn't know what to say or ask, unsure of what I mean.

That makes two of us. Though it's becoming clearer.

"Sure, you'll leave?"

My lips curl at the end. Not really a smile, not really a grimace. I slip off the bar stool, making sure both feet are on the ground. I don't want this ass to see just how drunk I really am.

"I'll get my shit out. You can explain to Kat."

I walk away, each step deliberate, making sure it hits the ground before I take the next one. I have no fucking clue as to where I'm going, and I kind of like that I've left Roger with the task of explaining to Kat that I'm not going to stay at her place, even though I think my present homelessness is a little more serious than him coming up with a white lie to cover his ass.

The further I get from the bar, the more I wish I had punched him and told him I was staying indefinitely.

Making it to the grand lobby, with its stone arches and terrazzo tile floor, I turn in a couple different directions, trying to figure out where a man who just gave away his accommodations and has no money actually goes. A sofa near a TV playing CNN silently with subtitles looks like a winner. I wonder whether Roger would be so kind as to get my stuff and drop it here. He did say he would put me up for a couple nights somewhere, didn't he? I might just pocket that money for drinks and camp out here until the wedding. The resort won't mind, would they? After all, I was infamous around here once upon a time.

My head swims in scotch as I stare up at the massive chandelier that hangs in this alcove of the lobby, wishing the damn sparkly thing would come crashing down and crush me in a jingle-jangled mess of glass and metal. I stare up at it until I fall asleep. Apparently, hoping for my demise has that effect on me. Don't ask me how long I'm out but when I wake up, it's dark outside.

And Harry's next to me.

"What the hell...?" I mumble, my throat scratchy.

"I guess someone saw us together today so they called me. They told me you fell asleep in the lobby. You were snoring. And drooling. It's bad for business, they want you out of here."

"I guess the jet lag caught up with me."

"The liquor caught up with you, shit for brains!" Harry fires back, his voice sounding a bit like the old Harry. "Let me get you a cab so you can get back to Kat's."

"Can't go back to Kat's..."

"What the hell did you do?" Harry snaps.

A feeble smile comes to my lips as I rub my eyes, my neck stiff.

"Goddamn you, Todd. Always have to play the fool!" Harry sighs, exasperated. "I'll get you a room here. You're going to be here most of the time anyway."

"Harry, I don't have the cash to stay here. The cupboards are bare, so to speak. That's why I was at Kat's."

"I didn't say for you to get a room, I said I'll get you a room. I didn't figure you had a pot to piss in or you wouldn't be sleeping here with your finger up your ass and that stupid look you always have when you don't know what the hell you're doing."

"What look is that?"

"Look in the mirror, Todd. It's there all the time."

There's the Harry I know and hate busting through that spray-tanned exterior.

As Harry pulls himself off the sofa, snarling out pissy comments under his breath, I grab his arm, stopping him.

"Before you go I gotta say something. And I want to do it before you go and do something nice for me. Which you might regret."

Harry girds his loins for my onslaught.

"Harry…" I continue, letting his name linger in the air between us for a long moment. "Carolina seems like a really nice person. Really great. And beautiful. But she reminds me of someone. You know who that is? She remind you of anyone, Harry?"

Even under that fake tan I can see Harry's face fill with blood to the point the veins protrude from his freshly-trimmed head.

"Don't piss me off, Todd!" he snarls in a low, almost cruel, voice.

"I'm not trying to piss you off. I'm trying to open your eyes. Good or bad, that's all I'm trying to do," I counter, taking a deep breath, ready to launch the depth charge and blow up his whole fucking world. "Tami! She. Reminds. Me. Of. Tami."

"Todd Fucking Cartwright---!!!"

"Way too close for you to be banging her, in my opinion. It's creepy, Harry. Goddamn, it's just not right!" I erupt.

Physically seething, Harry scowls at me, spittle flying from his tight lips as he screeches, "You are the meanest, dumbest asshole I have ever known!"

While I'd like to argue with his adjectives, I really don't want to do it with him standing over me, his nostrils so wide with anger I swear I can see up into his brain. Besides it's probably true. And having met some of his buddies from back in Chicago, that's saying something.

"She does. I know you know it. You can't not! That giggle, come on, Harry; you have to hear it, its Tami's."

"Tami laughed just like her mother, Evie, you nitwit! If Carolina reminds me of anyone it's Evie, NOT Tami. Bad as I was in my marriage, I still always found Evie beautiful and alluring."

I want to say that this mea culpa makes everything all right but we're far from that threshold.

"Harry, she's easily twenty years younger than you. She's not even my age, is she?"

"So?"

"So? I don't know, you tell me. When did this new Harry emerge from his cocoon and become this tanned butterfly in khaki slacks? Did she pull this Houdini act on you? Changing you from a horse's ass into a stallion?"

"I was tired of how I looked. I joined a gym, got a trainer. I bought some clothes, went and had my hair styled…"

"Harry, you don't have any hair!"

"I have some and it always looked like shit. I was tired of looking like shit, Todd. My exterior was copying my interior. So to help me change my interior, I changed the exterior. Nothing wrong with self-improvement, jackass. You should try it!"

"At least you can still recognize me, Harry."

"You say that as if it's a good thing."

Owww. That cut deep.

"Did you do this for yourself or for her?" I ask.

"Did you change for yourself or for Tami?" he returns volley.

Damn him, he's winning this verbal knife fight. The look in Harry's eyes transforms from anger to empathy. Something rare for him. At least the old him.

"Yes, Carolina has that special something other women I've loved in my life have had. I know she's younger than me. I know all of it, Todd. Do you think I'm some rube that doesn't realize things?"

I sit back and sigh, wishing I hadn't slept off most of my drunk.

"Why is she marrying you, Harry?"

"Why don't you interrogate her?" he snaps. Then realizing what he said, he immediately waves his hands in my face. "No! Don't you dare! You leave her alone or I will kill you!"

"Second time today someone's threatened to do that. I'm very popular. Look, Harry, I'm not trying to be a bitch here, I'm trying to look out for you. I'm surprised when I get word you're getting hitched, I'm surprised you wanted me here, I'm surprised when you show up looking like an old GTO with a new paint job, rims and a spoiler, and I'm surprised when the woman you're marrying reminds me of your daughter and isn't much older. What am I supposed to think? Especially when you and I have the fucking history we have!"

"I decided to live life, Todd. If you don't want to be happy for me and Carolina, well, it would fit right in with how you do pretty much everything. I hoped you'd be a different person when I saw you again. But you're back to the person you were when I first met you."

"Worse."

"Have it your way. Worse. I wanted you to come down here and celebrate with me. Celebrate me getting married, celebrate me being happy. Celebrating life, including your own, for Christsake! If you can't do that, go back to wherever the hell you were. I don't need you ruining this for Carolina. That would be unforgiveable." Harry looks down on me, his eyes equal parts sad and mad. I remember that look. It may not have been on a tanned face with the little, crinkly hairs all trimmed and neat, but it's like I've gone back in time to the lowest point in my life.

That's when the harshest realization I've ever had hits me. The lowest point of my life wasn't then, it's right now.

"You're right."

Harry looks at me as if I'm speaking ancient Arabic.

"You're right, Harry. I claim I'm not being a bitch but I'm being a bitch," I say emphatically. "All of this...you, her...it's out of sorts for me. And I can find the gray cloud on a sunny day. Because for me, there's always a gray cloud."

"Not this time," he says, a pale but buoyant smile sliding onto his lips like they've been sprayed with Pam.

"I'm happy for you. Seriously. You deserve happiness, and if Carolina is that happiness, damn it, Harry, I'm proud of you," I say, adding with a smirk, "And I hope I look as good as you at your age."

Harry's smile grows. "You'll be fucking dead!"

We both laugh. Harry sticks out his hand. I shake it.

"Dinner? Viola's?"

I nod. A smile comes at the memory.

"We're going to make a hell of a week of it, Todd."

Again, I only nod.

"We'll finish with a bang, not a whimper. Maybe tonight you and I can get up and dance together, show them how it's done," Harry chortles wisely.

This fucker is nuts. And it looks like I'm joining the circus.

## THE NEW ME

Five days. I can do this. I can be the guy who survives the wedding of my never-to-be father-in-law to a woman who reminds me in bits and pieces of my dead fiancée. Easy-peezy lemon-squeezy, as a girl I dated in high school used to say. She was easy-peezy and there was lots of squeezy.

Like many guys, I haven't changed much since high school.

I catch a ride with one of the bartenders to the other side of the island to retrieve my gear from Kat's. Arriving, Roger's truck isn't in the driveway so I will get a partially clean getaway. Knocking, Earl opens the door.

"Hey. Didn't Mom give you a key?"

"No," I answer, moving past him into the living room. "She here?"

"No. She and Roger went to dinner. I think it's something special, like their anniversary or something."

Yeah. The four-hour anniversary of him banishing me from his kingdom.

As I move through the kitchen to the small room behind it, I ask, "Which anniversary? I didn't think they knew each other that long."

"They haven't," Earl replies, staying a few steps behind me. "Maybe he's counting in dog years or something."

I smile as I grab my bag, throwing the few things not inside on top and zipping it.

"Where are you going?" Earl asks, leaning against the doorjamb.

"I'm getting a room at the resort. With Roger here, I'm kind of in the way."

"Now you know how I feel," Earl muses.

The bag zipped, I turn toward Earl. From the expression on his face, he means it.

"You know you're the man of the house," I tell him with direct sincerity.

Earl shifts on his feet uncomfortably. He shrugs a couple times as if he's mulling that concept. I don't live here, I don't know what's going on. But I do know he's a young teen and it's been him and his mom for a long time.

"Whatever," he finally responds dismissively. "He likes my mom. Probably more than she likes him. And a lot more than I like him."

"Your mother has never had great taste in men," I remark with self-deprecation that he doesn't understand.

Walking past him, I can't believe this kid is almost as tall as I am and how uncomfortable he seems in his body. When I was his age, I hated that everyone treated me like I was older because I was bigger than everyone else my age and matured a little earlier. The kids my age were scared of me which I attributed to my big forehead, thick brow and the whiskers that started filling in on my jaw long before some of their balls dropped. It all combined to make me look angrier than I probably was. Or more accurately, wanted to be.

Other kids made fun of me. Never to my face but I knew it. I remember wanting more than anything to be friends with some kids my age but it never happened, so I found trouble with kids a few years older. I was easy to talk into doing the dumbest thing possible, often taking the fall which I felt I deserved for being both the youngest and the stupidest. I'm not sure what Earl's deal is but I sense he's not the most popular boy at school. And on an island, I imagine that can be a social death sentence. There's nowhere to go to get away from it. No starting over.

I want to tell Earl it'll all work out, but truth is, if I'm any example, he'll never really get completely comfortable being the big guy. His body will become his tank, protecting all the bullshit going on inside. And when he lashes out, it will be effective, giving him a false sense of his place in the world.

"So, what about you? You got a girlfriend?" I ask, heading back through the kitchen to the living room.

"I'm thirteen."

"So," I say, turning back to him, "I was interested in girls at thirteen."

"How do you know I'm not interested in guys?"

"Are you?"

"No. But it was worth saying for the look on your face."

I like this kid.

"I got some stuff to do, man. So I'll let you bail," Earl says, turning around to head back down the hallway to his sanctuary.

"Bail?"

He turns back around and looks at me with a shrug. "Mom said you always bail."

"I don't always bail," I answer, my feelings hurt, "Your mother knows that."

"Whatever. Didn't mean nothing by it. It's cool," he says before shuffling down the hallway to his room. I hear the door shut.

Debating whether I should go knock on his door to let him know I'm a better guy than my reputation would lead him to believe, I opt to let the rumor fester. No point stirring up any more shit. Besides, he's not used to my boundless charm and creamy smooth personality. I'm an acquired taste, and probably much better as his monster than a friend to a thirteen-year-old.

Walking out of the house without a goodbye to Earl and unsure whether Kat knows I'm 'bailing' on her hospitality, I take in her small cottage. Kat's raised her son in this little place. They aren't living the high life but they survive perfectly fine. They seem happy other than the normal teenage angst and ennui. Unlike me, Kat always possesses contentment, as if she is exactly where she should be in life. There is an acceptance of what life throws at her and she handles it with ease though it's doubtful it's ever been easy. No one raising a kid alone has it easy. Especially when you're a working mother.

In spite of Earl being unusually large for thirteen, an age where hormones collide with bad choices, he doesn't seem as big of a prick as other teenagers I have known. Unlike me, there's a gentle sweetness to his hulkiness. Maybe I had that once but it was beaten out of me. But I appreciate it when I see it. Earl wears his insecurities on his sleeve and hasn't harnessed the power of being big yet. That will come with age and a few more bruises. From the little I've gleaned from mother and son, I would never refer to their relationship as typical but it certainly isn't out of the ordinary considering the circumstance. Until Earl is on his own, he and Kat will always be dubious of one another, all the while making sure the other knows that home is their safe haven.

"All da way over to Viola's he cursed you, Mr. Todd," Tomas relays, rattled at the one-sided conversation he had with Harry while driving him and Carolina to dinner. "He kept warning…I don't know who…dat you better not be late for dinner."

I am.

I had to get back to the resort from Kat's which meant sticking out my thumb. After ten minutes of only one car driving past and not stopping, I returned to Kat's and borrowed one of the mopeds from the side of the house, hoping her earlier offer hadn't expired. Holding onto my bag with one hand and steering with the other, the narrow seat crawls up my already aching ass like a string bikini. And once back at the resort, I had to stand in line behind the tourists checking in to get a room pass and hey, I have a lot of body to shower and dry. As I got downstairs, showered, changed and ready for the evening, I found Tomas racing through the lobby searching for me per Harry's demand.

Embarrassingly, I have nothing to give Tomas for the ride. He laughs it off, but I feel like shit. I regret all the booze I drank at the airport and on the planes because most of my cash was allocated to getting loaded — although I probably wouldn't have made it down to the island without it — but now there's not a cent to my name and it's humiliating.

"When you can, Mr. Todd," Tomas says, shaking my hand.

"That might be never, Tomas."

"You are always rich in spirit, Mr. Todd," he answers, smiling as I step from the cab.

I wish I possessed an ounce of his optimism.

Viola's. There was a new coat of paint haphazardly applied to the outside walls but the door that leads inside still squeaks loudly as if to comfort guests with its familiarity. I feel giddy as the spicy aroma filling the building tickles my nose. Hearing the tinkling sound of plates and glasses fraternizing with the voices of people enjoying themselves and the sexy, joyous live music from the trio that plays in the corner, I'm overcome with a sense of repose I don't often feel.

"I remember you," a voice says, as I search the packed dining room for Harry and Carolina.

Viola. Regal elegance still radiating from her dark, glistening skin.

"You remember me. Uh-oh. I think I behaved pretty well last time I was here."

"You danced."

I did. The first night I was ever in this place was magical. I was healing from my beating, stitches still holding me together but I got up and danced. The entire evening, from the people to the meal, even Harry's constant scolding, was one of those nights that lingers in your memory, always bringing a forlorn smile. As long as I live, this place will always be special to me.

"Your friend is over there, anxiously awaiting your arrival," Viola purrs, her eyes holding bemusement at Harry's impatience, as she points to a corner table which four people crowd around.

I wind my way through the tables and bodies, moving toward Harry who finally spots me and stands, his hands going into the air as he calls to me, "Please tell me you're not going to be late on my wedding day."

His words cause everyone else at the table to turn. Tucked back into the corner next to Harry, Carolina smiles. But with them are Kat and Roger. Kat smiles, Roger forces something onto his lips he must believe is a smile but more resembles a pit bull that lost a dogfight. He locks his sights on me trying to get me to lock mine on his which I refuse to do. Fuck him.

"Look who else was here!" Harry exclaims, as I make it to the table. "I insisted they join us."

"How's that for luck?" I respond, kissing Kat on the cheek and shaking Roger's hand with my back to him before greeting Harry and Carolina.

The only open chair is on the other side of Kat. Perfect. As I sit, the tension at the table rises noticeably. Harry, playing host, slaps me on the back.

"What took you so long?" he quizzes.

I grin idiotically for a moment, letting the question graze me like a bullet as I reach past Harry and touch Carolina's hand. Luckily, the vibe in this place keeps me mellow, as if Viola has opened her home to me and told me to take my shoes off and relax. A great hostess, she sets the mood of this place.

"Forget me, Harry," I announce. "I want to know more about this beautiful woman." Turning to Carolina I ask, "You stole this guy's heart. Something some of us didn't even know he had."

Both Carolina's and Kat's laughs are tinged with effort but Harry — knowing me under very different circumstances and having weathered much worse from me — laughs unbridled. Roger sizes me up, wondering just how big a dick I can be. Maybe he should sit next to Harry and listen to a few of my war stories as told by the master while Carolina and I talk.

Carolina lays out the basics of her life — she was raised in Georgia, though her mother was a native South Carolinian, thus her name, but she moved to Chicago when she was almost thirty. She works in marketing and has been freelancing for the past couple years. She met Harry a few months ago and something clicked and they've been together ever since. Through it all she giggles sweetly, which causes me to twitch each time. Not unnoticed by Harry.

It all sounds generic and rehearsed. I sense Carolina is spoon-feeding me what she wants me to know. It's not that she's hesitant or cagey but being a master of providing selective history, I sense she's designed this story with Harry's approval and is being careful to stick to the script. Much like the heavy makeup and the tidal wave of hair, she has created a charming mask to keep anyone from seeing what she doesn't want them to see. She can be anything she wants to be, and tell me what she wants me to know. She and I will never be more than we are right now. On opposite sides of Harry. And he seems pleased; so fuck it, I can handle a charade for a few more days! I'm not the one marrying her.

Harry orders a second bottle of wine for the table. I've never seen him so bubbly. I watch him closely and every time his eyes travel to Carolina, there's a subtle flicker, a warmth that even my stone-heart feels is genuine. His entire being glows. God, I remember that. I crave to feel that again. It's been so long now I can barely grasp I ever touched it, like the fingertips of someone trying to save me that never actually grabbed hold before I fell. I can't help but be happy for Harry. The old goat has done what I failed to do. He transformed himself into someone people actually enjoy being around. He found a woman that loves him and he clearly loves her back. Even though I suspect pieces are missing, if the end result is Harry's contentment, who am I to judge? Okay, I judge. But damn it, he has everything I once had!

That I still want.

I cannot begrudge him his happiness; after all, I know just how rare a gift it is.

I would love to know what she sees in Harry. What made them click. Especially Harry, pre-transformation. How did she know he was a diamond in the rough and not just some fossilized animal turd? But tonight isn't the time. I'll find a moment before the nuptials to privately quiz her about her attraction to Harry, though I sense this is a woman who would take in a stray dog if she found it on the street. I mean any man can look at her and look at Harry — even with his new, shiny veneer — and know he's the lucky one of the couple. But I need to know she loves him for him. Whichever him that is. I'd hate to find out she took him on as a project. There's only two results to that endeavor. One, the project is a failure and they break up out of frustration. Or the project is a success, in which case, the fixee no longer has any need for the mechanics of a fixer. Maybe I'm overthinking this, but I truly want this relationship to be about more. For Harry. For Tami. If something goes wrong with this relationship, I know Harry will never venture into the deep, murky waters of the relationship pool again.

"How do you and Roger know each other, Kat?" Carolina asks, deflecting the conversation from herself as the next bottle of wine arrives at the table.

Now it's Kat's turn to relay her story. I find myself not listening. Glancing around the restaurant, I don't see Viola who usually floats through the place, greeting people and talking to each table. Thank God we are here and not one of the over-priced, chi-chi restaurants planted inside each and every hotel or resort along the beach. If I were having to endure being odd-man-out in a place I didn't feel comfortable, I'd lunge at that bottle of wine and rip the cork out with my teeth. But here in Viola's, I'm content sipping from my glass, soaking up the aromas that breeze through the dining room and the energetic conversations and laughter erupting from each table. Hell, I can be my own significant other. I'm pretty sure I'm going home alone anyway. Though you never know, the night's still young.

Once Kat finishes her story to my complete disinterest, mostly because I think Roger is a douchebag, Carolina points at me.

"And you and Todd know each other too, don't you, Kat?" she asks harmlessly.

"We're…old friends," Kat answers, her look a mixture of amusement and discomfort. Thank God she's already tossed back a couple glasses of Pinot. Being slightly lubricated keeps this moment from being too awkward.

"Did you meet here on the island?" Carolina quizzes, oblivious to how much a few of us at the table want to drop this line of questioning.

"No, no," Kat throws off casually, "We met back in the States."

Sensing there's more to the story, Carolina leans in and smiles. "Oh…?"

While I wait to see whether she has the balls to go there, Kat slams down what's left of the Pinot in her wine glass and responds, "Fourteen years ago, I waited on him in a cocktail lounge, we slept together and he left without saying goodbye."

Carolina breaks up laughing at Kat's brazenness. Harry, on the other hand, his face puckers up like he's just taken a pill and it's dissolved in his mouth instead of going down.

"Why don't I find that a surprise?" he utters, looking directly at me.

"In my defense, I was young," I answer as Roger shifts irritably in his chair. Which might be the only thing I'll enjoy about this.

"You're still young, Todd," Harry retorts, not ready to give this up. "Not as young as you act most of the time, but you've got plenty of living to do. I was just hoping for something a little sweeter, you know, something out of the ordinary for you."

"I never deviate from my path, Harry."

Kat raises her hand and continues, "Takes two to tango, Harry, and back in the day I tangoed pretty hard myself. Not something I'm proud of but not something I regret either. If you're going to be mad at Todd for anything be mad at him for not remembering me when he saw me here last time you two were on the island."

"That doesn't surprise me either," Harry says with a sad shake of his head.

"But in his defense, he was pretty much a big, fat mess then," Kat states with a grin.

I raise my glass.

"Cheers!"

Carolina laughs, which makes me like her more.

"Do you remember every guy you ever slept with?" I ask Kat.

She thinks a moment, her head tilting. "Most, I guess. Yes. Most."

"But not all."

"I'm not on trial here," she says, her head darting in Roger's direction, "Be nice, Todd, I just pulled you out from under the bus."

"And I appreciate that. I admit, I do not remember every woman I've had sex with. Sorry. Don't," I say, turning in Carolina's direction. "Prior to Tami I was pretty much as Kat would describe me, a hot mess. After Tami I was pretty much as Harry described me, a big, fat mess. The common denominator is me being a mess. The only time I wasn't was when I had the unconditional love of a woman who for some reason thought I was the best thing since potato chips in a can. I can't explain it, even after musing on it for the last five years. But she did. And her belief in me changed me."

"It did," Kat chimes in, "And you're not a total mess now, Todd. You're a mess but you can no longer be a total mess because you know what it's like not to be one thanks to her."

This causes Harry to smile. Which in turn causes me to smile. Damn. She's right. I'm just a partial mess because I know what it's like to be loved. I'll take that. It's not exactly the penthouse of compliments but it beats the view from the basement.

"That's so sweet," Carolina says to Kat, "I can see why you and Todd are friends."

I can't help but look directly at Kat who is looking directly at me.

"You're lucky too," Carolina says to Roger, patting his hand as if he's the odd-man-out and not me.

Roger lets a hard smile cross his lips, which never part. "I am," he answers without elaborating just as plates of food are set down amid all of us on the table.

Douche. Roger better not try to grab the last plantain or he'll find my fork driven through his hand.

The server smiles and says, "Enjoy!" before retreating to the kitchen.

Glancing around to compliment Viola, I notice she's still missing in action from the dining room. The heady combination of the spices in the meats and vegetables, mixed with the wine makes me sit back and allow everyone else to serve themselves first. I don't remember seeing Harry enjoy himself more. I know he appreciates me accepting Carolina and despite my reservations and suspicions, I won't pepper her with questions to try to find the chink in her armor.

Even Roger's occasional disapproving glances bounce off me like my t-shirt is made of Kevlar. He should be kissing my big, black-and-blue ass. I haven't said a word to Kat about being persona non grata at her house, which judging from her mood she doesn't know a thing about yet. Let Roger confess if he's man enough. Can't worry about it, I'm not the one sleeping with him.

My belly full, my mind at ease, I feel better than I have in a long, long time. Coming back to the island may not be the horror story I envisioned. I have a few friends at this table. I've forgotten what this feels like having opted to travel the world, never staying long enough anywhere for anyone to really care about me, insulating myself from judgments. I also make sure they never get close enough to care about me. Being a modern-day nomad is a safe but selfish existence.

People get up from their meals and dance. Obviously a tradition that has stayed at Viola's, and it only adds another tier of joy to the evening. For the first time since I can remember, I'm not looking for an escape route. This is where I want to be. With these people. Hell, I'm actually enjoying myself. I've almost forgotten what that feels like. It amazes me that I've drifted so far from this feeling that it feels almost foreign.

Excusing myself from the table to use the restroom, I nudge Harry to order another bottle of wine before meandering through the dancers, stopping to dance with a couple young ladies, then an older woman, then a group of people, on my way to the bathroom. With each stop, Harry gives me the thumbs up, like I'm putting on this performance for him. But I'm doing this for me. Because it feels so damn good.

Harry, Carolina, Roger and Kat dance together as I slip out from the dining room and into the narrow hallway leading to the lone bathroom in the back. The bathroom in use, I hang out in the dingy hallway just outside the kitchen waiting my turn.

Through the window in the swinging kitchen doors, I can see the staff hustling plates of food the chefs have prepared onto trays to be carried out as more servers enter, a continuous loop of movement from the kitchen to the dining room. Watching them work, I smile. Their routine is almost musical, each person in sync with the others, never bumping into one another, never a mistake. It's like a band that has played together so long they can riff on the music and it is seamless, never losing its rhythm.

The bathroom door opens and a beautiful woman steps out, giving me a smile. If I were on the hunt, this would have been my opening, but not tonight, tonight I'm a team player. As I turn from the window in the kitchen door, I stop. Peering back in as I crane my neck, I see Viola having an argument in the corner of the kitchen, the men washing dishes watching uneasily. I only see the guy she's face to face with from the back, but from his build and long, wavy hair, I know exactly who he is.

Staying at the window, I observe, battling the urge to plunge through the door, grab Michlean by his overly-product-filled mane and shove his face into a large pot of boiling water. Unfortunately, I'm not drunk enough to throw all caution to the wind and though it aches me, I stay vigilant at the door, my eyes on his back, as Viola steps away from him stiffly. He snaps his fingers at the eavesdropping kitchen staff, ordering them back to work. Viola returns with an envelope and hands it to him. Michlean peeks inside. Even from my point of view I can see cash. Though I can't tell what denomination, there's a lot of it. Satisfied, he holds up the envelope and says something to her before slapping her across the face with it.

    My breath catches in my throat and just as I'm about to shoulder my way through the swinging kitchen door, Michlean turns and walks directly for it. It's a have-your-cake-and-eat-it-too moment as I duck down into a linebacker's stance just under the window where he cannot see me. As I feel his hand pushing the door open, I charge with everything I have, smashing him back, my bruised legs pumping like a locomotive. Crashing through the door, Michlean flies back, splaying out in the middle of the kitchen floor as I trample right over his sorry ass. The money from the envelope flutters through the air and spreads across the floor. Startled, everyone else backs toward a wall, even Viola, who one would think is hard to fluster. She stares at me in shock.

    Groggy but livid, Michlean attempts to sit up but the bottom of my sandal lands on his neck, pressing him down. Fuck this piece of shit! I don't care how powerful he believes he is, he's a grade-A asswipe and if there's one thing I hate in the world it's that. While my behavior is often suspect, there are lines I will not cross and things I cannot tolerate. I've seen this guy in action two too many times now not to step in. My better sense is having the shit kicked out of it by my rage but right here, right now, that's how I want it, come what may.

His eyes take a moment to focus as his hands go to my leg, trying to push my foot off his throat.

"Your Momma didn't teach you how to treat a woman, did she?" I spit out, leaning more of my weight onto his neck.

"You're dead," he gurgles from the floor.

"You mentioned that this morning and I'm still alive with my foot on your neck," I respond, again applying more pressure. "Karma don't like men that hit women."

His eyes travel down his body, which sends a cold shiver up my spine as he continues to use his hands to push on my foot, trying to keep me from crushing his throat. He lets go of my foot, his hand grabbing at his pants leg. Spinning, I see the bulge under his pants near his ankle. My survival instincts being what they are, I quickly kneel on top of him and shove my hand up his pants leg, finding a holster strapped to his calf. Yanking at the Velcro, I pull it free, slide the gun from the case and point it at him.

"You would have shot me, wouldn't you, you pumped-up little bitch?"

"And watched you bleed to death," he snarls as I pull my foot off his neck.

A swipe of blood from where he bashed his head as he fell wipes across the floor when he sits up. The first thing he does is straighten his shirt over his wide chest and arms, as if it's automatic for him to intimidate others using the size of his body. Being a big guy myself, turning myself into a Kodiak bear and growling is not an exercise that's unfamiliar, I just find it comical that it's the first thing this guy does.

"That your money?" I ask, looking toward Viola.

Her eyes go to Michlean as if asking his permission what to say or do.

"Pick it up," I add, before he can answer.

"You heard the dead man, pick up your money!" Michlean growls more at me than her.

Viola slips around the both of us and picks up the cash, sliding it back in the envelope which lays a few feet away. As she stands, her eyes lock on mine.

"I don't think you know what you're doing," she speaks softly.

Not the first time I've heard that today either. And she's probably right but that's never been my main consideration when something boils me into a frenzy. And this fucktard sitting on the kitchen floor isn't the first person in line who wanted me dead. Harry led that parade for a while and look at us now. I'm giving him away at his wedding.

Not that I discount the warnings I've been given about this guy. I know when I'm fighting a pole cat. And if I didn't cross a line with him this morning, judging from the kitchen staff's fearful, wide-eyed stares, I certainly did tonight.

One I might not be able to walk myself back from.

My mind races. I don't know how to deal with this from here. I've never taken something to this end before, one where the consequences could be lethal. For me. If this guy is all that and a bag of bullets, I don't have the wherewithal to fight him and whatever army he has at his command. My grand skill, my ability to buffalo my way to safety, might not work with someone who truly wants me dead. There's danger and then there's really fucking stupid. I think I've stepped in a big, gooey pile of the latter.

Michlean climbs warily to his feet, his eyes never leaving the gun in my hand. I sense he's not sure just how crazy I am. I'd like to keep that advantage. I could shoot him dead, but there would be a boatload of witnesses, and I don't know who might be pro-Michlean and anti-me among the kitchen staff.

"You are a huge pile of shit!" I growl, which elicits a chilling laugh from Michlean. "You really get off humiliating women, don't you? Well, shit stain, your mommy issues end today. I don't ever want to see you near this woman again," I continue, pointing to Viola as I feel the first drops of sweat rolling down my head to my back. "I'm on this island for quite a while and if I find out you've come after her, they'll have to hold the annual Easter egg hunt a little early to find all the pieces of you I spread on this island."

"Not if I kill you first," he threatens effortlessly.

"You are smart enough to understand I'm holding the gun, right? Your gun. Wrap your peanut brain around this, I'm giving you a chance to deal with this like a man," I say, hoping that offending his intelligence and masculinity will curb this battle. "Are you a man, Michlean?"

"You'll find out."

"You're one more smartass answer away from dying on this floor. Stay away from this woman, stay out of my way. Can you handle that?"

"You're a big target," he responds.

Guess he's not smart enough or man enough. Great. Now would certainly be the time to jump to Plan B if I actually had a Plan B. I'm painted into a corner. A place where I often lose control. Desperation only serves to piss me off even more. But I have to keep my shit together here and de-escalate this mess before I have no choice but to shoot this bastard in the face. Taking a deep breath, my mind spins like the drums of a slot machine trying to devise an exit strategy. But all that pops into my head is that I want to beat this bully senseless.

I have always hated bullies. Admittedly, I am a professional jackass, but I've never been a bully. I grew up the son of one. So it burns my gut like a bleeding ulcer when I see anyone prey on others. I have a pretty dark soul and it grows mean when confronted by this type of subhuman. I wish when I had met him this morning I had gone apeshit and put his sorry, pathetic, woman-beating ass in the hospital. It would have saved me from this semi-public spectacle. There are too many eyes in this kitchen, all cemented on me. If I do anything too stupid, I'll be spending a lot of time on this island. In an eight-by-eight cell.

"Outside," I command, waving the gun at the glowering prick in front of me. Whatever I'm going to do, I can't do it here. So no one on the kitchen staff has thought to whip out their cell phones and record my dubious heroics to post on social media. I need to be a ghost before anyone does. The Constables would be here posthaste and if the gossip is true about Michlean paying them off, they wouldn't be on my side.

I march Michlean past Viola toward a back door propped open by a trash can to let in some cool sea air. As I walk past it, I kick the trash can out of the way, letting the door close. No more eyes. He and I end up near the dumpster, the incessant hum of flies the only thing between us. His eyes still size me up, trying to gauge exactly how far I want to take this. Something I haven't even decided myself.

"Okay fuckhead," I bark, tired of him looking for a weakness to exploit. "There's a couple ways we can play this. Most mean you end up hurt or dead."

"You got that in you?" he dares with cold assurance.

I automatically smile. Surprising even me. This schmuck doesn't know me. I'm not by nature a man who can kill. But if I sense you are coming for the people I love, there would be no hesitation. I'd have nightmares the rest of my life and there would be a cloak of self-loathing I'd have to shoulder, but I'm already paying for hundreds of past sins, killing this prick wouldn't even make my top ten.

"I have this compelling urge to fuck you up. Bad," I snarl, moving at him, causing him to cross his arms over his chest defiantly as he takes a step in retreat. "I've been accused of having a death wish. It's caused me to think about my life. The conclusion I came to…I don't really give a stinking fuck. Living's great and all, but dying…" I shrug before continuing, "I've had all that's important to me taken away, so I'm probably long overdue. You don't scare me like you do these other people. The world will not miss you."

"Then shoot me."

We lock eyes. I am big on looking people in the eyes. I find it is more intimidating than the size of someone's shoulders or arms. Most people do not want to be looked at directly in the eyes. It threatens them. I enjoy the sense of insanity that staring unblinkingly into another person's eyes creates.

"I don't want to," I answer. "I want you to walk away. With your tail between your legs, but alive. Because I don't give a shit about you. Not even enough to kill you. You've got some little island empire to run. Have at it. Just leave the people I know alone."

"Work for me," he answers, standing taller, bouncing his biceps in his tight shirt, letting me know he's nervous too. "You're new to the island. Judging from your looks, you came with a bag in your hand and little else, running away from something or someone, wanting to start over. You need money. Unless you got yourself a sugar mama or daddy, you're going to need a job. I have a few things a man of your size and attitude would be right for."

I kind of liked it better when he was spouting off about killing me.

"I'm not working for you. Ever. There's a lot of things a man of my size and attitude can do for money," I sniff. "You got balls, I'll give you that, though I'm guessing the testosterone you've been shooting into your ass has shrunk them up quite a bit. I'm offering you an out, you going to take it, raisin balls?"

"If I take it, you're going to trust that I'll stick to it?" He smiles.

"Your word isn't worth spit. But I know a hell of a lot more about you than you know about me. I know how to get to you. I know how to get to what's important to you. And I have no vested interest on this island," I lie. "So you want the out, or you want to take this to hell?"

"Todd..." I hear behind me.

Jerking my head around, Harry stands off to my right, at the corner of the building.

Fuck! Bad timing. This I don't need.

"Go back inside."

Michlean eyes Harry, who takes a step toward us, his head craning in Michlean's direction.

"That you, Michlean?"

Michlean smiles, his eyes darting back and forth between me and Harry, making a connection.

"Harry Everett, yeah, it's me. You know this guy?"

"Sure. He's---"

"Shut up, Harry!" I snap like a barbed whip, cutting him off, "Go inside."

But Harry can't. He cannot leave well enough alone, his ability to size up a situation pathetically underdeveloped. It's why I abhorred him throughout my engagement to Tami and it's now about to come back to bite both of us in the ass in a big way.

"What are you two talking about?" Harry asks.

"Your friend is threating to kill me, Harry," Michlean utters, enjoying how the power dynamic has just shifted by the arrival of our mutual very short friend.

"What?!"

"He wants to kill me. Move a little closer, Harry, he has a gun."

As Harry does as Michlean asks, his eyes widen and he bellows, "Todd! What are you doing?!"

"Shut. The. Fuck. Up. And. Go. Inside."

"Your name is Todd," Michlean remarks coolly.

"Good God, will one of you boys tell me what is going on?" Harry continues.

Right now no jury in the world would convict me if I pumped about a half-dozen bullets into Michlean and one into Harry. I might be doing him a favor since he's just put his own life in danger. As well as Carolina's.

"How do you know this son-of-a-bitch?" I ask, trying to curtail Harry revealing any more information about me.

"Michlean is in the suite above us at the resort. We met him in the elevator," Harry responds before turning it back to me, "Where did you get a gun, Todd?"

"I took it from this piece of shit. He was shaking down Viola for money."

Harry's head twists from side to side like he's keeping tempo, from me to Michlean and back.

"I can't believe it..." Harry mutters astounded.

"Yeah, well, then you probably wouldn't have liked it when I ran into him this morning, smacking the crap out of one of the young girls he pimps out."

Having always had a clear sense of right and wrong, Harry stiffens.

"Is this…true?" Harry asks Michlean, as if quizzing his own child about a dirty magazine found under the bed.

"Tell me about Todd, Harry. He's not a big fan of the truth, is he? He saw me come out back to have a smoke and not having a fucking nickel to his name he thought he would rob me."

Immobilized by confusion, Harry stammers, which pisses me off. How could Harry doubt what I just told him? I'm a lot of things but he has to know everything out of this scummy liar's mouth doesn't compute.

"For Christsake, Harry, you don't believe me, ask Viola! How could you entertain anything this fuck says?" I wave the gun at Michlean, almost hoping it will go off.

As Michlean laughs, Harry shakes his head and licks his lips. It's as if you can see the truth percolating in his head like my grandmother's coffee pot. But now he has no idea what to do. His presence has made a bad situation a hell of a lot worse and he knows it.

"I'm…I'm going to get to the bottom of this," Harry mutters, backing away until he disappears around the corner, leaving me alone with Michlean.

"Now I know something about you," Michlean cackles.

"Offer's still on the table. You walk away, don't fuck with the people I know, stay away from me, we both go on with our lives."

"And if I don't, one of us is dead," he threatens.

"Exactly," I respond, not taking his bait.

Michlean's biceps continue to bounce as he silently mulls. In the bleak light, his half-smile is more menacing, his eyes hard to see. Taking a step back, he glances toward the parking lot.

"Your car's right there," I point out, knowing.

"It's a small island. We will see each other," he says, moving out of the light and deeper into the shadows as he turns to walk away.

"Better hope not."

Would it be wrong of me to shoot him in the back when I had every opportunity to shoot him in the face?

I take a deep breath as if I'd been holding mine throughout this entire unpleasant event.

Fuck! More than fuck! This is an epic clusterfuck! As I listen to the engine of his Camaro rev before peeling out of the parking lot, I tuck the gun into the back of my shorts, pulling my shirt over it. I'm gonna need it. With Harry and Carolina staying in the room below Michlean. How can I protect them? Hopefully Harry can be convinced to change resorts for his and Carolina's safety. I'm grateful Kat's face and name stayed out of it. That would have really cooked the goose.

I lean back against the wall to try regain my mental bearings. I dread going back inside and having Harry glare at me the rest of the night. Who knows what tale he spun to everyone at the table. Kat will freak out. She sent up a flare about Michlean that I ignored. But what was I supposed to do?

Even when I'm doing the right thing, I end up doing it the wrong way. And it comes back to sledgehammer me in the back of the head. Maybe I should have stayed on the sidelines. But a guy hitting a woman always causes me to respond irrationally.

Thanks, Dad! Because of you the horizon has shitstorm written all over it.

## REACTOR MELTDOWN

Walking back through the restaurant, Viola catches my eye. I mouth the words, 'I'm sorry.' She nods with an odd look I can't decipher. Fear? Gratitude? Pity? And then I see Harry. He's not exactly scowling, though I am sure if Carolina weren't flanking him and Kat and Roger weren't across the table, he would be.

But hell, he has a right to be enraged that I cannot be counted on to simply show up, smile and be supportive. No, I had to find a way to jackboot his wedding plans, kicking them over and over until they are bloody and beyond repair.

Harry hates that. He's the guy who plans dinner at breakfast, breakfast at dinner, and lunch would be the same every day. There is a rhythm to Harry, which—at least until recently—was unwaveringly staccato. There were only minor variations, often too subtle to notice and usually unintended. Harry never likes being blown off-course. When Tami met me I was the hurricane that buffeted him in different directions. A big part of the reason he hated me so intensely is because I threw him off his game.

And I imagine I pretty much accomplished that trick again. Ta-da!

But he doesn't want Carolina to know because as I return to the table, she smiles.

"Where have you been?" she almost purrs, her vowels sounding even more southern, probably from the liquor.

"I had a....I was dealing with…some stuff. A phone call…" I respond, failing at not stammering, matching her smile as if nothing is wrong.

Kat throws me a disbelieving side-eye, recognizing an ass-covering when she hears it. She catches my off-kilter vibe like she's plugged into the same socket, knowing whatever went down while I was gone, it wasn't savory and somehow Harry was involved.

"It's getting late. Maybe we should get home," Harry chirps in a clipped tone.

"One more drink, Harry. We're celebrating love tonight," I counter.

"Another bottle," I call as the waitress passes by, raising the nearly empty wine bottle before pouring what's left into my glass.

"We both work tomorrow," Roger says, his hand slipping over and covering Kat's to emphasize the 'we'.

He stands before Kat has a chance to respond. She pastes a smile on her lips, scoots her chair back noisily as if making a point — though I am unsure whether it's aimed at me or him — and stands up.

"I guess that means we're going," Kat remarks, obviously not thrilled about leaving or about being told when to leave.

Roger and Kat thank Harry and Carolina; there are handshakes and kisses all around, before Roger excuses himself to use the bathroom. Once he disappears down the hallway, Kat's eyes land on me like a wrecking ball.

"What is going on?" she asks pointedly.

Instinctively, Harry and I glance toward each other, playing chicken as to who is going to say something.

"The looks you two are giving each other are taking me back a few years. It wasn't much fun then and it's not now," Kat continues.

His hands flying into my face, Harry erupts like a grenade in a foxhole, "You had to find a way to ruin my week! I debated and debated trying to find you because I knew, I knew, I knew this is what would happen. Part of me hoped you wouldn't actually make it down here," he nearly shouts.

"It's nothing I can't handle," I lie.

"Oh bullshit!" Harry spits, his face curling into fury.

"What happened?" Kat implores, talking over the both of us.

"He was outside…" Harry says, leaning over the table to talk more closely so he's not overheard, "with a gun on the guy staying right above us at the resort!"

Carolina gasps, tipsy and frightened. "That nice man above us?"

Putting two and two together quickly, Kat surmises what's happened before asking.

"Michlean?"

As I nod, Kat's face drops, her eyes darting back and forth nervously.

"Where did you get a gun? Please tell me you didn't bring it into my house," she asks sternly.

"He had it strapped to his leg. I yanked it from him before he used it on me."

"This morning?" Kat questions.

"A little while ago," I respond, "He was shaking down Viola for money. Then once he got it, he smacked her across the face."

"He what?" Harry reacts, teeth clenched, moral outrage turning his face red beneath that fake tan. Harry may be a bastard, even when tanned and nattily dressed. And he and I share little other than a love and a loss. But like me, he has a special aversion to bullies. Hard to gauge but his may be even stronger than mine. This guy was raised with a very clear sense of right and wrong, even though most of the time it's misdirected.

"He hit her?" Carolina gasps, grabbing hold of Harry, her blonde curls flying in all directions as she shakes her head in disgust.

"She gave him an envelope with money in it. He slapped her across the face with it."

Harry pours himself more wine, his eyes searching the crowd until he finds Viola talking with a table full of guests. Glancing toward the front entrance and then back toward the kitchen, her body is noticeably more rigid than her usual languid easiness.

"I am pissed about you getting into the middle of things when you don't know what the hell is going on!" he snaps, waving his glass at me as he speaks in a paternal, level-headed tone as if to impress Carolina with his coolness under pressure, "But I wouldn't have let that go either."

Harry then spins, facing Kat. "What do you know about this guy?"

"I know nobody messes with him…present company excluded apparently," she says, looking over at me. "Whatever's illegal or under the table on St. Carlos, he has his hands in it."

Harry weighs her statements, putting credence in her words.

"We have to get you on a plane. Tonight," Harry then announces to me.

Rearing back in my chair to get a clearer look at his face, I feel my face scrunch up like I've got my head caught in a pickle jar.

"I'm not going anywhere."

Harry's eyes narrow at me as if he smells something rotten and it's coming from me.

"Goddamn it!" he starts, "your life could be in danger. Mine and Carolina's lives could be in danger."

"Maybe we should move to a different resort, Harry," Carolina says, concern etched in her voice.

"Whoa! Whoa! Everybody take a big breath and calm down. This guy's bark is a lot bigger than his bite. Come on! Harry, I came back to this island to see you marry this woman."

"Be hard to see us get married fifty feet underwater with an anchor around your neck," Harry counters.

"Not only do you have this guy killing me, you know how he's going to do it," I laugh. "Harry, I'm not leaving until you're married. This douchebag doesn't intimidate me."

"Well then what are you going to do about him?" Harry asks, as if I have all the answers.

"Kill him, I guess," I say casually, trying to bring a little dark levity to the moment, but instead it numbs the conversation.

"I'm joking for Christsake! But I'm not running. Not in my make-up. I don't know this assclown but I gotta think that if he wanted me dead, he would have already walked back in the front door with about six friends and done the deed. I'm sorry I got you all involved. You're right, Harry, I was bound to fuck up your wedding one way or another. And there's still plenty of time for me to make an even bigger mess of it. But I'm here. I'm not leaving. So, pour me more wine and let's enjoy the rest of the night."

As Roger returns to the table to collect Kat, she turns to me and asks, "Why don't you come home with us? It'll save Harry having to drop you at my place and then drive all the way back to the resort."

My eyes lock on Roger's. I smile, pleased as punch for the shift in conversation, more than happy to turn the spotlight over to this weasel.

"I got him a room at the resort," Harry responds, sensing the hostility between Roger and myself.

"When did this happen?" Kat questions, surprised.

"I need him this week," Harry lies, "and I can keep an eye on things," he adds, taking Kat's hand reassuringly as if he's in charge now, "Keeping you and Earl out of it."

While I appreciate Harry tamping a lid down on Kat's concern, by doing that he lets Roger squirm out of the situation he created and stand silently like an angelic choirboy.

"After what just happened, does anyone think this is a good idea?" Kat argues.

"What just happened?" Roger quizzes, confused by the tension at the table.

"Nothing you gotta worry your pretty little head over," I remark.

Kat studies Roger and me, unsure but suspecting something more is behind my move as her eyes narrow in my direction. "I wish you would have talked to me first."

Again, I'm the bad guy.

"We should call it a night. There's a lot going on and I know I for one am exhausted. It's been…very eventful," Carolina says, giggling timidly.

I pretty much knew I wouldn't be getting another glass of wine. Harry's always been a dog with a bone; he wouldn't let any of this go, and now he's got Carolina to worry about.

"Harry's right, Kat. It's better I'm not there with you and Earl, You and Roger have a nice night."

Kat's not stupid. She knows there's animosity between Roger and me, and Roger is not about to admit to asking me to take a hike. He can tell how pissed off she is at me, he's not about to get himself dirty. I'd love to make the chickenshit wriggle on the line but considering everything that's going on, he's hardly worth it. If I hadn't had my life threatened I'd probably make him sweat a bit, teasing Kat with the truth, just to add a little more verve to the evening, but I've fulfilled my quota of turmoil for a while. He cursorily shakes my hand, not once making eye contact. I like this gutless bastard less every time I'm around him.

Harry signals the beautiful, young woman who waited on us to bring the check. She steps over with a smile and says, "Your meal is on the house."

Every set of eyes at the table searches the room for Viola. She stands near the door, her arms gently folded across her chest, taking in the restaurant. When she spots us all staring in her direction, she allows a whisper of a smile onto her lips. A smile loaded with gratefulness tinged with fear.

"Should have ordered another bottle of wine," I satirically mutter.

I don't know much about St. Carlos but I've had a bit of experience bribing a Constable for a hooker, and I know bad shit happens even where the water is warm and the drinks are cool. I've never been one to let my guard down other than in an attempt to get laid. And I've been taken down at those moments, wearing the scars to prove it. So, I don't minimize Michlean's influence or doubt for a moment that it's real. But I don't shy away from it either. I have an advantage. I don't have a lot I would miss or that would miss me if something bad were to happen to me. Problem is I have no idea how to mine this advantage other than to keep digging myself in deeper until I do.

## LET THE GAMES BEGIN

As Harry and Carolina walk to a waiting cab, Kat stays out front while Roger retrieves his truck from the parking lot. Gentleman that I am, I stay with her but she doesn't say a word, keeping her back to me while she waits.

"Pissed much?" I ask, cutting through her not-so-subtle silence.

"I'm not pissed," she glances over her shoulder at me, still not turning to face me. "You think you're safer with Michlean living above you, then stay there. I'm no longer amazed that trouble always finds you."

"I'm seldom amazed," I respond with a sliver of a smile, trying to yardstick how angry she is.

"Todd, has there ever been a time in your life where there hasn't been some crazy situation that's gotten out of control? Some crazy person, not including yourself, that wants to harm you? Something you're trying to run away from, something you're trying to avoid, or something you're trying to injure because you're pissed off? Has there ever been a time?"

Wow. Judgement stings. I mean, I love Kat and there was a moment in time that we connected. Okay, two moments in time. But we haven't seen each other for five years and in my estimation I am doing the right thing here.

"No," I say honestly, "probably not."

That shut her up pretty quick.

"Do you like your life that way?"

"I'm used to it."

"Don't you want to get off that ride?"

The answer should be obvious considering how twisted I get over most things. I'd love to turn off the noise, empty the clutter from my head and lessen the acid that burns in my stomach. If only it were that easy.

"I try, Kat," I say. "Do you think I went out searching for a problem with this guy?"

"And yet it found you."

"If you're going to fault me for anything, fault me for not walking away."

"Todd, all I want is for you to not get hurt anymore."

"Why do you care?"

Finally she turns to face me, her head cocked, looking at me like I'm a loon. It takes her a while to answer as if she's positioning varying responses in some kind of order.

"Because I might be your only friend."

Again, ouch. Probably true but damn, it hurts hearing someone say it out loud.

Roger pulls up and I open the truck's door for her. She climbs in.

"I'm trying to do the right thing here. And for me that's making sure you and Earl are safe," I reassure her.

"I'm not scared of Michlean," she answers.

"I meant safe from me."

She goes silent again, her eyes burrowing in.

"Look at your life, Todd. When do you---"

"Grow up?" I ask, cutting her off.

"Wake up," she says with a shake of her head.

"What are you talking about?

"Todd, Jesus..." Kat sighs, again using her favorite form of communication, a shake of the head. She tries to shut the door but I stop her.

"Don't drop hints and then act like I'm too stupid to figure them out. Say whatever you're saying."

Furious with me, she glares, snapping under her breath, "Earl!"

"Earl? I'm doing this for him! I'm doing this so he'll be safe," I respond, glancing in at Roger who feigns like this has nothing to do with his sorry ass.

Kat's mouth falls open. I can actually hear her breathe.

"Christ, Todd, do the math!"

She slams the door and Roger drives off.

Staring at the truck's tail lights, I can't wrap my head around this woman. She talks in hieroglyphics. Good luck, Roger, you're in for a lifetime of Rubik's Cube conversations. Kat is always so direct about everything else but when it comes to her feelings — or more to the point, you understanding her feelings — she won't come right out and say what she means. It's got to be a contest. As if you're not worthy if you can't figure out just what the hell she's saying.

And I can't. Earl? What's some large, lumbering thirteen-year-old have to do with anything? I wonder if he spends his days trying to jigsaw his mother's comments into a coherent statement. No wonder the kid locks himself in his room. His head probably hurts from talking with his mother who won't come out and say what's on her mind.

I'm not fucking Kreskin!

Maybe I should have just told her that her boyfriend doesn't want me around. He's scared. He's jealous. He thinks I'm a big asshole. He thinks I'm bad for her, he thinks I'm bad for Earl and will somehow prevent him from getting close to Earl, who has made it rabidly clear he doesn't want anything to do with Roger. Me, at least I can get Earl to crack a fucking smile. I know what it's like growing up big. That dumb grin that curls at the end of his lips, I used to have that smile myself. Over the years it's transformed into a snarl but I remember when it had at least a modicum of innocence in it. Roger will never get close to Earl. He knows nothing about him. I am the one who could break through to the boy because I *was* him.

I was him.

I was him. Holy shit! I was him.

The air I'm breathing gets caught in my chest as a stabbing pain starts somewhere in my cerebral cortex and works its way south into my heart. I can't get another breath, feeling like someone's just wrapped my head with Saran Wrap. I can't feel my hands or my feet. Earl. Me. Earl and me. Me and Earl.

As Harry hollers for me to come join them in the cab, I'm busy doing Kat's math in my head. Thirteen years old. Means conception was fourteen years ago. Fourteen years ago I was twenty-five, maybe twenty-six, traveling around as a rep for Mason and Lembrick and---OH SHIT. Oh shit. Oh shit, oh shit, oh shit!

"Go without me, Harry," I hear myself say, though I can't feel my lips moving.

"What?! Todd, get in the cab," Harry orders.

I shake my head and walk off in the other direction; with each breath I take, I shake more. Fuck, that's my kid! My kid. Finally getting out of the light of Viola's, to the safety of complete darkness, I lean against a tree and fight not to lose control. I'm not even sure what I'm feeling entirely, there's so much pinballing around inside of me. I'm shocked, yeah, I can sense some of this is shock. But there's elation, fear, anger, embarrassment, all of it swirls around like it's all been jam-packed into a blender and set on high.

It's not pureeing easily.

Kat's home can't be but a few miles from here. A few miles of inky black roadway. And that's what I want right now, darkness. Darkness that will allow this information to settle in. Though I have no idea what I will say to Earl, or for that matter Kat, who I am sure by now is regretting leaving me breadcrumbs to follow to their logical conclusion. But if nothing else, I have to be sure. I have to know for sure, from her mouth.

It's somewhere after one in the morning when I finally find Kat's house. A few cars passed me as I walked on the side of the narrow road; one guy stopped and asked if I needed help. All I could mutter was "You have no idea," which caused him to speed off.

I approach the house, unsure whether I should knock or find a place to bunk down at least until sun-up. But as I step closer, I make out a figure plopped into a beach chair in front of the house.

Kat.

"This a coincidence? You being out here?"

"I figured you'd figure it out. Though I thought you'd be a little faster about it, I'm getting chewed up by mosquitoes out here."

"I walked from the restaurant."

"Afraid of the questions Harry would ask?"

"That's always a given. I needed to think. Well actually, I was hoping an oil truck or something large would come and take me out on the two-lane. Sort of God's way of telling me it was okay if I didn't deal with this."

We both go silent for a moment, Kat's eyes illuminated by the moonlight, a light breeze blowing her hair.

"Why didn't you tell me?"

"Exactly when was I supposed to do that?"

"When I got here. At the bar today. Five years ago. Thirteen years ago. You could have found me."

"I didn't decide I wanted you in Earl's life until Harry called and asked me to find you," she says. "I debated and debated. I thought you'd be smart enough to see it when you met him. He looks just like you. And worse, he's beginning to act like you. Truth is, I wasn't sure I was ever going to tell you. I'm still not sure it's the best idea."

"Does Earl know?"

"He suspects."

"Fuck! Even he's smarter than me."

I look at the house, knowing my actual, real-live son is inside. I wonder just how big of an asshole that kid thinks I am.

"You didn't think I had a right to know?"

Kat lets go with a tired laugh. Dropping her face into her hands, she rubs her eyes before looking up at me again.

"Did you plan on getting me pregnant?" she asks. "If I had told you fourteen years ago, would you have cared? You were nothing more than a good-looking asshole. And that was fine. I didn't expect or want anything from you. I was actually relieved when you disappeared without wanting my number. And I was on the pill. I thought I was protected but apparently I'm the one in a million. So what was I supposed to do, Todd? Would you have come running?"

Pushing herself up from the chair, going as close to face-to-face with me as she can, Kat can only shake her head.

"And when I saw you here five years ago, you were a total mess. Even worse than you are now and that's saying something. I appreciated what you did for Earl then but you were in no shape to find out he was your son. Not after losing the love of your life and all the other shit that went down. I wanted to tell you but couldn't. If I hadn't caved, you wouldn't even have remembered we had slept together. But you weren't the same asshole I had sex with in that horrible hotel room. You changed. So I crumbled. If I hadn't, if I'd just kept it to myself that we knew each other before, no one would have ever made the connection to Earl and I wouldn't be apologizing now."

As tears well up, Kat's eyes stay on me.

"I don't want anything from you. Earl and I are fine. So don't think I told you because I want something. I...I guess it's just time. I've always hated secrets and I'm terrible at keeping them. I figured that five years ago when you saw him you might put it together. And then earlier today when you met him, as big as he is, with some of your ridiculous mannerisms, I thought the light bulb would go off. But..." she trails off, shaking her head. "...I chalked your ignorance up to always being pre-occupied by whatever mess is swirling around you at any given time. I figured with you staying here, being around Earl, you'd eventually put it together. But you bailed on that too."

"Goddamn it, I didn't bail!" I bark. "I was...it's for the best."

"Well, now it's out there. And when you go, I'll sit Earl down and tell him. Just don't expect Father's Day cards."

Kat bursts into tears. I want to join her but I need to let her have the moment. I reach out for her but she slams her hand into my chest, pushing herself away from me.

"No, no..." she whimpers, turning away from me.

I want to hold her but I know that's the wrong thing to do. And I don't know what the right thing is. I try to contain my breathing as I feel regret reaching up from inside my guts and squeezing my heart. I begin to cry too, covering my face.

Jesus, when did I turn into this guy?

Are there emotions that are too pure to be shared?

I know there are moments in life that are beyond my capacity to deal with. I've lived through enough of them to make that statement honestly. I haven't really cried in a long time. I thought after Tami, I would never cry again; there was nothing left for me to give. But as rivers of salty water drop off my cheeks onto the ground I'm reminded that there's still plenty of pain left inside that hasn't been tapped, pain that can pound me into submission.

Seeing me sobbing, Kat gasps. "I'm sorry…I'm sorry," she utters.

I grab her. Pulling her to me. This time she lets me, falling against me as we both weep until self-control finally catches up to our emotions. As the warm, moist air blows softly as if to comfort us, I use my shirt to wipe the tears off her face. I then wipe mine roughly as if to grind them into my cheeks.

I'd like nothing more than to go in and look at Earl sleeping. To soak him in safely, when he couldn't look at me, couldn't confront me. I want to see me in him. To know. But with Roger snoring away in the next room, entering Kat's house is not a particularly intelligent option. That will have to wait for another day.

"I'm going to go," I announce.

"Let me get my keys, I'll drive you."

"No. You got your guy in there. You should…" I point toward the door.

"He's fine. And Roger's---," Kat stops herself, uncomfortable. "It's late, you shouldn't be walking. Let me get my keys."

I make it easy on her. I give a wave and back out of the yard. As I walk away, I hear Kat call my name twice but I don't turn around. I may not like her taste in men but that's her deal and I'm not going to kick that hive. Even I'm smart enough to know I'll be the one that looks like the asshole if I say anything.

Then I hear her call to me, "Did Roger ask you not to stay with us?"

Nope, nope, not turning. Not my monkey, not my circus, not my monkey, not my circus, not my monkey, not my circus…

"Goddamn it, Todd! Did Roger ask you to leave?!"

I stop. Damn it. What's the matter with me? Go, go! But I don't. I have to say something. Turning, Kat walks about fifty yards behind me. She stops too, the distance between us never lessening.

"Do the math," I voice, before turning to continue in the direction of the resort.

I don't hear her following me any longer.

A few more miles on foot can't hurt me. And a few more hours alone will do me good. I can use the silence to try and sequester my feelings and focus rationally on what just happened, boxing up the emotions I'm feeling so I can deal with the ones I need to and ignore the others.

Over two hours later I climb the stairs to the front entrance of the resort. My eyes shift with concern, hoping I don't run into Michlean or anyone associated with him. It's nearly three in the morning, I figure even pimps and hookers sleep.

As I cross the lobby toward the elevators, I spot Harry sitting at a small table near the windows that overlook the pool area. He has a glass in front of him, the ice melted, condensation dripping down the outside of the glass. It's been on the table a while which means he's been there a while. He doesn't notice that I made it back and part of me wants to pretend I don't see him and continue on to the elevators. But if he's waiting to see if I make it back and I know he is, I can't leave him perched down here all night.

"You can go to bed now, I made it back."

"What'd you do with all the money you had?" he asks.

"What?"

"You had some money when you left for Europe. What did you do with it?"

"It's been five years, Harry. And it wasn't like it was millions of dollars. I think I did pretty good spreading it out."

"Didn't you work?"

"Of course I worked," I answer, falling into the chair across from him. "I did lots of things, went lots of places, met lots of people. When you do that money washes through your hands."

"What happened? How'd you end up…like this again?"

"Your daughter grew further away from me every day. Without Tami…this is me," I respond honestly. "I'm sorry you're involved in this shit. And Carolina. I don't mean to ruin her wedding…even if it is to you."

At least he chuckles. Some parts of the new Harry I actually enjoy.

"Carolina doesn't know what to think. She's scared, which I can't blame her. I'm assuring her everything will be all right. She has such a good heart," he says, then asks, "What do you think of her?"

Yippee! Another bomb to defuse. It's late, I'm tired and there's no fucking way I'm going to say some shit that will cause this bomb to go off in my face.

"She's lovely," is all that tumbles out.

Harry stiffens, pissed. He starts that twitching thing he does when he is trying to put a lid on his anger but can't quite seem to get it under control. His eyes are bloodshot. Wine and the late hour.

"Just what the hell does that mean?" he pounces.

There's the old Harry I know and tolerate.

"Don't get your Jockeys in a knot, Harry. I like her. I don't know her but---"

"She told you all about herself!"

"I'm not interviewing her for a job, Harry. I don't care where she's lived, how you met. You're asking me what I think about her and I'm telling you all I know is the *Reader's Digest* version. Truth is, I don't have to know her. You do. If you're happy who the fuck cares what I think?"

"The point of getting you down here was so you could get to know her. Not that you haven't tried to screw that up."

I mull his words a moment before I sit back, my hands dragging down my face, pulling my skin with them, exhausted. Today has been filled with enough confrontation. I just don't have it in me to participate in another.

"Do you really give a shit what I feel about this marriage, or her for that matter?"

He leans back in his chair as if to see me better. The expression on his face fluxes from sour to direct.

"Next to me, you're the person who knew Tami best. And I would want to believe she'd be happy about this."

There are a thousand things I could say, the most obvious being, "she's dead, Harry. Live your own goddamn life and keep Tami out of it," but considering the hour and all the shit the day has rained down, not the best idea. Especially because the same forlorn sadness I remember from five years ago is being held captive in his eyes.

"Harry, Tami would want you to be happy. If you're happy, you know she's happy."

Harry doesn't speak. He stands, his eyes downcast. I feel my heart drop. It's been a day filled with that.

"Harry…you're happy? Right? I mean, you want to get married?" I ask, sudden trepidation clogging my throat.

He doesn't answer for a remarkably telling second but then looks down at me, a weak smile bending at the end of his lips.

"More than I have a right to be," he says.

Why can't I just take him at his word? Ever since I arrived, something has been off. And I'm not just talking about the new look and faux-attitude adjustment which reminds me of someone extoling the virtues of a cult they joined. There's something else. But I've never been really adept at picking up clues. Earl is proof of that. But Harry and I have always had a connection, deeper than most friends, certainly deeper than most in-laws, maybe because of a finish line we never got to cross. Our relationship was forged out of true hatred. Something so deep it crawled into our DNA and altered the chemicals in our brains. It was ugly. They say you have to hit rock bottom to recover. Harry and I hit rock bottom, and I am here to tell you the bottom is jagged and rough and it will tear the living shit out of you until you don't recognize yourself. We stayed in that hell for a long time.

Even when I left St. Carlos to travel the world, I can't say Harry and I liked each other. We had come to an understanding. And while at my most vulnerable, I fancied that we had become friends. But recalling all the horrible things we said and did to one another reminded me that people who have done that to each another never fully recover from that sort of internal damage. You heal but there are always scars.

"What, Harry?" I ask knowingly.

"What do you mean what?"

"There's something more you're not saying. Is there something about you and Carolina I should know before you tie the knot? I just told you Tami would be happy if you're happy, but not if it's based on a lie. She's not pregnant, is she?"

"Pregnant! God no!" Harry gasps. "No. Nothing like that. I mean nothing at all. I was going to ask you, you seem like you have something on your mind. Want to tell me?"

"Some asshole wants me dead. Don't you think that's enough?"

"I know you, Todd. You react differently when the danger's physical rather than emotional. There's something else."

Touché. Thanks for playing hot potato with my secrets. I think I taught him that move.

"I'm going up to my room. Goodnight, Harry," I say, standing, facing him.

We hold our eyes on each other suspiciously, both lousy poker players, especially when it comes to something emotional.

"Don't clear out the minibar. It's expensive."

"Everybody needs a hobby, Harry," I say, leaving him standing there as I walk away. The saints are with me for the moment, because he doesn't move. He won't be sharing an excruciating elevator ride with me.

He doesn't want his secret exposed as much as I don't. Apparently, Harry and I have something else in common.

## NUCLEAR FAMILY BOMB

The curtains are cracked just enough to let in a strip of sunlight that's determined to burn my corneas through my eyelids. They've redecorated the rooms since I flopped here on my non-honeymoon and the way I am most comfortable in a bed also puts the morning sun in direct contact with my face. I barely slept last night but I did pass out for a few hours thanks to the minibar which beckons me like a siren luring me toward the rocks.

Lying there, my mind can't help travel to Earl. Fuck. I was hoping by morning I would have some grand revelation as to how to deal with this personal A-bomb. But at least I'm not waking up at Kat's because I wouldn't even be able to look at Earl. Guilt gnaws at me even though my better sense, slim as that is, tells me I'm not at fault for anything other than being blind and blindsided. I have this kid that's sorta-kinda mine but not really, who I have only met twice, briefly, in thirteen years. I have no right to be his parent. I'm not even sure I know what relationship I want with him. And I'm sure he'd resent me taking a stab at playing the father. It would piss me off if I were him.

Parenthood. It's never even entered my psyche. Even with Tami, I never went that far ahead. It was all about her. I imagine we would have started a family but my total focus was on her. Children would have come after I was sure I was staying the course, being the man she helped turn me into. The man I turned my back on since leaving the island.

I swing open the curtains to let the sun overpower the room. Peering out at the ocean view, I can't help but search the horizon for a beautiful woman swimming out toward the sun. I would love a sign right now as to what I should do. Tami would know. If she had lived and this had come to light, Tami would be the one taking me by the hand and leading me to the right actions. She'd open our life to Kat and Earl. She would instinctively make them at home; she and Kat would become best friends. She would instruct me on the ways to be a good parent, thirteen years after the fact.

But I'm completely bankrupt as to what I should do. And that makes me itch for a drink.

Squeezing my hands into fists over and over, I struggle to prevent myself from dashing over to the minibar and begin a day of inebriation. I'm sure Dr. Buzz would have answers for me. They'd be completely fucked up but I'd probably follow them to the letter and screw up this screwed-up situation even more. I'm funny like that.

The phone rings. Good. At least it means I can distract myself from the allure of the minibar, even though I know that whoever is calling isn't calling with good news. Picking up the phone, I hear Harry breathing on the other side of the line.

"You up?"

"I picked up the phone, didn't I?"

"You can't just say yes? You always have to be a prick?"

"Force of habit. What's going on, Harry?"

"Breakfast. Meet me downstairs."

My eyes keep watch to see if Michlean is anywhere in my path to the dining room. Probably doesn't get up this early. And if he does, he's in the gym, I imagine, not standing in line at a buffet, ready to pile up the bacon and sausage and smother a few biscuits in gravy. He seems more like a protein shake and egg-whites kind of guy.

I don't see hide nor hair of my mortal enemy, but Harry is tucked into a small table in the corner. When he sees me, he stands and marches toward me.

"I ordered us both the buffet."

He does know me. At least a little.

Harry hands me a plate as we get in line as they are bringing out another tray of scrambled eggs.

"Buffet is pretty damn good here," Harry says, dishing a load of eggs onto his plate.

"Ease up, tiger, you can come back for seconds," I answer before asking, "Where's Carolina?"

"Shopping for a dress for the wedding. She and Kat."

"Kat?" I respond, surprised, hoping she doesn't spill any information I'd prefer to tell Harry in my own time.

"Yeah. They made plans last night while you were being the hero. Kat knows the shops on the island," Harry answers before sending me a look as I throw the bacon and sausage onto my plate. "What, you trying to give yourself a heart attack?"

"Yeah. My life hasn't been exciting enough. I thought I'd try Russian roulette with pig fat."

"Changed up my diet. Trying to eat cleaner. Closer to the grain," he says, selecting a bran muffin. "It's made a big difference in how I feel which affects my mood. You should try it."

"Not getting the necessary amount of grease, liquor and coffee affects my mood. Leave me alone, Harry. I've been picking out my own food since I was four. I eat what I like. Got a metabolism like a roadrunner," I say with a smile, tearing open a couple biscuits and ladling on the gravy as he winces.

"Friday. Noon. On the beach," Harry states.

"Okay…" I answer with my mouth full.

"You and me need to find something to wear. I'm wearing all white."

"You a virgin?"

"Fuck you! Carolina's request. She wants me and her in white. So you can't be in white."

"Because I'm not a virgin?"

"Will you shut up with all the virgin shit? It's a big day for Carolina and a big deal for me."

Harry relays the rest of his wedding plans. He's gotten hold of a minister who will marry them, and then it will be a private dinner with me, Kat, Roger and "that kid of hers."

"Earl," I correct him.

"Right. Earl. Keep forgetting his name. I've never met him. He a nice kid?"

I am not sure whether Harry knows more than he's telling, but I can't help feeling like I'm being played, like he's fishing for an answer.

"Yeah. Good kid. Thirteen, which you probably don't remember, but it's a tough age."

"I don't remember what I had for breakfast yesterday; rest assured I don't remember what it's like to be thirteen. But I'll take your word for it, since I don't think you've matured much past that. Got to be hard for the kid, not having a father."

He's yanking my chain. Got to be.

"Yeah," I respond, clamming up by shoving a piece of bacon into my mouth and crunching it loudly, my eyes searching Harry's face, hoping he gives himself away.

But when he quickly changes the subject, telling me he hasn't seen Michlean this morning, I am not sure whether he's messing with me. Harry tells me most mornings he usually spots Michlean somewhere around the resort.

"Probably at the gym or out finding some other woman to slap around. As long as we give a wide berth to the assclown, all is good," I respond, stuffing my face.

My belly filling, I'm feeling pretty good. Even the idea of going shopping for clothes with Harry doesn't fill me with dread. I want to look natty for his big day. Harry's phone rings and seeing it's Carolina, he answers.

"You find a dress?" Harry asks with a sweet smile.

But his smile quickly evaporates.

"Slow down, slow down…what?!" he barks into the phone.

Oh shit.

"Okay, okay…we're coming!"

Harry hangs up as he stands.

"Let's go," he says, throwing some cash on the table for a tip.

Before I can ask why, he's literally jogging out of the restaurant.

## THANK YOU FOR NOT SMOKING

I can't believe it until I actually see it.

It's not the smoke that causes me to hold my breath; it's an icy fear that prevents me from exhaling. Rage surges through me and I have to keep holding my breath so I don't erupt.

There are three fire trucks, spraying water over the smoking ashes of what's left of Viola's. The lights from the Constables' cars dance through the thick, gray smoke.

In the crowd, I spot Kat holding Carolina. Pushing through the onlookers, Harry and I get to them. Both have tears. Kat's eyes lock with mine and I know exactly what she's thinking. Did my taking on Michlean last night cause this? I'd love them to discover it was a freak accident: a burner left on, bad wiring, someone accidentally tossing a still-lit cigarette into a trashcan. Something else other than what I know in my heart it is. Arson.

Searching, I spy Viola talking with a Constable. I get Harry's eye and nod in her direction. Feeling our eyes on her, she turns to us briefly with a look that warns us to keep our distance. When she finishes speaking with the Constable, her gaze returns to me, nodding me toward her.

"I'm going to kill that piece of shit!"

"Not your fight," she says.

"He made it mine."

"No!" she answers sternly, surprising me. "He's a monster. To fight him, you must turn into a monster too. Men who become monsters do things that boil over into things they cannot control. You shouldn't even be here."

As she speaks, I see Gabriel walking out of the remains of the still-smoldering building, his gray streak of hair catching the sunlight and actually shimmering. As Viola turns away from me, I march in the Constable's direction, crossing under the yellow tape.

"Back on the other side of the tape," he orders before recognizing me.

He straightens up. The last five years haven't been kind to him. He's clearly still a drinker, his eyes rimmed with a watery redness that he'd probably like me to believe is caused by the smoke. He smiles, still wide and disarming for a man of the law.

"What are you doing back on St. Carlos?" he asks, sticking out his hand for me to shake.

"Harry's getting married," I respond, taking his hand. "What do you think caused the fire?"

His eyes narrow at me. With years of experience, intuition is simply second nature now.

"Why the concern, Mr. Cartwright?"

Behind me, Kat, Carolina and Harry move up like a posse. Kat and Carolina remain on the other side of the tape as Harry joins me.

"You tell him about that son-of-a-bitch?"

"I'm getting there," I answer.

"Welcome back to the island, Mr. Everett," the Constable says with a smile. "I hear congratulations are in order."

"Yeah, yeah, thanks," Harry rattles off, getting to the meat quickly. "That kid that stays at the resort, Michlean, the son-of-a-bitch set this fire."

The Constable's brow raises in Harry's direction, allowing a better view of Gabriel's bloodshot eyes. I imagine he wakes himself up with bourbon in his coffee.

"Whoa, whoa..." Gabriel mutters, his eyes slowly moving from Harry to me. "First, we don't know if the fire was deliberately set. Second, I've not heard he was associated with this."

"Well, I'm associating. He was here last night," Harry pipes in, "He tried to extort some money from Viola, then he hit her. Todd stopped him."

Gabriel's shoulders raise, the slight hunch in his back as if he's carrying a load of laundry down to the river disappears as he stiffens uncomfortably.

"And how did you do that?" he asks me.

"Pretty much how you think I did it."

"You have a hard time making friends on the island, don't you, Mr. Cartwright?"

"Not just here," I answer. "Look, he and I got into it a couple times yesterday, once when I saw him smack the shit out of a young woman who wasn't exactly jumping for joy that I came to her rescue, and then last night when he took money from Viola and smacked her. No, he doesn't like me. And I know he greases the palms of the law down here---"

"Whoa, whoa, Mr. Cartwright!" Gabriel commands, his hand going up in my face. "As my father would always say, do not let your mouth overload your ass."

We take each other in silently for a moment, me stewing, trying to get my rage tamped down, sensing that Gabriel is wary of the other Constables' prying ears.

"You telling me it's not true?" I ask, playing the only ace I have.

"I am telling you he's not putting money in my pocket," Gabriel speaks in a low, hushed tone, "If he were I'd be wearing better slacks. This island is filled with all sorts of people doing all sorts of things. Truth here is relative to the source."

"That son-of-a-bitch burnt down this restaurant!" Harry sidles around me, getting into Gabriel's face. "We told you why. Go get him. Question him."

"You believe we will get the truth?" Gabriel counters.

"I believe you can put his nuts in a vice and sweat it out of him," Harry answers.

It's clear from the expression on Carolina's face that she's never seen this side of Harry.

"Let us find out the cause of this fire before making accusations," Gabriel says, putting his hand out as if stopping traffic.

Harry and I trade an unconvinced glance but we both know better than to push. Our history with Gabriel was brief and half a decade ago. We are visitors on his turf. He's wise to the underbelly of the island in ways Harry and I never could be.

Walking away, the four of us stay silent. Every inch of my body surges with rage. Carolina has a confused fear plastered on her face, her eyes snapping toward Harry, hoping for some reassurance that I'm not about to stir up a revengeful pot of trouble and beat the ever-loving shit out of that fuckbag, who I am sure had this restaurant destroyed to make a point.

A point that I unfortunately helped sharpen.

We still have to do the pre-wedding clothes shopping, something none of us are in the mood for now. As we push through the gathering crowd to get back to the cars, Kat sidles up next to me.

"Last night when you said do the math…" she begins, but I shake my head, stopping her.

"I need to cool off before we get into any deep discussion about anything. Kat, don't let me get into the middle of your life and scramble it up only to leave again in a few days. Because I will if you let me. And like most things I cyclone through, it won't be me picking up the pieces."

Harry and I ride silently in the back of the taxi he hired. Two usually barking alphas hushed by our inability to react, leaving neither of us with anything to do but brood. Why can't I mind my own business? Why does a man who creates so much shit himself jump into the middle of other peoples' piles? I know I'm no hero so the only motivation I can wrap my head around is that if I can right some other wrong the checks and balances of my life will teeter closer to even. Truth is, all I've really done is drag everyone I know on this island into a dark tunnel with a guy who is shaping up to be a sociopath.

"We're in a pickle," Harry says, the first to speak.

"This is my fault," I admit.

Harry turns, his sympathetic eyes taking me in a quick moment. He then nods. "Yep. It probably is."

"Thanks," I mutter.

"Well what the hell do you want me to say? You always have your puss someplace it shouldn't be. You never think of the big picture. I was hoping after everything you went through with Tami, something would have resonated in your heart over these last five years. Something to make you more reflective and thoughtful. With a life plan. But I can see none of that happened. You've wasted these last five years, five years you could have made a positive change in your life; instead you wandered around like a goddamn gypsy pulling the same stupid shit. Carolina thinks I love you because of the way I talk nice about you, but I don't. I don't love you, I worry about you. That's all. I have for five years. Because Tami would have wanted that. But it doesn't mean I like you, Todd. Because to like you, you'd have to give me reason. But you seem incapable."

Harry's words plow me in the gut. It's all true so I can't argue it on its face, and it sucks that it took him less than two days to figure out that the last half-decade of my life has been one giant swirl of the toilet. All leading to a less-than-glorious now. But I wish he hadn't said it. Speaking it out loud digs deeper to the bone. Will I ever get out of this pattern or will I eventually run out of gas and crash? I've already scraped the ground a few times in a spectacularly ugly fashion. How many more miracles does one guy get?

Though there is a dank, stinky cloud of gas hanging over the afternoon of shopping, the women internalize it, capping off the morning's scare as Carolina tries on clothes for the wedding. But it's there, in her eyes, which appear gaunt today. You can pretend, but you can't escape dark truths.

Never being wishy-washy about what he wants, Harry quickly settles on a white linen shirt and white linen pants. He looks like a lounge singer in an off-beach nightspot, especially with that bullshit tan. But I'm not going to say anything, not after that flaming bucket of truth Harry doused me with in the taxi.

Tossing me a pair of tan pants and a loose-fitting shirt a few shades lighter, Harry waves me toward a changing room. "This is what I want you to wear."

"Brown?"

"Tan. It's subtle. I wouldn't expect for you to get it."

"I'm going to fade into the sand."

"That's the idea. The spotlight should be on Carolina."

He could ask me to put on a turquoise thong and a bedazzled half-shirt and I'd probably mutter "what the hell?" and go with it at this point. I'm still not one hundred percent invested in this union of Harry and Carolina and Harry doesn't want to hear from me. He's pissed off at me but can't justify being outraged because what I did was at least on the side of right, regardless of the consequences. And if he wants me to blend in with the sand, I'll blend in with the sand. In a few more days, I'm off this island.

As Carolina continues trying on dresses, I can see Harry is getting antsy.

"Wanna give the women some space? Let's find a place to get a drink," I offer.

He nods almost before I get the sentence out.

Bar Esmeralda, with its hinged plywood doors that attach to the ceiling, leaving it open from end to end, feels touristy-Caribbean, even more than the resort's bars, which try extra hard to give the tourists their fantasy of what island life is actually like. But Harry and I are clearly the only non-locals in the place. They eye us like we're INS. I'm too caught up in my own drama to care who is looking at me as Harry waves to the bartender to bring two shots of whiskey and two beers.

"If you see anything out of sorts here, don't get involved, I might like to come back," Harry utters as the beers and glasses of whiskey are settled onto the bar in front of us.

Picking up the shot of whiskey I down it in one gulp. The heat from the liquor warms my insides, like someone wrapping a parka around me after being lost in the Arctic. The feel of a glass in my hand is my security blanket.

I can't help but smile as I marginally relax.

"I don't know what you're smiling about. You got a target on your back. And you put one on my back."

"You honestly think that guy is going to do something to me? Or you?"

Harry takes a gulp of his beer and then downs the shot.

"Yes," he says with absolute assurance.

"I wish I'd never come back here," I respond before thinking.

"Why did you?"

"I owe you. I owe Tami to be here. But since coming back I've been haunted by visions of the woman I love. I fucked up everyone's life I'm close to, and I'm...I'm..."

I go silent. Harry turns to me on the stool, demanding I finish the sentence with a look.

"You're what?"

"A dick. A gigantic dick."

"Everybody knows that, Todd."

"I'm a father, Harry! A fucking father!" I blurt out, wishing I had another shot in my hand rather than a beer.

Harry squints as if he can't see me even though he's sitting right next to me.

"A father of what?" he says with smug glee.

"A billy goat, Harry! I fucked a goat!" I woof at him. "A person, goddamn it! A real, live human being, you fucker! You like getting me worked up, don't you? Bastard!"

Harry's tan, shrew-like face screws up into a dark temperamental funnel but then he bursts out laughing. He laughs so hard he begins to cough, choking on his own jolly.

"I know," he huffs between coughing fits.

Turning to him, I can't even find the words. I can sense my lips are moving but nothing is coming out. I might be going blind at this moment as I can't get my eyes to focus. I'm going to melt off this rickety bar stool and puddle onto the floor if this wily prick doesn't start talking soon.

"First day I got back on this island, I saw Kat. Her son had some doctor's appointment or something and was waiting for her at a table in the back of the bar. I took one look at that kid and knew. Jesus Christ, Todd, how could you not have known when you saw him? That big, lumbering lox looks just like your sorry self. Poor son-of-a-bitch. He's in for a lifetime of misery."

"You knew…before me?"

"Why the hell did you think I told Kat I wanted you to come down here? Do you really think I needed you here for my wedding? As I said in the cab, I don't even like you much. You disappeared on me. Fuck you! I don't need you here. And thank you for proving me right as to why," Harry stops his rant only to take a drink from his beer. "Carolina doesn't know you. And from the stories I've told her she was terrified of ever meeting you. But when I saw that kid, with that dumb look on his face, that mouth that always seems to be hanging open and those eyes, Christ, you can totally see it in the eyes. For someone who thinks Carolina resembles Tami, you are painfully oblivious to the obvious."

Harry takes a slug from his beer again. I pick up my bottle, my hand shaking, unsure whether I want to down the whole thing, or smash it off of his head.

"I confronted Kat and she denied it," Harry continues, "She wasn't happy I demanded she find you and get you down here. I told her either she get you down here or I will, because the kid is you. Well, maybe not as big an asshole as you, thank God, but he looks just like you."

"Yeah, I can sort of see that now," I mumble.

"Poor kid. But we aren't talking about him right now; we're talking about your favorite subject. You. You have a son. And you needed to be down here to deal with it. That boy deserves a father. Even one as shitty as you will turn out to be. It will at least help him put a picture together and there won't be any lingering questions."

Harry drains his beer bottle before signaling the barkeep for two more.

"I was a foster child," Harry continues, "My mom gave me up when I was four to a couple who took me in. I always suspected the reason they took me in was because the man who raised me was actually my father. But he died of a heart attack at work when I was eleven. Didn't get to ask him. My mom…the woman who raised me, didn't know. At least she said she didn't. But I always thought, you know…"

Harry's voice trails off, the lines that had been absent from his forehead with his new look, were back, scrunched up into waves of contemplation and regret.

"And I wasn't going to let that boy go through his whole life not knowing. Not fair to him."

"Or me," I add.

"Piss on you. Who cares about you? You should have been smart enough to see it. And yes, Kat should have told you, but in all fairness to her, last time, coming off Tami's death probably wasn't the right time to lay this news on you. But now…Christ, that kid is almost a man, almost as big as you," Harry states, his head shaking as various thoughts both past and present bombard his mind, "he deserves to understand."

"I don't know what I can give him," I utter in all honesty.

"He doesn't want nothing from you. Except to know for sure. Just don't go trying to be a 'dad' or anything as pathetic as that," Harry warns. "Let him take the lead instead of you trying to foist your big asshole-self into his life. All he wants is to know. That's all."

"I have some sort of obligation."

Harry sighs like I'm the dumbest person he's ever met.

"This is why Kat didn't want to tell you. Let me explain it as clearly as I can. It's. Not. About. You. There! Get it? She doesn't want you being obligated. And neither does that kid. So stop that shit right now, Todd, or I'm going to knock your teeth out of your head. I'm telling you, just acknowledge the kid and let him and his mom take it from there. They've made it without you for this long; they will survive without you acting on your so-called obligation."

I drop my head, staring down at the opening in the top of the beer bottle. This has been my view of life for too many years. Looking down at a drink. It has become where I feel safest, as if I could crawl down into that sanctuary of cool libation and my worries would swim away on the foamy head. It's not reality I have a problem with, it's living in the world that baffles the shit out of me, that I can only seem to survive by drinking and crawling between some random woman's legs, working through my pain with a mix of prowess and aggression. I *want* to grow up. Grow past this fucking nonsense that only makes me feel better in the short run and certainly fixes nothing in the long run.

But I can't see any way to do that. As if all the drinking and fucking has addled my mind into believing it's all I'm worth. I know there are plenty of men who would tell you this is enough. I absolutely wish I was dumb enough to believe you don't need anything more. But I do. I had it once. For a remarkably short time I owned it and embraced it. But now, I can't see any way to even get my arms around it, much less pull it to me.

If Harry knew the emptiness I feel, he'd scoff at me. Tell me to buck up and be a man. But I've been a man for so long, I've pretended to be strong and bold and devil-may-care, but I can't sustain that.

"I should have never come back here!" I say, sitting up tall on the stool.

"You said that. And if you're going to start feeling sorry for yourself, I am going to smash this bottle off the bar and stab you in the eye with the jagged end," Harry says.

"Harry, I don't know what I'm doing. I'm the same guy I was before Tami walked into my life, only older and more pathetic. How can that be? She was so powerful in my life. She made me want to change. And I did. You may have never seen it, but I did. And now…"

"I saw it. And I hoped you would keep changing but some people don't, Todd. I think it was you who said they just become more of themselves. And you have."

He holds up his beer to me. I pick mine up and ineffectually tap it off his bottle.

"Some people need a dump truck full of dirt to hit them in their sorry asses. They have to have a reason to change or they don't. Maybe this kid is your reason to change."

As we drink, I feel someone standing behind me. Harry turns first, the bottle in his hand, ready for a come-what-may battle.

"Yeah," Harry snarls in the direction of a man whose skin is deep as dark chocolate. There are pockmarks on his face from acne that went untreated when he was a teenager. His eyes are bloodshot from the booze and mistrust.

"Whachu need man?"

"What do you mean what do I need?" Harry repeats, wagging his beer bottle in the air. "We got what we need. Thanks."

"Mainlanders who come here are looking for something else."

"We came in here for a few drinks, pal. If we needed anything else, we would go to our man, Michlean," I joke, knowing at least Harry will get it.

The black man's eyes narrow harshly. "Fuck you!" he spits at me. "Michlean. Dat piece of garbage. I'd like to slit dat rich boy's throat."

"Whoa. Don't hold back, dude…" I respond, reaching out to stop him from walking away.

He turns back to me, his eyes venomous now. "Tell him dat Antony said that."

"I'll be sure to pass that along if I see him again, Antony," I say, spinning the stool around to face him. Every pair of eyes in the place are on Harry and I. "Why do you hate him?"

"Why do I hate him?" Antony parrots, looking back at the other men occupying tables in the bar. "Because that rich, muscly white boy took our business. Dis island is ours! Not his! He came here and got involved in our gambling. Got de high-rollers in love with his girls and his drugs and then he took our business. We had da cards, we had da tables, we had da wagering. He took it. And we sit our asses in dees chairs and remember what we used to have. Dat's why I hate him."

"You want it so bad, take it back," Harry says as if it's elementary.

"Fuck you! You tink we don't try that? He hurt anybody he don't like. We got families," an irritated Antony responds. "You two white men get out of here. Dis is our bar. We don't want you here."

The other men dotting the tables in the place stand up. It's fourteen against two. Odds are not in our favor. Especially when my other half, while mean as a rabid badger, is short and old.

Holding my hands up as we slip off our stools, I smile. "We come in peace. We actually don't like Michlean any more than you do."

"Less, actually," Harry adds.

The men weigh our statements and sincerity, sizing up Harry and me as they slide behind Antony in a show of solidarity. The disdain on their faces openly suggests they would like to drag Harry and me behind their cars through the streets of St. Carlos.

A couple of the men whisper something in a local island dialect I can't understand, as if debating whether or not we are on their side or playing them on Michlean's behalf.

"You want us to go," I say, casually turning and grabbing my beer off the bar and downing it. "Best of luck, guys. Just so you know, we're on Team Bar Esmeralda."

Harry and I walk out of the place carefully, not sharing a word until we're outside, as the men all continue to whisper to each other, glances going to and fro, making me more nervous each second.

Once outside, Harry asks, "Should we run?"

"You know, even in my most fucked-up state, I'm still faster than you, Harry."

"So what?" he remarks.

"This is what…" I answer, turning around and walking backward, looking at the men now congregating at the entrance to Bar Esmeralda.

"This old fucker here," I yell in their direction, pointing at Harry. "He's Michlean's daddy. Gives every hooker Michlean brings to the island a little test run. He's the reason your sorry asses are out of business."

With that I bolt, leaving Harry flatfooted, his head turning like an ill-timed metronome between me dashing away, and the gang of men eyeing him from the door to the bar.

"You-son-of-a-bitch!" Harry yells at me over and over, as I distance myself from him, his body practically waddling as he gives chase in my direction.

Thankfully the men don't come after us because I wouldn't be much help in rescuing Harry. I'm laughing so hard at the harsh panic pasted on his face, I can barely breathe. As we take refuge in the clothing store where Carolina has finally selected the dress she's going to wear to marry Harry, both of us fall against the wall, him trying to get his breath and me still laughing. It takes nearly fifteen minutes for Harry to finally stop breathing hard, all the while staring daggers at me. His lips move, forming curse words, but his breathing is so strained he can't get the sound out. Gathering himself enough, he moves closer to me, speaking in a raspy growl.

"If you feel someone drive a screwdriver through your brain while you sleep tonight, you don't even have to open your eyes to know it's me."

I laugh even harder, starting to hiccup. Harry hunches his shoulders, putting some distance between himself and me. Watching Harry shit his pants a little after all the garish truths he dropped on me today is worth whatever it's going to cost me.

Paybacks are always a bitch. I know that better than anyone.

## VIEW FROM THE BALCONY

Carolina hangs up her dress in the closet in her suite so as not to wrinkle it, while Harry opens the sliding doors, letting in the cool ocean air. I should have curled off and gone to my own room two floors down, but I wanted to get a moment alone with Kat and she wasn't making it easy, moving away from me every time my shadow crossed her.

"What time you working 'til tonight?"

"Close," she says with suspicious abruptness.

"You mind if I go to your place and talk to Earl tonight?"

The events of the last two days weighing on her, she pauses before answering. She's still not behind this, but the cat is not only out of the bag but carousing the neighborhood.

"Fine," she lies with a dramatic sigh.

"Is Roger going to be there? I don't want to---"

Kat rolls her eyes at me, shutting me up.

"It's my home. If you want to talk to Earl, talk to Earl. I said it's fine!"

She abruptly exits Harry and Carolina's suite, pulling the door closed with a bang behind her, just to put a period on the moment.

I stand silently, my back to Harry and Carolina who have a front-row seat for the show, staring at the door, again unsure of what I should do.

"Do you want us there with you?" Carolina asks from behind me. "For moral support."

Turning to her, I'm surprised and touched by her sympathetic concern. It's foreign to me. Not just because I don't know her well, but because it's been so long since I've seen it in anyone's eyes. Much less directed at me.

Harry's right, this is about as nice a woman as one will ever meet. Which only boggles my mind more as to what's going on with her and Harry. I still can't rectify who she is with who he is, knowing what I know about Harry.

"No. I gotta put on my big-boy pants and deal with this alone," I answer.

"Yes you do," Harry agrees.

Carolina admonishes him with an acute look but that doesn't daunt Harry.

"Let the boy know you're there for him," he continues, "He'll probably resent you at first but as he gets to really know you…he'll resent you infinitely more."

"Harry!" Carolina gasps, her blonde mane of curls spinning as she slaps him lightly on the arm.

Eyeing them both incredulously, I blurt out, "Why the hell are you two together?"

The words hit my ear as I say them but not as I mean them. Especially to Carolina. She hasn't been around Harry and me enough to realize that's how we always talk to each and only take a percentage of it personally.

Hell, he's said far more hurtful things to me today and I'm still hanging around. But now I'm punched in the face with their silence. *Ouch,* I think to myself, *this is going to fucking hurt!*

Carolina turns to Harry, her eyes begging him to take that question. He scowls at me from across the room, the curtains billowing around him as if he's about to break into a passionate aria, filling the room with a high-C that will shatter the mirrors.

But instead he turns away from me, looking out at the ocean.

Come on, Harry, level me with some snarky comment, but don't turn away and leave me here in silence, looking at Carolina whose feelings I just hurt. She's too good for this. Too sweet. Too small, almost frail, for the kind of bullshit Harry and I inflict on each other. I don't want to hurt this woman.

"We've been over this, nitwit," Harry mutters, pulling the curtains out of his way and stepping out onto the balcony.

Carolina and I hold a gaze on each other. At this moment, she looks more vulnerable than I've ever seen her and she wasn't exactly steely-spined to begin with. There's a longing in her eyes that feels like she wants to tell me something but won't. She turns and looks back at Harry but he keeps his back to me, staring out, as if he's looking for Tami like I always do when something roils me and I don't want to cope. But she's not there.

I didn't intend to cause a scene with what I meant as a barb. But now the smell of something putrid on the inside can't be covered up with perfume.

"You going to talk to me, Harry?" I ask, moving past Carolina to the balcony door.

"Don't you have a kid's life to ruin?"

"What the fuck is going on, Harry? Come on, level with me," I hammer, stepping out next to him, the sun hot on my face.

"You don't have to believe me, Todd. No skin off my back. I adore Carolina, I'm marrying her and she wants to marry me. Enough said. Now get the fuck off my balcony and go be a shitty father to that kid, so there's yet another person in your life who resents you! We're one shy of a baseball team."

"Does she know the kind of dick you can be?"

"I'm not a dick to her. I don't have to be."

"You're a fraud to her. Which is pretty dickish if you ask me. The tan, the haircut, the clothes, the bright shining teeth. Jesus, you're a counterfeit hundred-dollar bill. I want to know why. Because I'm not buying this line about you changing. You can't fool me; I've seen you at your absolute worst. I've borne the brunt of it. Something else is going on. Are you dying, Harry?"

He laughs. "That would be your fucking dream, wouldn't it? You'll be the one dying when I throw your big, fat ass off this balcony."

"I've fallen further and lived," I say, looking over the railing with a smile.

He goes silent again but I can feel him seethe. He's not going to tell me anything. I know Harry, he loves to hear a good secret but he's pretty stingy with his own. As I turn to walk back inside, Carolina dabs tears from her eyes.

"I don't know how you two can talk to each other that way. I never met Tami but I can't imagine she would like it at all."

"You're right," I respond, looking directly at her face. Beneath that sprayed-on tan, there is a darkness under her eyes as if she hasn't been sleeping, the wedding preparations taking their toll. And now me…

Or that she's getting married to Harry and realizing it might not be the sanest decision she's ever made.

"Why are you marrying him?"

Her smile grows sunnier and she giggles Tami's giggle, simultaneously wiping away tears.

"Because we're perfect for each other. Why else?"

"A green card. Maybe Harry came into some money, I don't know. But you're not the beautiful girl who took the short bus to school every day that Harry found selling matchsticks on a corner. So there's something else."

"Were you this suspicious when Tami fell in love with you?"

"Yeah. I was. Still have trouble believing it."

"I feel sorry for you, Todd."

"It's how I suck people in," I reply. "Harry didn't want me anywhere near your wedding, but he couldn't help but meddle in my life, trying to do what he thinks is right."

"He warned me about you," Carolina says, with a disappointed shake of her head.

"Did he? Then he should have warned you that as much as I can't stand that prick standing out on that balcony, I was in love with his daughter and she cared about him deeply. So I'll say this, and I don't mean any disrespect, Carolina, because I would say this to anyone in your shoes, but you fuck that man over in any way, shape or form, and you will find me so far up your ass, you'll start believing I'm your third lung."

She stares at me for a long moment. I'm not sure whether she's going to cry or slap the shit out of me, but I can see anger and understanding collide in her eyes.

Then she wraps her arms around me in a hug. I instantly freeze. This is completely unexpected.

"That's love, Todd."

I stutter and stammer, unable to get out a full word. I'm often confused but rarely addled. This I will remember. Because I'm addled to the point of stillness as she won't let go of me.

"Don't worry about me. Or Harry. I know Harry far better than you think I do. You shared a short time with him and it wasn't positive or healthy for either of you. He loved his daughter and he knew you weren't the best match for her. Maybe you knew it as well. So please, don't transpose any negativity onto my relationship with Harry. I know how Harry can be. But I also know his heart. He deserves his slice of happiness. And if us getting married brings that to him, I'm proud to be his heaven."

"Is getting married to Harry your heaven?"

She steps back, still touching my arms but looking up into my eyes. They are dull and still watery with tears.

"I was just starting to like you, so don't be nasty," she says, surprising me again. "I've got nothing to lose by hurting you either. Okay?"

And with that, she moves out onto the balcony and takes Harry's arm. She glances back at me once, dismissively, before speaking softly into Harry's ear. They continue murmuring softly to each other, their secrets locked between them.

Heading for the door, I stop at their bathroom. I've been holding it since the clothing store. Before I head down to the bar, I'd like to drain the dragon so I can get right to business. As I push open the door, there's piles of makeup and hair products littering the counter, some of these I suspect are Harry's. And then, clumped together as if trying to breed are at least a dozen amber prescription bottles, of which I'm sure one is Harry's blood pressure medication and another is Viagra. As I step into the bathroom, Carolina sweeps past, ducking under my arm and into my way. Again, she smiles. The warmth replaced by an indignation that could scorch the paint off the walls.

"Leave a girl a little mystery," she declares, pointing to the door leading to the hallway.

As I step out into the hallway, I look back to see Harry standing at the opening to the balcony. He remains still. Carolina pulls the bathroom door shut behind her as she announces, "Goodbye, Todd," and shuts the door to their suite in my face.

Sorry, sister, there's more than a little mystery to you and why you're marrying Harry. And if I didn't have to pee so bad, I'd bang on the door until one of you gave me a good goddamn explanation as to what the hell is going on. Because the more I see you together, the more I'm not buying what you're selling.

## TROPHY DADS

Standing out front of the resort, Tomas pulls past all the waiting cabs and over to the curb, allowing me to crawl in and fall into the seat.

"Where to, Mr. Todd?" Tomas asks, his voice happy.

"Over to that house you dropped me at the other night," I answer, my hand going to Tomas's shoulder to give it a squeeze before adding, "I've alienated pretty much everybody on this trip. Might as well have my kid tell me to piss off."

Tomas glances over his shoulder, confusion on his face. "You have a child?"

"Apparently so," I sigh, wrapped up in what I'm going to say to Earl.

Tomas smiles joyously, saying, "Well that is reason to celebrate! Across the island it is!"

God, I love this man.

The entire ride I rehearse what I'm going to say and imagine how the conversation will unravel. Though it is a fool's effort since nothing ever goes as cleanly as the scenario you create in your head. After you tick off your list of talking points, the reaction only throws off your game more. But it's a questionable habit I've gotten into, pre-living inevitable confrontations. And it works about as well as armchair quarterbacking in whatever dust-up I've been involved in. Both are a waste of time.

The analysis of life is often as much a folly as preparing for it.

Tomas lets me off in front of Kat's house. After thanking him I add, "If you don't hear from me in about three hours send the Constables to pick up my body."

Tomas's brow deepens over his eyes. "Are you being serious, Mr. Todd?"

Smiling, I tell him I will call him, which returns the smile to his lips. "You will do wonderfully," he says, waving as he pulls away.

I can hear Earl inside, though my knocking doesn't bring him to the door. Headphones or earbuds. Has to be. I never see anyone under twenty-one without them. Back in the day we just cranked the stereo as loud as we could when no one else was home. It's no surprise why this kid seems incapable of holding a conversation. But I bet he's a hell of a texter.

Seeing through the curtains that he's gone into the kitchen, I jump up and down at the window until Earl finally peers out. He doesn't move until I point toward the door. At least he understands basic hand gestures. Then again, maybe his mother has warned him about letting strangers into the house. And in truth that's all I really am to this kid.

Opening the door, he nods, headphones still attached to his skull. I point to the headphones and loudly he grunts, "Oh," before pulling them off.

I have a moment to look at him. Really look at him and see what I was blind to before.

He's big. Like me. His face is long, his brow dark, bushy, like mine. His nose is definitely not mine, more Kat. But his mouth slides off to the left into a lazy smirk, a look I have perfected, which he battles by keeping a perpetual teenage frown on his lips. The eyes are blue, Kat's blue, not mine but the shape is mine, the dark lashes mine. This is what I should have noticed. I'm big on looking people in the eye. But Earl being uncomfortable with me gazing directly into his eyes, he turns away, an awkward side-to-side amble which matches how I moved as a kid.

"My mom's not here," Earl announces, clearly wanting to end this moment.

"I didn't come here to see her," I say, "I came to talk to you."

Earl's face scrunches up like I farted chili.

"Man, don't give me a lecture about how I act toward my mom. I get enough of that from Roger," he says. "I love my mom. She just gets on my case all the time. But I don't need nobody telling me how to act with her."

"Not about that," I say, taking a deep breath. "Do you know who I am?"

"Todd Cartwright. I mean, that is your last name, right?"

"Yeah, but I mean who?"

"You mean like who as in like a friend of my mom's."

"Fifty percent of the time we're friends, I think the other half she thinks I'm an asshole."

"Yeah, I sort of get that from her too. I mean about you, not me."

Great. Confirmation.

"I'm talking about who I am to you."

"What do you mean?"

"Oh fuck!" I start my confession, wishing I hadn't led in the way I have. So much for pre-planning. "Earl, I'm your father," I say, sounding a little too much like Darth Vader.

The expression on his face shifts dramatically as if he's not sure whether he wants to break into a rare smile — or an even rarer cry. His nose twitches, signaling that he's fighting his feelings. Bouncing the weight of his body back and forth between his legs, he tries to settle himself but he can't.

"Yeah. I sorta figured," he says, moving away from me so I can't see the emotion locked in his face.

"You did?"

"Why else would my mom want you around? I mean you aren't sleeping with her. I've seen you like twice in my life. Why else would she let you stay here? Even if it was only 'til Roger went all dark warlord and kicked you out."

"You know that?"

"Figured," Earl shrugs as if to tell me I'm ignorant to simple logic. "He's a noodle. What do you expect?"

"You figured I was your father but you never said anything? To your mom?"

"No. I don't really care, you know. I mean, someone has to be my biological father. Tag, you're it!"

He definitely inherited my snarkiness gene.

"I didn't figure it out until last night," I admit.

"Seriously?" he laughs. "Dude, you can't be that stupid!"

"Apparently I can. I never thought of myself as a father. I guess I thought if I did have a kid out there somewhere, which is always a possibility if you don't use protection when you have sex—so always use protection to save yourself from really screwed-up, awkward moments like these—but I thought if I *did* have a kid, I would just know. Something kind of magical that would happen between me and my kid."

"Child support. That would be kind of magical."

I almost laugh. Yep, he's definitely mine.

"I don't know where we go from here. I don't know where your mom wants me to go. Well, I kinda do…" I joke. "But I want you to know that I know, and if you ever need me for anything, I'm…I'll be around. I don't know what else to say. Just if you want me around, I'll be around."

Again, he shrugs. Not that I should expect him to throw his arms around me and howl, "I missed you, Dad!" even if that is what I secretly want. I want him to make this easy on me. Not that I deserve it.

A surprise father can wish, can't he?

"I need a new X-Box. I mean if you want to be that kind of dad. But you wouldn't need to stay here if you were rolling in the dough, would ya?" Earl opines, taking a few steps away from me and leaning against the doorjamb to the room. "No offense, dude, but I've made it thirteen years without a dad so I figure I'll keep going with or without you around, you know."

Not sure if he intended his comment to be a conversation ender but it has that effect. I'm out of cogent things to add, not that that has ever stopped me before, but I do not want this moment to devolve into each of us muttering the word "okay" at each other, waiting for the other to say something or disappear.

Then wishing I could kick myself, I nod, muttering, "Okay then..."

Earl angles the headphones back on his head, and tromps back to his bedroom, closing the door without another word.

I'm not sure how I could have handled that any differently but I feel a sense of emptiness. I assumed it would be more emotional. Maybe he'd cry. Maybe he'd yell. Maybe he'd chew me a new asshole. I don't know what to expect from any thirteen-year-old, much less one being confronted by his biological father for the first time. At least he didn't take a swing at me. If I were him, I probably would have. But I have Daddy issues out the wazoo.

We learn our ability to parent from our parents. We learn how to be men from emulating or reacting to the men in our lives. No big surprise why I suck. My example of fatherhood was worse than a failure. Thankfully, I didn't end up being my father but genetics being genetics, I certainly inherited some of his traits; those are the things I hate most about myself. And when your life is all about extending your adolescence well past its due date, you have no impetus to gain any actual adult skills. If Tami had lived, I imagine we would have a couple kids by now against my better judgment. The extent of my parental ability would be summed up in the sentence: "Ask your mom." It would have been comical, ugly and tragic rolled into one, and my kids would be the bonanza some shrink hopes for to finance a retirement villa.

By the time my kids got to Earl's age, they'd hate me. At least Earl doesn't appear to hate me.

So far.

But the truth is out in the harsh light of day. Dying of thirst, but it's out there. And now I have someone's name to put on that life insurance policy I shouldn't have let lapse. Maybe I should be mad at Kat for withholding the truth for so long. Maybe I should be mad at Harry for sticking his nose where it doesn't belong. But the person I'm most pissed off at is myself for my willful blindness.

After calling Tomas to see if I can hitch a free ride back to the resort, I step outside of Kat's and pull the door shut, making sure it is locked. It's more comfortable to wait outside. I feel awkward standing inside with Earl hunkered down in the back bedroom.

Staring down the road on this warm afternoon, I realize this side of the island doesn't get a consistent ocean breeze. The tall grass across the street hangs over as if it were a drunk man snoozing on a stool. Without a breeze the air is a stifling mix of salt, stagnation and humidity that makes you realize you're breathing. The resorts and the rich are perched on the side of the island where the trade winds cool everything to a comfortable level, the smell of stagnation tempered by the aroma of suntan oils and brazed meats on grills in the restaurants.

Tropical music is piped in everywhere over there. Here no music plays except the sound of the occasional squawking bird, noisy insect or car engine. The out-of-control vegetation isn't trimmed and managed; it grows like the hair of a mountain man. And while the homes are all painted Caribbean colors, they refuse any of the glamour of the resorts.

As I vacantly stare across the street, the grass suddenly moves, yanking me back from my thoughts. A well-driven Ford van skids to a stop in front of me. The side door slides open and four black men, two of whom I recognize from Bar Esmeralda, leap at me. I take a step back and prepare myself but they don't seem interested in a fair fight. Especially when the first guy brings a gun up from behind him.

"Get in!"

"I told you, Michlean and I aren't friends. And I was bullshitting you about the guy I was with. It was a joke. You know, ha-ha, a joke," I chatter, trying to jerry-rig a way out of this mess.

I feel it before I register what's happened. Lights blast in my eyes as if I'm watching a sunburst. I feel warmth trickle down the side of my face as my hand goes up to protect myself and my step wobbles. It registers that he's cracked me across the face with the gun.

"Get him in de van!" he orders again as I feel hands on me, rushing me toward the Ford. Knowing if I get in that van, I'm probably not coming out alive, I rear back and grab one of the guys, slamming his head through the side window. I come around quickly, backhanding another as I charge yet another like a linebacker, picking him up and pile-driving him into the side of the van until he screams.

I feel the butt of the gun hit me over and over on the top of the head until my knees buckle. Turning, the last thing I remember seeing is a scuffed-up boot coming full-force toward my bleeding face.

## I'M A PEOPLE PERSON, DAMN IT!

I've never been tied up before. Okay, except in bed. Twice. Suffice it to say I didn't enjoy either time as much as I anticipated. But being claustrophobic and more than a bit panicked, I'm pretty close to losing my mind as I groggily awaken to find myself bound to a metal chair in an airless, dusty building where the moist heat gets more intense as the late afternoon sun beats down on the corrugated roof. I battle the rope and twine they've tied me with, perspiration rolling down my face, my shirt and shorts drenched in sweat.

Judging from how haphazardly I'm laced up, these guys aren't professionals, which may or may not be a good thing. I'm not gagged, which makes me believe I'm somewhere where people can't hear me scream even if my mouth didn't feel like I'd stuffed a bag of cotton into my jowls. Out of the side of my eye I see dried blood caked onto my face, melting away with the sweat and dripping onto my shorts. My head throbs with each heartbeat. I don't know how long I've been out but my body aches from head to toe.

Especially my head.

Struggling to focus, to get a picture of my location, I glance side to side, searching for one of my captors. No one. Which at least for the moment is a good thing because whatever limited amount of oxygen circulates in this sweat box, I want it for myself.

Why the fuck would these guys kidnap me? Do they think I'm worth something? That's a greater fear for me than actually being worth something. Because sooner rather than later they are going to discover that not only do I have literally no assets, I am a liability. That I've pissed off everyone I'm even remotely acquainted with on the island. Being worth nothing and having no one that would readily come to my rescue pretty much assures me of being dumped into a hole and covered with wet cement as part of one of the new buildings on the island.

I am having a hell of a time adjusting my vision, worse than any hangover I can remember. Getting pounded in the head with the butt of a gun will do that to you. I've been smacked upside the head with hard objects a time or two in my life, my last visit to this island for example, but I never remember anyone pounding on my head over and over with a metal object until I buckled into unconsciousness. Another horrible event off the bucket list.

Soaked in flop sweat and straining against the twine, I feel the bindings give and take, burning into my skin as I scrimmage them up and down, back and forth. When a door opens behind me, I instantly stop moving, trying to turn to get a surreptitious look at whoever is entering, their shoes padding across the crumbling concrete floor. I steady my breath. I need to keep my cool. I still don't have a limb free, so I'm not in any position to bargain.

The guy from the bar, who cracked me on the head with the gun, moves warily into view, examining the gashes in my head.

"I conked you pretty well," he says, his voice dripping with his island accent.

"How do you say 'Go fuck your ugly mother' in island-ese?"

So much for keeping my cool.

"I could beat you in da head again. You want that?"

"Not really," I huff, the throbbing veins in my head so debilitating that getting knocked unconscious again might not be such a bad thing. "What do you think you're going to do with me? I don't have any money. No one I'm with has any money and even if they did, they wouldn't be spending it to save my ass. And my demise is pretty much a foregone conclusion in most people's minds. A matter of when, not if."

"We're going to use you to get Michlean," the man says with a smirk.

I laugh at his absurd declaration.

"I told you, we're not exactly kissin' cousins."

"I don't understand half of what you say."

"He doesn't like me, dipshit," I reply with flat sarcasm.

The man smiles wider. "I know. I saw you."

Even with my brain verging on oatmeal, I foggily recall seeing this guy's face from the other night. Even in the bar today, he felt familiar. Viola's. He and at least one of the other men at the bar today were working in the kitchen. They witnessed my confrontation with Michlean.

"Nice to see you found a legitimate occupation to fall back on," I snort. "You and your pals fucked up. Michlean isn't going to give you crap for me."

"No," he avers confidently. "We are going to take you to his room and kill you. Den we call the Constables to find your body there. We say goodbye to Mr. Michlean because there are many people who saw you fight, including your own friends, who know he wants you dead."

He grins like a three-year-old boy who just figured out how to wipe his own ass.

Even in a damaged state, I'm never one who lays back to see how things play out. Especially when I'm fighting the mania of being bound to a chair in this hellhole and the motherfucker who pounded my head with a gun stands only a few feet away. No matter how completely asinine his plan is, it contained the word 'dead,' and has my name attached. Even if he's caught and goes to prison for the rest of his life, or Michlean finds him and uses piece of him to troll for sharks, I'm still dead. This is fucking go-for-it time.

"That's the worst plan I've ever heard," I launch quickly, the heated sarcasm spitting toward him with each word, my mouth working infinitely faster than my mind. "Think, chowderhead. That fucker lives at a resort. A resort, you imbecile! Even if you could get me into his room without anyone seeing me, which is pretty doubtful considering I weigh about as much as two of you and your friends put together. Even if you beat me unconscious, you'll never be able to drag my ass up to the penthouse of that place. You need a pass card to get on his floor. Even if you have me bound and gagged in a giant fucking bag, you think four sweaty, stinking black men, in your ratty ass shirts and flip-flops aren't going to pull an audience as soon as you walk in the place? Security will be crawling up your ass in a heartbeat, you dope!

Then you think you can fire a gun inside a hotel suite and no one is going to hear? Jesus, were you guys high when you made up this genius plan? And if you think I'm going down without a brutal-ass fight, you're even dumber than that look on your face, and let me tell you, Prince Dumbass, it's a pretty goddamn stupid look. I plan on ripping out your entrails and strangling you and your friends with them before I'm dead! I promise, I will kill at least one of you before I go. And I'm going to make at least one more suffer so bad, you'll wake up every night screaming because I'm going to haunt your fucking dreams!"

I laugh, forcing the maniacal maybe a bit too hard, but at this point I don't have a thing to lose and I am pretty close to a manic state anyway.

"Even then," I pop off before he can speak, "what makes you think you're going to be able to scam Michlean? That rich, little cocksucker has already proven to be a lot smarter than you and your friends. He's living at a fucking resort surrounded by thousand-dollar-a-night hookers while you guys are scraping leftover rice off of plates. He took your business right out from under your nose and you think you're going to play him? Only the most stupid person would believe that's going to happen. And I think the dumbest person is the one standing in front of me."

The guy rears back, reaching behind him and pulling out the gun he beat me in the head with.

"It's time you shut up!" he demands.

But that would shift the power back to him. And I feel safer not letting that happen.

"Even if your plan works, Michlean can make it all go away and you and your Scooby gang are going to be standing there with your dicks hanging out. You might be the only people that don't know but Michlean shoves cash into the Constables' pockets to give him wide berth. You think he can't make a dead body in his hotel room disappear? Even one as big as mine?" I answer, continuing to endure the pain of the twine as I let it cut deeper into my wrists hoping the blood and sweat will lubricate my freedom.

"He owns this island, pal. Owns it. They're going to use you and your gang for chum. He'll be sitting in the captain's chair, a big-titted hooker on either arm, laughing his ass off as he watches you and your friends die a vicious, horrible death one after the other."

He tries to look like he's not distressed at the words I regurgitate at such a rapid-fire staccato that he's finally catching up with what I'm saying. I can see in his eyes, I have frightened him enough that he's rethinking at least part of his plan. I'm praying it's the part about killing me. I can't let this go, I have to unseal my fate.

"I could have helped you get this motherfucker! Handed him to you! But no, you think you're smarter than everybody, you and your equally illiterate drinking buddies. Let me tell you something about coming up with plans when you're drunk. They only sound good to other drunk people. Your colossally moronic plan is going to get you and probably your whole family killed! You fucked up! You aren't smarter than him! You aren't smarter than me! Accept that!"

"Who's tied to da chair?" he asks, trying to regain some of his whittled dignity.

"You think because you're not that you're in charge?" I fire back, feeling my sweaty, bloody right hand slipping from the trusses.

"Remember that little son-of-a-bitch I was in the bar with today? He may hate me but he's looking for me by now and that little barracuda is mean and nasty. Like a hungry wolf waiting for some dope like yourself to take down and gnaw on. You do anything to me, that bastard will bury you and your pals up to your necks in the sand and then use a four iron to knock your fucking heads off your bodies. He's that crazy! Untie my ass right now, I'll make sure he never finds you. And you and your friends can get off this island before the shit hits the fan."

From talking so fast, the blood pumping into my head causes me literal anguish. I'm woozy again and short of breath. I don't want to pass out, not now, now that I got an arm loose and have this douchebag on the ropes trying to figure out whether what I'm saying makes sense, which *I'm* not even sure it does. I fall back onto the chair, relaxing my entire body for a moment, exhausted from struggling, my wild rantings and the loss of blood.

As I slump, trying to regulate my breathing, relaxing allows my right hand to slip completely from the ropes. Sitting up quickly, my eyes go to the guy in front of me, hoping I haven't given away what could be my only hope of dodging death in this island sweatbox.

"So, what's it going to be?" I ask. "You going to work with me, or are you going to take your chances on your own?"

His dark eyes flit side to side, contemplating my offer, as if he's picking from the cafeteria menu and can't decide whether I'm serious, desperate or just fucking crazy.

When he once again swings the gun up at my head, his face knotting up into a pitiful rage, I get my answer. I guess my diatribe didn't quite cut through the slab of fat he calls a head. No time to negotiate. With my feet still roped to the chair legs, I lift my body, half-leaping, half-falling at him, my freed right hand coming around quickly with everything my weakened body has. Surprising him, I plow my knuckles into his cheekbone. He's stunned more than injured but it's enough to knock the barrel of the gun from between my eyes, wobbling him like a delirious prizefighter. The gun clatters to the warm concrete as he stumbles to the floor with it, falling to his side like a deer hit by a dump truck.

I fall with him, the chair and my body slamming hard to the concrete.

Seeing his hand slither toward the gun which is impossible for me to reach, I realize I have one asset at my disposal. The chair I'm tied to.

As he goes for the gun, I rock my body as hard as I can, blood now pouring into my eyes, using my legs to crank the chair over—the chair and my big, fat ass—crashing down toward him like I'm pulling some kind of professional wrestling move. His eyes widen as he sees my great, big body lumbering downward as he gets his hand around the butt of the gun. But he seriously miscalculates the velocity with which my body with a metal chair attached will fall. As he tries to swing up the gun, I crush him.

The gun fires, the smell of powder snaking up my nostrils. Realizing I'm not hit, I slam one of my knees into his groin. The air erupts from his lungs like popped balloons. We are literally eye to eye as his mouth opens and he gurgles out a long, sinewy moan. Before he can regroup and shove me off of him, I crane my neck back and slam my head off of his with all the piss and vinegar I have left. Blood splatters everywhere as his head cracks against the concrete, his body softening into semi-consciousness.

I grab the gun from his fingers and rock back and forth until I can roll my body and the chair over and I'm lying upside down, staring at the ceiling, astronaut-style. I'm not sure whether I should let go of the gun and try and untie myself, or continue to hold it in case the gunshot brings reinforcements. Laying there a second, catching my breath, no one comes to the rescue. I tuck the gun into the waistband of my shorts where I can quickly grab it if necessary. I use my right hand to wrench the ropes until I can snake my left hand free.

Untying my legs, I'm finally free of the chair. I roll off onto the dirty concrete, trying to get the feeling back into my lower limbs before I attempt to stand. Looking over at the unconscious guy, I actually feel sorry for him. I'm sure me landing on him broke some of the misguided dope's ribs. I understand the anger at losing your livelihood. Not to the extent you crack some other dope's skull and kidnap him, but I get it. This guy had nothing to lose at this point. And he and his equally boneheaded posse thought they had some ingenious plan to turn the tables on their rival. If they had any sense, they would have shot me dead the moment the gun came out in front of Kat's home. Earl wouldn't have heard it.

Standing, I stagger, wiping blood from my eyes. I'm positive I have a concussion which I've been prone to since receiving the beating I took last time I was on the island. My wrists are bleeding, the skin rubbed off, and my ankles are black and blue. Add to that, I am hungry, need to pee and crave a drink. But I'm alive, upright and have the gun.

Winner-winner chicken dinner!

As I stumble out of the building, the sunlight only compounds the agony behind my eyes. Feeling my pockets, my phone, which has been with me through thick and thin, is MIA. That means hiking until I find someone willing to take pity on a guy soaked in sweat and blood. Hearing a rattling engine, I drag my ass to the side of the building and watch as the van the guys threw me in pulls up in front of the corrugated metal warehouse. The three pals crawl out and head into the building. Grabbing a sharp piece of metal out of the dirt near my feet, I rush at the van and jam the metal into one of the front tires. Nearly threadbare, the tire pops easily, giving me time to do the same to the other front tire. I want to open the door and piss on the driver's seat just to make a point but it's smarter to make myself scarce; there's still three of them and one of me, and any moment they will be dragging their buddy out of the warehouse, racing him somewhere to recover from the injuries he sustained when the big guy fell on him. I need to be long gone from this place.

Pulling myself to the road that leads into the compound of warehouses, I glance in both directions, trying to figure out which way is the closest to anywhere. This island isn't that goddamn big but right now I am in the middle of nowhere. With dusk approaching, I figure to my left is east and to my right is west. I pick west and hope like hell it's the fastest way to a hospital. Considering how soaked my clothes are and caked my hair is, I've lost a fair amount of blood and am sure going to need at minimum stitches and antibiotics. These rope burns on my wrists and ankles itch like a motherfucker. I'm feeling no panic but I need to get the hell out of here. At least the road is paved because as faint as I am, walking on uneven ground could put me right on my face. Only thing that makes me nervous is I cannot see a car coming in either direction and this road is flat and hot. Fifteen minutes ago I was tied to a chair awaiting execution, now it feels like I'm the last man on earth.

That is until I catch a 'thump, thump, thump' growing more pronounced behind me.

I'll be damned if these psycho dumbshits aren't driving that van on two front flat tires. Worse, they're gaining on me.

My hand instinctively grabs the gun stuck into my shorts. The last thing I want to do is shoot any of these idiots. But if it's me or them, I'm picking them to eat metal. Checking to see how many bullets are in the clip, I find eight. Good. Two bullets apiece if necessary. If I shoot the gas tank of the slow-moving van will it explode like in the movies? Are these guys dumb enough to stop when they know I have a gun? Maybe they have guns. And a lot more ammo. Besides, I'm a punch-thrower not a marksman and my vision is too hazy for a gunfight.

Clearly they can see me walking on the side of the road; since there isn't anywhere else I can go unless I want to hike through chest-deep grass hiding God knows what. Unlike much of the island's coastal areas, there isn't the dense vegetation here, but rather expanses of high grass that would make it easy to follow anyone running through it and difficult for anyone to see out of. I get caught in the middle of this; I won't know which way I'm going. And who knows what kind of animals use this high grass for cover. I might be ready to pass out but I'm not irrational. I'll take my chances on the pavement with the dumb motherfuckers before I'll take my chances in chest-high grass where something could eat me.

The sound of the flattened tires smacking the pavement with increased pronunciation, I turn and walk out into the middle of the road to face them, O.K. Corral-style. If we're going to do this, let's get it done. I'm too tired and hurt to run. I'm hoping this really, truly stupid move will intimidate the shit out of them.

Though they are probably falling over themselves laughing inside that ugly van.

They stop the van in the middle of the road about twenty yards from me, three of them stepping out. The guy I fell on must be too injured to join the posse. One down, three to go. They move to the front of the van, squaring off with me without a word. I raise my gun so they all can see I'm armed.

Each of them pull out a gun.

Fuck! Not unexpected but still, fuck.

As my hand goes to my face to wipe the bloody sweat dripping into my eyes, I call out to them, "We going to do this?" I've never been in this kind of situation before and the only thing I can come up with in my addled state is to spout some Eastwood-esque bullshit. I mean exactly what does one say in a shootout?

I'm probably not dressed appropriately either.

This gunfight would be more of an even match if I could actually focus my sight and this stinging sweat dripping down my forehead wasn't causing me to blink continually. One of the men raises his gun in my direction. I raise mine in his direction, hoping they suck as badly at this as I do. I prepare myself to fire and then dive into the tall grass, which—regardless of what could be living in there—makes more sense now that the guns are out.

Preoccupied with men pointing guns at me, I don't notice the dark, shiny SUV speeding up behind them until the sound of metal slamming and crumpling echoes in my ears, and their already injured van launches forward like a baby flung from its parent's arms as they trip down a flight of stairs when the black SUV smashes into the back of it. Before the three men have a chance to react, the van plows into them from behind. Two are knocked to the side, guns clattering to the asphalt, the guy in the middle is knocked on his face, the van rolling over his legs as he screams in pain.

I'm spitting grass out of my mouth before I even realize I've thrown myself off the pavement and into tall grass on the side of the road, watching as two of my kidnappers stagger to their feet to assist their buddy trapped under the van. From around the back of the van, two men appear. I recognize Michlean right away, the other musclehead obviously being in his employ. Both have guns. Both have them aimed at the three men.

"You fucks burned down Viola's restaurant!" Michlean roars at them, firing a bullet into each of their legs, crippling them without warning. The men writhe on the hot pavement, holding their bleeding legs.

"You take away a piece of my income and destroy the best place to eat on this goddamn island?! I should kill the three of you and leave you for the birds to pick apart," Michlean says, sauntering up until he's standing over them. "You thought you were going to pin that fire on me and get your action back, didn't you? That was your plan?! If you stupid shits didn't run your business so poorly, it wouldn't have been so easy for me to come in and take." He bites each word as if tearing it from the bone, kicking each of them as he does.

One of the men holds up his hands, waving them frantically at Michlean. "We have da man that took your gun at de restaurant! We were bringing him to you!"

Oh shit…

Michlean smiles. Slowly he looks in my direction as he holds up his gun and fires two more shots. These two fly through the windshield of the van, shattering it.

"Get off this island. Or I *will* kill you!"

The two men climb to their feet, keeping their weight on their good leg as they hobble over to their friend trapped under the flat tire. One of them slides his body along the van until he can pull himself into the driver's seat. He puts the van in gear and flops the front tire off his friend who sobs in pain. The two injured kidnappers then assist the third to the van, blood trailing each slippery, limping step. The trio climbs in and steps on the gas, the van thumping down the two-lane.

Michlean turns and waves his gun at me, directing me to stand. Aware that he could shoot me just as many times lying in this high grass as he could if I were standing, I crawl to my knees and then up to my feet, stutter-stepping out onto the pavement.

Eyeing me up and down, Michlean chuckles as he snorts out, "Oh, how the mighty have fallen!"

He waves his gun at me again, directing me to drop mine. Considering there are two of them both armed, I have little choice so I toss the gun to the asphalt.

"Jesus. They beat the shit out of you, didn't they?" he continues, laughing.

My eyes narrow. Even in my weakened state, a smartass response percolates in my head. But this guy could kill me and toss me into the grass, never to be found, so I have to keep my sarcasm holstered.

"They planned on getting me up to your suite and killing me there, then calling the Constables," I relay.

"They wanted to frame me for murder too?" he chortles again, enjoying the hell out of their failed scheme. "Damn, if they gave points for trying, those stupid bastards would have me doing twenty-to-life in some sweaty prison."

"I think they might hate you more than I do," I respond.

Michlean sniffs like he could care less who hates him, most especially me.

He points his gun at me for a moment causing me to stiffen. He then waves it to his SUV and commands, "Get in!"

"If you're going to kill me, do it here," I respond, shaking my head. "I'm over people driving me around to fuck me up."

His silence is almost painful. But then a smile whispers onto his lips as he says, "You are one pig-headed son-of-a-bitch! Kick the gun over here."

I toe the gun in his direction. Michlean picks it up and points it at me.

"I could unload the clip into you and make sure those clowns take the fall."

"Yeah, you could," I answer almost blithely, having come to some sense of fate.

He responds by throwing my gun over my head out into the tall grass. "If I wanted you dead, tough guy, we wouldn't be talking. They took the fun out of messing you up. Look at you. But you having the shit beat out of you and me not taking any heat for it, good to be me, sucks to be you."

As if I couldn't hate this guy any more than I already do.

"I'll drive you to town, 'cause you're going the wrong way and it'll be dark soon. You need to get your head checked out. Split wide open. Probably see your brain if you had one."

He holds up his gun, and then makes a display of placing it behind his back. He nods to his minion who does the same. They move and get in the front of the SUV. Still leery I stare at him through the windshield a moment until he calls, "Last chance."

Beggars can't be choosers. I've proven that ad nauseam and I'm awful sick of begging. I stagger to the rear door, open it and climb in.

## RATHER THE DEVIL YOU KNOW

Climbing into the back seat of the SUV, there are two of Michlean's working girls strapped into the seats, wearing little more than bikini tops, sarongs and idiotic smiles. Enthused by all the excitement, they seem unable to grasp the reality that their boss just shot two men.

"Girls…" he commands, waving the girls closer to one another.

"There's only one seat," one of the girls protests.

"Both your skinny asses will fit there. Move."

They scrunch over, leaning away from me, not that I can blame them since I'm covered in blood and sweat. They rub their hips against each other playfully, giggling, as they settle into the seat. Maybe it's me but I'm more partial in a social situation to crusty, old hookers who smoke Camels and toss off bitter one-liners over girls who will eventually grow into those women but now behave like endowed bimbos on their first porn shoot.

Handing me a bottle of water, Michlean says, "You probably need that."

Taking a couple long gulps that empty the whole bottle, I gently touch the top of my head, wincing.

"Fuck, I might have brain damage," I announce out loud, my eyes closing.

Michlean chuckles again. "You're funny."

Yeah, a boatload of laughs. I open my eyes to find him craning his neck to look at me. The other two times I've been near this guy, I haven't had a chance to actually take him in as I like to do with people that either become friends or enemies. In those moments all I recognized is he was modestly tall, steroidally muscled and good looking in that Prince Charming sort of way. He is one of those lucky bastards who won life's trifecta. Born rich, confident to the point he needs his ass kicked, with quality genetics. His face is European, but without the inbred appearance of many of the wealthy, powerful Europeans whose lineage seems to have come from only a few strains. Michlean's face is feline, with thick lips and a dark brow. Teeth have been done, expensively, professionally. Damn, I want to look like this guy! I'd feel better about looking at him if I had messed up his face when I had the chance. He needs some character. Not many men are born this handsome.

Between his money and his looks, this boy has never gone home alone from a club. Not that I do all that often but the girls that go home with me do it because they're drunk. Girls that go home with him do it because they're sober and hope the sex is as good as he is good-looking.

The girl near the other door peeks around her friend with a smile. "You really think you have brain damage?"

"Jesus Christ, Tiffany, shut up! No, he doesn't have brain damage. At least any more than he started with. He's making a joke. You girls are as dumb as the shoes you wear," Michlean chastises.

Automatically, I want to stop him from being a dick to her. But in the back of his SUV is probably not the best time. And in all honesty, she does appear to be pretty stupid. And at least he's not smacking her around where I would feel obligated to say or do something and probably get killed for it. I need to learn not only to pick my battles but when to pick them as well. I've never been good at either.

"So you didn't burn down Viola's?" I ask, my eyes closing again.

"Why would I? I get a cut of her business and she does the best business on the island. I don't know what kind of insurance she has but even if I have to loan her the money, I want her to rebuild. You got this misconception that I'm some sort of thug. I'm a businessman. I'm in the pleasure business, and often it isn't very nice. There's limited product and always someone trying to horn in on it. You have to know who has your back and whose palm to grease."

"Both are expensive."

"Money changing hands is the real circle of life."

"How old are you?"

"Twenty-eight," he answers, stretching his large shoulders.

"Fuck! I'm over a decade older than you and I never learned that."

He smiles. "Most men don't."

"I'm always late to the party," I add. "And sometimes I never even get invited."

"Then you crash," Michlean says. "Something tells me you've done that a time or two in your life."

I nod slowly, not wanting to scramble my brain any more than it is. "Sometimes I'm not a very good guest though. I've been known to drink too much and pretty much make an ass out of myself."

"I can be a pretty mean prick too," he answers.

"No shit!" I snark in his direction.

"It's the testosterone. Fucks with my head. When I'm off cycle, I'm a sweetheart."

"I doubt that but I'll take your word for it 'cause if you're on it now, I can attest that, yes, you're a genuine asshole when you're on it. I can let a lot slide, but I've never been good at watching a guy humiliate a woman. Probably the one thing that's gotten me in most fights in my life, and I'm not really that great with women myself. But I draw the line there."

"I'd tell you you're noble but I sort of get the sense you're just a big dope with a lot of problems."

Like I said, a genuine asshole.

Peering out the window, I realize we're back on the resort side of the island. The guy driving flicks on his turn signal. They drive me up to the emergency entrance of the small two-story hospital and stop.

"Why?"

"Why what?"

"Why didn't you just kill me?"

He shrugs his shoulders. "Because someone like you, it's more painful to let them live. I've known guys like you my whole life. Their own worst enemies. Ten years from now, who knows, I might be one. With a cracked skull and little else."

Stung, I close the door. He hangs out the passenger window toward me.

"We're square now. You didn't kill me, I didn't kill you. But you fuck with me again and I won't hesitate. And if I can't get to you, I can get to the old man, his woman, the bartender or her kid," he says, the look on my face grinding gears from easygoing to enraged which he seems to enjoy. "Yeah, I know about her too. I know all about all of you. So, stay on my good side. And when the Constables question you, leave my involvement out of it because that would make me come looking for you and I know right where you'll be."

He pounds on the side of the SUV and it peels away.

He's right. About a lot of things. Mostly that I should have killed him when I had the chance.

Walking into the emergency room, every eye locks to me instantly. I guess I do look like I've been savaged by a pack of wild boars. Quickly, an attendant rushes a wheelchair over and almost shoves me down into it. They don't take me to the front desk to ask if I have insurance (which I don't), money to pay (which I don't), or even if I have a name, which I do. I'm taken directly to the O.R. and helped onto an examining table, a sheet paraded around me for privacy.

"An admitting nurse will be by in a moment," the orderly says, checking my blood pressure. "Is there anyone you want me to call?"

"I'm not going to die, am I?"

"You would probably already be dead if you were," he answers, gingerly checking my head.

"Okay, then call the Resort Club, ask for Harry Everett or Kat Brennan."

Nodding, the attendant exits.

I should have asked him for something for the pulsating torture in my head. The rest of my body was pretty badly mauled but I need to get this head checked out. After my last disaster on St. Carlos, I've needed to be more delicate with the thin layer of sheet rock protecting my brain. I was warned then to avoid getting hit in the head, something I really haven't heeded considering the shit I've done in the five years since, but this is the first time since being smashed across the head with a board I can remember my head aching this intensely.

By the time Harry arrives, sans Carolina, I've had my head X-rayed, which showed a skull fracture along the same line I had my last island ass-whipping. And a CAT scan to check for any possible brain damage.

Harry pulls my doctor, Doctor Colon, aside.

"You don't need a CAT scan to know the dumbass has brain damage. He's lying there in that bed, isn't he?" Harry speaks loud enough for half the hospital to hear. "You just need to find out whether it's old or new. This stupid gorilla has been brain-damaged since I met him."

At least this time he doesn't want to hold my hand. But he does call Gabriel, the Constable, who arrives in my room with a smug shake of his head.

"If I knew someone who would take the bet, I would have wagered you'd end up back here," he remarks. "But I give you credit, Mr. Cartwright, I would have bet it would be during your first twenty-four hours on the island. So congratulations. Now, do you want to tell me how this happened?"

Relaying the story of my abduction by the men who burnt down Viola's, Gabriel nods. his eyes narrowing as he grumbles, "We'll find them."

The smirk that washes across my battered face says something different.

"You know something more, Mr. Cartwright?"

"I know you're not going to find them."

"Did you do something to them?"

Harry's eyes shift to me, suspecting before snapping back to my defense. "Does he look like he did anything to four men? Good Christ, look at him! They won, he lost. His brain is a mashed potato. Go look for these sons-a-bitches. Put them behind bars," Harry demands.

"They're gone," I insist. "I lived, their error. They don't want to be caught, they're ghosts by now."

"There's something you're not telling me, Mr. Cartwright," Gabriel probes.

"Gabriel, I know I'm a little fucked up but what kind of effect do you think it would have on this island if I went to a couple of the big tourism magazines and told my story? Tourist kidnapped and held for ransom on St. Carlos. Head cracked open. Had to fight for his life. That could scare the honeymooners off, you know…"

Gabriel's eyes stay on me for a long time as if he's trying to figure out whether I'm bluffing, pulling this out of my ass, or just being a dick. He turns to Harry whose shrug suggests I'm not kidding. My story doesn't pass the sniff test because as Gabriel surmised there's a few elements tossed to the curb. He's experienced enough to know that, which is why a less-than-subtle form of blackmail seems necessary to put the kibosh on the questions. For my own sake, leaving out Michlean's participation in my rescue is good for business, both the island's and my own. I make too easy a target lying in a hospital bed and I can't even imagine explaining to Harry and Kat that Michlean threatened their lives as well. No. This piece of the story disappears with the kidnappers.

Cutting her shift short, Kat arrives just in time for the CAT scan results, which come back negative for any actual brain damage. Though I do have a concussion and a couple rows of stitches in my head, I am expected to survive this beating without having to be fed through a straw the rest of my life.

Harry bows out to head back to the hotel and check on Carolina who isn't feeling well. Kat parks herself next to me on the only chair in the small room. She keeps glancing at me, forcing a smile and then turning away.

"If I didn't know better, I'd guess you're pissed off at me," I half-state, half-ask.

"Then you don't know better."

"Why…what did I do, other than get my fat ass kidnapped? You blame me for things that aren't in my control. There's enough to get heated at me for, not the shit that falls on me."

"It's just…it seems everywhere you go, bad things happen, Todd. You think that's fate, karma, you're the bad penny…what?"

"It's life," I snap back. "My life. Yeah, some of it I create but not all of it. Sometimes, guys like me, bad luck's the only luck we got."

"You're unbelievable, Todd!" she chastises, standing to pace back and forth at the foot of the bed. "You accept the negative side of everything as your truth so that you're not disappointed when it happens. And it happens because consciously or unconsciously, Todd, you want it to. Because more than being happy, you want to be right. Do you know how cynical that is?"

Wow. Wasn't expecting this conversation. But she's pissed and I can't escape it. I'm glad the Vicodin is starting to kick in or I might just rip these tubes out of my arms and drag myself out of the building. Again, Kat is the last person I expected to jump on my case. I've never been anything but good to her; well, as good as someone who pops in and out of your life after years being elsewhere can be. Yes, we share a kid but she's not obligated to me and I didn't think I was obligated to her. We are friends. At least I thought we were.

Does she think I get up every day and do the happy-dance over squandering every chance I've had in my life? Christ, even Michlean thinks I'm too pathetic to kill. I've had one good thing in my life, the love of a woman I didn't deserve. That was taken away from me and I pissed away any residual goodness she entrusted me with, as if her life and her death didn't matter. I can't truly be happy for Harry's good fortune and I have no idea how I'm supposed to act toward a thirteen-year-old who clearly thinks, and rightfully so, that I'm just some bad choice his mother hooked up with a million years ago resulting in his unfortunate genetics. Even Kat, a woman I should be closer to, maybe even have feelings for, I can't. Part of it is the exhaustion locked in every look she gives me; part of it is I know she deserves better. I'm still not done being a ridiculously overgrown, ridiculously petulant adolescent. Even I'm aware that I feel sorry for myself for transforming into such a monumental douchebag after I was given the chance to crawl out of that.

"Why are you so judgmental?"

"I'm not. I'm asking you to look at yourself. Without any cynicism or smugness. Honestly look at yourself and what you want from life."

"I haven't been right about most things in my life, Kat. A few but certainly not most. You're right, I have come to expect the worse. And yeah, it happens more often than not. In some ways, walking through shit is the only way I know I'm alive. I don't know when I got so off-track. I can't blame Tami's death; I was a mess before I met her. I was only on an even keel for the short time I had her in my life. I want to be the man Tami saw in me. I just don't know how to get back to that."

"Easy. Stop making Tami your crutch."

What did she just say to me?

I don't have to say a word; Kat can see the shock on my face at her words.

"You blame her," Kat continues, her words hitting me harder than the butt of the gun against my head. "Like you can't be a good person without her. That's bullshit, Todd, and you know it! But you keep bringing her into the mix so you have an excuse. Hell, I never met the girl but she's damned if she does and damned if she doesn't. If you find your way back to being a decent guy, it's because of her; if you don't, it's because of her. Let her go, Todd. Stop keeping that girl hostage."

"What are you saying?"

"It's you and only you. Man up."

There are a lot of ways to take that. None of them complimentary.

I lay there, silent. She stands there, silent. My insides now match my battered outsides. Kat allows herself a deep breath. She can see in my eyes that her words have destroyed me.

"I'm going to go. Earl's probably eating something out of a can. I'll tell him what happened. And…I'm sorry," she says, quickly kissing me on the forehead and just as quickly striding for the door.

"You shouldn't be," I answer, stopping her for a second before she disappears from the door, never turning around.

Kat leaves me alone with her words lingering in the room, like the stale smell of cigar smoke at my grandparents' home after a Sunday night dinner when I was a kid. Being left alone with my thoughts is not the best company for me right now. I hear Kat's words over and over in my head as if on a loop designed to hypnotize me. Kat's right; I've taken Tami hostage. Tami loved me. And that was more than most men get in their lives but I'm not happy with that; I've used her death as a justification to deflect culpability. I dump the liability for my behavior on her dead body.

Tami should be ashamed of me.

I am.

## THE DRAPES DON'T MATCH THE RUG

My eyes pop open and I sit up in bed. She smiles at me, warmly enough for me to believe she's happy to see me. Tami, beautiful as ever, her presence relaxes me and I feel my head fall back to the pillow.

Thank you, Vicodin, for bringing her to me.

"You just can't help yourself, can you?" she asks with a bubbly giggle.

I can't help but smile, even though I know she's chiding me. But it never hurts when she does it. Tami never hurt people, not like me when I get a few drinks and a bad case of the ass, where I work with precision to tear the shit out of someone.

"No," I say softly, humility echoing in that single word.

"Todd...you know why I'm here?"

"To save me. Again."

She smiles with a mix of pathos and regret.

"I can't do it alone!" I beg.

"Let me go," Tami says.

I feel a breath shutter as I pull it in.

"Don't say that," I implore her. "I can't."

"You have to, Todd. That was our plan, that I would be free to roam your heart. But I'm not free. And neither are you," she says, looking into my eyes. Even in the darkness, her eyes shine like a place I never want to leave. "We are both missing so many wonderful things."

Tami leans over and kisses me softly on the lips, her eyes connected with mine. I feel her hand slip around my arm, clasping me tightly as she smiles.

"No...please," I murmur, "don't go."

"It's all right, honey," I hear a voice say as I feel the cuff slip around my arm, waking me. The nurse was checking my blood pressure as she has been doing every four hours. She hands me a paper cup of meds and I toss them down my throat before she leaves.

With any chance of sleep in the crapper, I sit in the semi-darkness, allowing what Tami said to me to collide with Kat's words. Thanks for teaming up on me, ladies! Goddamn, whatever drugs they got me on are working against me. I can't sit in this boxy room all night awake, again letting my internal pity party go into the wee hours. I twist my body and sit so that my feet hit the floor. I need to walk, I need to move.

Though I'm sure I'll get a ration of shit if someone sees me, I slip out of my room, peeking down the empty hallway. Wherever the nurses are, they aren't here. I shuffle down to the large windows in the waiting area. There will be lights on outside so I can stare at more than the dark. I've been living in that long enough, I know what it looks like.

As I stare out at the parking lot from the second floor of this two-story hospital, everything on the other side of the glass seems still, as if even the air isn't moving. The palm trees that dot the perimeter of the parking lot, probably planted by Roger, remain still, the sea breeze nonexistent. I stare out, searching for some sign of movement, of action, something to look at that isn't still life when I hear the siren.

An ambulance races into the parking lot and up to the emergency entrance on the first floor. I watch as the EMTs race from the vehicle and move to the back, swinging open the back doors. Another poor soul on a gurney being rushed into the emergency room, life and death in the balance. From where I'm perched, he appears to be bald and slightly built. Old, his arms frail and thin. I watch as the gurney is pushed through the door, disappearing inside just as another man emerges from the back of the ambulance. He's also smallish, also bald, wearing a simple white t-shirt and slacks. I can't get a look at his face but even without seeing it I sense the look of fear. Rushing toward the sliding doors, his gait, a mix of a waddle and a stride, is familiar but I cannot register why. He stops at the emergency door and turns, as if to get one last breath of fresh air. He looks up, unaware I'm staring down at him.

Holy shit, is that Harry?

Can't be. Who's the old guy he's with? What the hell are the meds they are giving me in this place? But the bald head, the tan, the walk, the defiant gaze, it's all the noticeable aspect of him, who else could it be? I feel a tightness in my chest, my breath quickening. If I had my cell phone I'd call him, hoping to hear a barely-awake hello and Carolina asking who it is in the background.

I head toward an elevator down the short hallway that runs perpendicular to the one I walked down. But as I push the button, I hear a harsh voice behind me.

"You should be in bed."

Turning, there is a tall nurse, arms folded across her chest like a parochial school teacher. I am closer to the elevator and could make a run for it, but she's got some long legs and could probably catch me in a footrace. Especially when I'm saddled with staples in my head and a throbbing headache that knocks me off balance when I attempt anything more than a slow shuffle.

"I saw a friend of mine downstairs."

"Visiting hours are over."

"I don't think he's here to see me. He came in the ambulance to the ER with another guy."

She nods dubiously.

"Seriously, I saw him."

"Patients often see things on medications," she says, her voice deep and purring in island dialect. "Especially those who don't rest. Would you like me to give you something so you'll sleep?"

"What I'd like is for you to walk me downstairs so I can be sure."

She smiles. It's not a nice smile. Understanding but not nice.

"I'm going to walk you back to your room and give you something to help you sleep through the night," she says, moving toward me.

"I don't want anything."

"And I really don't want to chase you around all night."

She takes my arm. I could put up a fight until she either overpowers me or I pass out. But if I fall and hit my already cracked head, I'm coherent enough to know that wouldn't be the best thing for my scrambled brain. So I let her lead me back to my room without a word passing between us. She gets me to the bed and stands there, making sure I climb in and lay back. She pulls up the sheet like I'm a three-year-old, tucking in the sides as if that would keep me there.

"If you leave the room again, I'll have to give you something."

I am in no position to do anything but abide.

It couldn't be Harry. The meds must have fucked with my softened brain. I see Tami, how could Harry be far behind? I need sleep. It's been a long couple days. Between having my head cracked open, to the women in my life—past and present—dropping wisdom on me that made what's left of my brain spin, I need to shut my eyes and not open them again until there's sunlight. Actually, if I could sleep for a few days, it'd be better.

When I finally open my eyes, there's a face staring at me. I recognize it, but it takes a while for me to comprehend.

"What are you doing here?"

"I ditched school," Earl says with a lopsided smile as he chows on a Snickers bar.

"You think that's smart?"

"Probably not. But I don't do many things that most people consider smart. Want some?" he asks, shoving the half-devoured Snickers bar into my face.

"You are my kid," I respond, waving the candy bar back.

"You got your head shaved and stitches," he says, the smile widening into an elated grin. "You look like my monster again."

His words make me smile.

"Mom was worried," he continues. "She told me she said something to you she shouldn't have. At least that's what she was upset about last night. Never know with her. Anyway, she told me you were in the hospital, and well," he shrugs, "I wanted to see you, you know."

I shrug back. Strange as it feels, I'm really glad Earl skipped school to check up on me. I can't expect him to be a son to me any more than I can ever really be a father to him. But I can be something to him. What that will be, time will tell. Right now I am just glad he's standing over me with that semi-dumb look on his face, chewing noisily.

"You sure you don't want some? I got another," he says, reaching into his backpack and handing me the second Snickers.

Relenting, I take it. "Thanks," I respond quickly, unwrapping it. "I am kind of starved."

"Yeah. Food in these places sucks, don't it?" he adds.

We both munch on our candy bars silently for a minute. Something about sharing this moment, chewing, feels right.

"I'm glad you checked on me. I'm still your monster. And if that's all I ever am to you, Earl, that's cool with me."

"It's one of the best things anybody's ever done for me. I mean, I still remember it. That kinda tells you something, doesn't it?"

I can't help but smile. It sure the hell does.

Earl sticks around for the better part of another hour. We don't talk about much, but even the casual nonsense we banter about, it takes fragments and bonds them together. The more he talks, the more I find pieces of myself. I don't believe he'll ever become the self-absorbed, sexually-addicted douchebag I've saddled myself with, but there's a lumbering charm to him, a sly sense of humor that creeps through with some coaxing. It's like me, only younger and better.

He has the makings of a grade-A smartass. And I mean that in the best sense.

After I convince Earl that maybe he should slip into school and get back to his classes, offering to write him a note, adding, "After all, I am your biological parent," — which elicited a hearty laugh from him — he says he'll see me later, and hulks his way out of the room.

Nearing ten o'clock and Harry's still not here at my bedside making everyone's life miserable, my mind shifts back to what I saw the previous night. Couple that with my body aching from inactivity, I push myself off the bed and settle onto my feet. With the nurse who threatened to pump me full of drugs off-duty by now, it's the perfect time for me to troll the halls of this hospital with my still-bruised ass hanging out the back of this gown.

Staying close to the wall like a Supermax escapee, I ooze toward the elevator, trying to be as inconspicuous as a six-foot-five guy with a black-and-blue ass twerking down a hallway can. I wanted to dress but my clothes are stained with dry blood which would call more attention to me than a hospital gown and a bruised ass. I crowd into the elevator, keeping my back against the wall and luckily, the elevator clears out on the first floor.

Spotting what looks like a kind-faced woman standing behind the reception desk, I waddle up and give her my best smile. She looks up, smiling, until she sees the staples holding my scalp together.

"What did the other guy look like?" she asks.

"Guys. They got theirs," I respond.

"Should you be down here? Especially with that gown not covering everything?"

"I got special dispensation because the whiteness of my ass has been known to cure blindness," I respond, making her smile, obviously more at my smartassiness than actually being clever. "I watched them bring in some guy into the ER last night in an ambulance. He was with another guy that I think I know," I say. "Can you tell me if the guy they brought in is still here?"

She sizes me up once again before checking her computer.

"Only patient admitted last night who arrived by ambulance is a woman."

"I could have sworn it was a guy."

"Room 111. Go peek in. She's still here."

After thanking her, I shuffle down the first floor hallway toward ICU. From down the hallway I hear a vending machine being pounded in the waiting area. As I pass the alcove with the machines, I spy Harry beating the shit out of the coffee machine. Opening my mouth to call to him, I stop myself. Was it him? Has he been here all night, or did he just stop off to get some coffee before coming up and badgering me?

I slip past unseen and slither my way to Room 111.

The woman at reception is wrong. It's a man. He lies in the bed, bald, his deep-set eyes ringed in dark circles are shut. The face seems familiar, gaunt. Tubes run in and out of his tiny body as a bank of monitors beep and gasp. Confused, I step closer as I keep my gaze on him.

"Oh shit!" I whisper.

My chest tightens, my head swims. Falling into a chair, I'm forced to take short breaths as if I cannot get one to go down my throat.

It's not a man. It's Carolina.

The massive mop of curls has been replaced by a cap of skin with clumps of wispy hairs, crinkled like the last dying survivors of a shipwreck. She seems tinier, even more delicate than before, like a baby bird that's been pushed from the nest too early. I was just with this woman. How could I not notice she was sick? What happened? This cannot be the woman Harry is going to marry in a few days.

I inch the chair closer. Her eyes never open as I reach out and take her hand. Overwhelmed, I fight tears. Not just for her but for Harry as well. He seemed so sure this was the woman with whom he was going to spend the rest of his life. Maybe she fell. Maybe she almost drowned. Could she have a disease? Where is her hair? This makes no sense. My head begins to throb again.

Bowing so that my forehead touches her hand, I try not to make a sound, not wanting to wake her. This is wrong, whatever the hell this is, it's wrong. It shouldn't be. She and Harry were going to have a life; he would take care of her. Looking up at her face, a broken angel painted up to appear as if everything is just as it should be, her head betraying her face, I have to look away, my shoulders heaving as I cry silently, my eyes closing tight, wanting to make this go away.

"What are you doing in here?!"

My soggy eyes jolt up, finding Harry standing at the door, coffee in hand. I've seen that look before, angry, defensive, feral. It was the look he used to give me every time I came over with Tami. It's the unobstructed face of hate.

"I..." is all I can get out before I stop trying.

Harry throws the coffee cup to the floor, the coffee splashing across the room as he rushes at me.

"Let her go! Let her go!" he demands, grabbing my hand and yanking it off of hers.

As I stand, he pushes me. I stumble, catching myself against the wall, knocking over the chair I was sitting on. Harry is quickly in my face.

"Goddamn you! You shouldn't be here! You have no right! You son-of-a-bitch! How did you find out?! How did you---?"

He stops speaking as if something lodges in his throat. The dye on his face mixes with his rage, turning his face almost grayish-red as his panicked, dark glare grills into me since he has nowhere else to turn, no one else to be furious with.

Harry's hands grab my gown, his fingers wrapping up in it until the front of the gown is balled into his fists. He lays his head against my chest and breaks into primal sobs that heave his body from deep within. I remember crying like this. From my core.

"I got you, Harry. Goddamn it, I got you…" I whisper into his ear, my hand around his back, pulling him to me. Harry buries himself against me, trying desperately to protect his soul from this abject horror.

## TRUTH IS, TRUTH SUCKS

His eyes rimmed so red they appear to be bleeding, his trimmed hair framing his crumpled face into a frozen spasm of anguish, Harry looks more like the old Harry as we sit across a small table in the hospital cafeteria. His hands shake as he picks up his coffee.

"Cancer. Stage four," Harry admits, hesitating with each kernel of devastating news.

"You knew this when you asked her to marry you?"

Nodding, Harry sips from his coffee and scowls.

"Should have thrown this cup on the ground too. Goddamn hospital coffee!"

He takes another wincing sip and sets the cup down, pushing it away.

"Carolina is one of the sweetest people I've ever met. It's been her dream to get married but cancer, she got in her twenties, been fighting it for fifteen years. Last year she went into the hospital again…stage four. The death sentence. She's been doing really well and then last night, she collapsed in the room."

"Her hair…"

"You thought that was real? What kind of dumbshit are you?"

"Obviously a pretty big one, Harry. How the hell was I supposed to know it wasn't hers? I mean with the hair and the tan, she looked thin but not sick."

"She didn't want to. But why the hell did you think she wasn't with us all the time? She was resting so she could do the things she really wanted to. The wedding…I wanted to give her that. I wanted her to have the one thing in life she wanted."

"Your daughter would be proud of you, Harry." I say with sincerity. "This is the most like her you've ever been."

That at least elicits a laugh.

"Fuck you, Todd! But thanks. I think she would understand why I'm doing this, no disrespect to her mother."

"Where did you two meet?" I ask innocently.

Harry pauses, taking another drink, his eyes darting around the room as if he's looking for answers on the walls. Hiding his feelings is not a skill Harry possesses, so it's not hard to figure that Harry doesn't want to talk about this. He probably thinks he can talk around it considering he was able to dupe me and probably a few others as to Carolina's condition, not that most of us understood how this older guy—no matter how suddenly spit-shined—landed an attractive, younger woman. The longer the quiet between us builds, the more I feel the itch to fill in the gap.

"Look, I don't mean to be in your business," I blurt. "But if you need to---"

"I met her in a support group. You know what that is?" Harry snaps like an alligator caught in a net.

"Yeah, sure. I should probably belong to about a hundred of them."

"Yeah, you should. One for being nosy," he states abruptly, standing defensively. "I'm going to go be with Carolina," he announces, telling me not to join him without having to say it.

I nod, understanding. If it were me, I'd want to be alone with the woman I love too, not have some guy with his ass hanging out trailing along.

"I'll...I'll see you later," I stammer.

As Harry exits, I feel compelled to call out to him.

"I'm sorry, Harry."

He stops in his tracks, his back to me. He turns sideways, trying not to let me see his face. But I've shed enough tears to know when a man is doing the same. He nods and slowly disappears from the cafeteria.

Death has become too much of a common denominator for Harry and me. While this isn't the contentious battle which consumed Tami's death, it's still a very dark sandstorm that engulfs what should have been a blessed and happy time for him. Harry can't buy a break when it comes to the women in his life. Watching him walk out of the cafeteria, that broken waddle, the shoulders slumped as if he's being crushed, the sides of his mouth curled down trying to pull attention away from the warm tears that lay on his lower eyelid, biding their time before they fall, I remember so well the Harry from five years ago. That's him.

And I'm powerless to do anything but feel sorry for him. Not something I'm entirely comfortable with. Or very good at. Harry's lost so much; this is another slice of the knife in an unnatural battle against realities completely out of his control.

Arriving back at my room, the new nurse gives me an icy glance which causes me to smile as I beeline for the bed, wondering if they have ESPN or the Playboy Channel and what time they're going to let me out of this place.

That's when I notice Kat leaning against the wall near the window.

"Where were you?"

"Went for a walk," I answer, climbing up into the bed.

"With your big, very bruised ass showing? Did they beat your backside with a board?"

"No...that happened a couple days before I got here. Not a pretty story," I offer, not wanting to tell her the entire surreal story.

"None of yours are," she grimaces.

I debate whether or not to tell her that Earl stopped by earlier but figure that should be something he tells his mother, otherwise I'll be snitching on him. And I cannot afford to detonate the tenuous bridge I'm building with the kid.

"Harry's here," I say, not sure she knows about Carolina and not sure I should say much about that either.

"I was working when the ambulance came last night. I saw them take her away," she announces. "I didn't know you knew, that's why I stopped by. I thought you should."

I'm not sure whether I'm being complimented by her concern for what I should know, or insulted that it's the only reason she stopped by. Knowing Kat for only small chunks of time over the last fourteen years, I realize for the first time she's not that young woman I conned into bed in Indiana. She's onto me. Probably even more than Tami was. Tami changed me, Kat recognizes me. She recognizes I've morphed back into a shit-heel, making it very clear she's disappointed but not judgmental.

Just observing. And hoping.

Kat's turned into this woman, even though exasperated by what life has thrown into her path she's kept a sense of humor toward it. There's still a freshness in her eyes that I lost somewhere along my journey. One can see the struggle in the tanned lines of her face but there's no air of defeat. Unlike Tami who always saw the good in people, most especially me, Kat sees people for who and what they are. And for me in particular, she has X-ray vision. There's a relief in being unmasked and still have the person not blatantly hate me. I don't feel any pressure around Kat to pretend to be anything other than my fabulously flawed self. Our relationship is comfortable. Even when she's spooning me a dose of 'grow the fuck up!'

"I have to get to work. I'm going to stop downstairs and see Carolina, see if Harry needs anything."

"Did you know her hair was a wig?"

"Yeah. I mean come on, who has hair like that?" she quips.

"It's cancer. She's dying."

Kat stands taller as if stiffening her spine will keep her from reacting emotionally. She nods in silence before asking, "Do you need anything? Other than to put on some underwear?"

"I'll be fine once they give me my walking papers."

"That today?"

"I don't think they want to keep me."

"Unless it's for a psychological evaluation. Then you might as well take up residency," she says as she walks out of my room.

Watching her exit, I remember that ass. Hers is memorable and even after fourteen years, it still looks good. This probably isn't what Tami meant when she told me to stop living in the past and live for the future, but hey, appreciating a beautiful ass at any time at least keeps me in the present. And I'm not speaking out of school, Kat knows it. A hot body is an asset when you're working behind a bar. Ups the tips.

Alone, I wonder why she and I haven't rekindled anything. I mean besides I'm sort of an idiot and what we had fourteen years ago wasn't anything but carnal. But even those never stopped women from falling for my crude charms. Most enjoy that I'm willing to be a loudmouth goof to get noticed. Certain women find that fearless, especially after they've pounded down a few drinks. Women read me much better than men do. And while some woman hang expectations around a guy's neck like a silk noose, women don't bother with that shit with me. What they see is what they get, and they usually only want it for a night. I'm not a keeper. In my adult life, Tami is the only woman who ever took me home to meet her father.

And look how that turned out.

But Kat's with Roger now, so it's moot, even if I believe Kat can do better. Than me or Roger. Me, the reasons are obvious. Roger because he has a passive-aggressive sneaky streak that runs down his back like a skunk. Granted, he was dead-on about me and I completely understand why he asked me to take a hike from Kat's place, but to never step up and admit it — to not talk it over with her first as if trying to protect her from the big bad wolf, when what you're really doing is trying to put a fence around your territory — sorry, that's crap. I know the pickings on an island are slimmer than other places but Kat doesn't deserve to be stuck with a guy who is looking to play the good-guy, the hero, but is afraid to step into a shitstorm when they hit. Because they do hit. And sometimes they hit hard.

And what is even more agitating about that is I suspect Kat knows who he is.

After being released, I stand out front of the hospital, giving myself a few minutes to soak up some sunshine before heading back under the garish florescent lights to hang out if Harry needs me. I tug on the starched scrubs they donated so I wouldn't have to redress in the bloodstained clothes I arrived in. I'm not looking forward to making a steady diet of coffee and vending machine garbage but I'm not leaving here until Harry does.

I never spent enough time with Carolina to know anything more about her than she wanted me to. Which I now understand why and why I assumed that blonde mass of curls on her head were actually hers. Harry never appeared, at least to me, to be the bleeding heart type who would go to such an extent as to marry someone just to give them a wedding. Yes, he would have walked through fire for his daughter, but I never saw him go the extra mile for anyone else. Carolina somehow broke through the rhino's skin and got to his heart. She got into his heart like Tami got into mine, and transformed him into someone a hell of a lot more tolerable to be around. For that reason alone this woman is special. Harry is no easy nut to crack. He's usually the guy cracking someone else's nuts.

"You look like Frankenstein," someone says behind me, laughing.

Turning, I find Michlean moving up the walkway toward the hospital, a bouquet of flowers in his hand, flanked by two large guys who look like they wouldn't have an original thought even if you rubbed their heads together.

"Are the flowers for me?" I ask, partially grinning but actually hoping he says yes.

"If this were a cemetery," he answers. "They're for Carolina. I saw them take her last night."

"You don't strike me as the type to give a shit," I counter.

"We all have an angel inside wrestling with our demons," he sniggers. "Yours doesn't know when to shut up." His chest flexes and he looks to the men on either side of him before turning back to me. "You didn't mention anything about me when you spoke to the Constable, did you?"

Studying him, I sense this big asshole is nervous about it. I wonder if one of the men he shot died or is talking to the Constables or worse, related to Gabriel or someone else in the department. This at least brings me a smile.

"You're safe," I respond, barely moving my lips as I reach up and grab the flowers out of his hand. "I'll let Harry know you came by. He'll be touched."

Walking back into the hospital, flowers in hand, my head swims. Life crests high sometimes in a perfect wave of bliss only to crash painfully onto the hard sand. Kat is wrong about one thing; I don't always *look* for shit to step in. And even when I don't, shit finds me. I just used to be better at coping with the disastrous piles I often found myself knee-deep in. But after spending years running away to avoid myself, I've lost any tolerance for dealing with the feces flung by life. There's nothing fair about dying. This I know from experience.

And having survived the other end of it, I can attest with complete certainty that often living is a lot less fair.

So does Harry. His life has been a series of cruel ironies. But even his Grinch-like heart isn't capable of this much anguish. He and I share something no one else understands. And as much as I would love to get the hell off this island, escape this raw, insane plague of death that's here, I need to be with him. To hold his hand because Carolina can't.

Stepping back into the room, I place the flowers on the table near Carolina.

"Where'd you get those?" Harry asks.

"Michlean. He's making sure we know he knows where we are."

"Stick a hose up his ass and fill that piece of shit with helium until he pops," Harry mutters, sighing and rubbing his face hard. His expression changes from anger to despondency. "I don't know if I can go through this again," he almost moans in a soft, deep voice that's being overtaken by his emotions.

I put my arm over his shoulder.

"Does every beautiful soul have to die early?"

"Not everybody gets what they deserve, Harry. You know that."

Sucking in a defeated breath, he says, "Let me die. Not her."

I know exactly what he is feeling.

"It doesn't work that way. Or you wouldn't be talking to me right now."

Harry looks up at me, our eyes locking. There's that mutual pain that will forever bond us.

For the third time in his life, Harry is going to have to bury a woman he loves. How does any man endure that? Once damn near killed me.

"Goddamn it!" Harry utters softly, seeming to accept that there's nothing he can do now but live through another cruel event. He doesn't control it, which is what we want to do more than anything, control what is happening. That's a man thing. And we have an incomprehensible time understanding that we can't. That admission is like stepping out into daylight for the first time after living your life in a cave.

Standing a little taller, I grab Harry by the shoulders. I squeeze the tears from my own eyes and pressure myself not to choke up as I speak.

"You know what, Harry, we might not be able to give Carolina time, but we can still give her her wish. We can make the wedding she wanted happen. Right here."

Wiping his eyes and nose with his shirt, he remains absolutely still, only his chest rising and falling. Finally, he pivots his head to look at me.

"Then let's fucking do it!"

## DOG AND PONY MINUS THE PONY

Okay, full disclosure. I have no flipping idea how to pull off a wedding. When mine was being planned, I did the only two things I was good at during the evolutionary stage. I sat in a recliner and I nodded. Tami handled the details; much as I'm sure Carolina handled the minutiae of her intended wedding to Harry. And I'm sure he is pretty good at nodding as well.

Now it falls to me. So I do what all good men do in situations like this.

I'm quickly on the phone to Kat.

"Hey, it's me. I need help."

"That's been apparent since you arrived back on this island," she quips. By the tone in her voice I can actually see her smiling.

I explain to Kat what I want to do, adding, "And if we pull this off, there needs to be alcohol at this wedding."

"You talk to the hospital, see what it will take for them to let us hold the ceremony in that room. Use some of that old Todd Cartwright charm if it's not run out. I'll get a couple days off and we'll pull this together for Harry and Carolina."

"Good," I say, hoping she can hear me smiling.

"Todd…"

"Yeah?"

"You're doing a good thing."

"You sound surprised."

There is silence for a moment and then she responds, "No. Relieved."

Marching into the Hospital Administrators office, I come face to face with an icy-faced woman probably a few years older than me. Her skin is so pale it appears almost translucent, something you don't often see on an island, unless that island is Iceland. How she survives the often brutal sun here is beyond me. Her happiest days must be when it rains.

Remembering Kat's words, I smile, attempting to pull focus from the stitches in my head and the bruises on my face, though I'm not above using those if I have to play the sympathy card. Introducing myself, I quickly read her name plate perched on the front edge of her officiously tidy desk. Greta (what a surprise) Helgadottir. As she takes my hand to shake it, unable to hide that she's off-put by my Frankenstein appearance, I look into the bluest eyes I've ever peered into. Like her skin, her eyes are so opaque it's almost like you can see through them. It's then I notice that while she's not really beautiful on this island she's certainly exotic.

Luckily for me and for her, my appearance is atrociously frightening or I'd be unleashing my fifteen minutes of charm on her for evil purposes. But that's not why I am here. And I can sense she's used to guys like me making passes at her. I can't take the chance that me trying to charm her has to do with anything other than getting her to give me the keys to the kingdom for a day, to pull off the wedding of Carolina's dreams. So I opt for Plan B. Sympathy.

Looking as pathetic as possible, I announce to her my strategy to have Harry marry Carolina in Carolina's ICU room, creating the wedding of Carolina's dreams. If Carolina can't go to the beach, I want to bring the beach to her. I want this day to be exactly what Harry planned on giving her with all the flowers and sand and sun. Harry and Carolina's big day will be a knockout, ridiculous, over-the-top, beach wedding. Greta listens patiently, her hands actually coupled together on top of her desk, like some elementary teacher listening to a student's fantastical tale about the fate of their homework that never made it to class. I get verklempt at my near-death experience being kidnapped and tortured by islanders, only to escape and find Carolina on death's door. Thankfully, Greta doesn't interrupt me, making it easier on me to give a speech rather than have a conversation. And while I'm awfully good at speeches, it makes me uncomfortable that she doesn't ask a single question. I can't tell whether she's being polite, or is just completely disengaged and waiting for me to finish so she can say 'no'.

After an almost breathless four or five minutes of talking, opening the barn door of my salesman skills like I was slipping on a greased wet suit, my head pounds from the vibration of my jaws. I wish I was up in my hospital room lying down, popping a couple Vicodin. Finishing, I give the lovely Greta my best smile, the one I used to use to close the deal with the last drunk girl at the bar, and then remembering to play the sympathy card one last time, I add with an injured look, "For Carolina…my friend. Who's dying."

Greta waits until she's sure I'm done and then lets a compassionate smiles fall across her lips before speaking. "Mr…"

"Cartwright. Todd. Just call me Todd."

"Todd…" she continues, her accent a very odd mixture of island and something Germanic in origin, "I envy your good heart…"

Oh shit, if she only knew...

"And as someone with an empathetic heart myself, I would love to say yes. But as the administrator of this hospital, responsible for the exceptional treatment of all our patients, to do what you are asking is out of the question. We can arrange for a simple ceremony, but what you would like to do for your friend, I just can't agree to."

"It's her last wish."

She looks down at her hands as her fingers lock and then unlock. I'm going to work her until I get a yes. Even if it has to get a little crazy.

"But what you want to do..."

"They had this beautiful ceremony ready to go this weekend. We just want to move it here. That's all. We'll set it up; we'll clean it up..."

"Aren't you a patient here?"

"Discharged this morning."

"You don't waste time."

I smile again, hoping that distracts her from my head which she keeps glancing at.

"Come on, Greta. I hope you don't mind if I call you Greta. What will it take to get you, as the administrator of this fine hospital, to loosen up your rules just this once?"

"I don't see how I can allow that," she responds tersely.

I hold up my finger with a smile so charming, the sides of my mouth hurt. "Let's say you could. What would I have to do? Me. Todd Cartwright."

Thinking a moment, Greta's eyes glance skyward as if saying a prayer.

"Ten," she says.

"Ten what?"

"Thousand."

"Dollars?" I ask in an 'are you fucking kidding me' tone.

"What did you think I was referring to?"

"I don't know…" I huff, "Push-ups. Kisses. Hours of community service."

"A ten-thousand-dollar donation to the hospital could change my mind," Greta states without batting an eye.

"I don't have that kind of money. And I can't go to a man whose fiancée is lying in a bed, dying in this hospital, and ask him for it. He's going to have to get Carolina back to the States and that's going to take a private medical jet. They're going to have more hospital costs for however long she lives. Even if he has it, I can't ask him. Come on, have a heart."

"I'm not unsympathetic. But you're asking me to do something that could set a precedent at this hospital. I need to show the hospital board there's a reason for allowing such an event to happen here. Literally in the ICU."

Sitting back in the chair, my hands go to my knees in defeat. As smartassy as I can be about things, which makes it seem I don't really give much of a shit, I truly want to give Harry this. And Carolina. While a simple ceremony in her hospital room wouldn't cost a thing, this will be the last gift this woman will ever receive. I want to her to have it.

"Give me a few hours," I request.

## BEND OVER

It takes everything I have to knock on the door. My gut hurts worse than my head. And my head is exploding. And my soul hurts worse than my gut.

Goddamn it! Goddamn it! Goddamn it!

The door opening, I'm escorted into the well-appointed suite by one of the guys who was at the hospital earlier with Michlean. He doesn't say a word to me, which I take to mean he is too stupid to talk. There are two sizzling women sunning their oiled bodies on the balcony behind Michlean as he sits in a chair watching some MMA fight on the big screen.

I'm signaled to sit across from him, the television behind me, so now I have to compete with a couple of guys beating the shit out of each other on the screen over my head. Perfect. But I'm a beggar and since I'm here, obviously not choosy about who I beg from.

"So you need a favor?" Michlean asks, his eyes locked over my head on the fight, a smug smile locked on his lips.

"Ten grand."

His eyes drop from the television screen down to my face to see whether I'm serious.

"Who do you think I am, First Caribbean International…?"

"I want to give Carolina Starren her dream wedding."

"She going to live that long?" he quizzes, his eyes returning to the screen over my head.

"Don't be a dick. The hospital is willing to cooperate if I can wangle a ten thousand-dollar donation."

"You can't tell me that guy's not juicing. Look at the size of him," Michlean comments to his guys who are also watching the fight behind me.

His eyes then fall back onto me for a second.

"What do I get out of it?" he asks without pleasure or malice.

"A tax write-off."

He bellows with laughter, causing one of the girls to pull her spectacular body off the chaise and come inside, strutting through the living space of the suite, topless, her enhanced breasts barely bouncing as she gives a smile before disappearing inside a bathroom. The other men in the room barely pay her attention, jaded by the number of times they've seen girls parade around showing off their high-end goods. Although I can't help but watch the free show. It completely sucks that I'm here, hat in hand, hoping against hope a douchebag will turn out to be at least a semi-decent human being.

Watching this girl cross a room isn't going to change that but it beats a poke in the eye with a sharp stick.

"I don't need a tax write-off. And I give to the charities of my choosing. Give me something else, Todd Cartwright."

"I don't got much," I volley back.

"You."

Come again?

He clearly can read the surprise on my face because he continues. "You're a big guy. Got balls. Not afraid of a fight."

I know where this is going and want to punch him in the face as hard as I can. I'd never make it out of this suite alive but still might be worth it.

"I asked you once before, come work for me," Michlean continues, all business. "You would be helpful running girls, running some coke, collecting debts. Not too many people would fuck with you. And you've proved you're willing to break some heads if necessary," Michlean adds, nodding, his eyes annoyingly bouncing between me and the screen behind me. "I got a load of Columbian coming in and need a man making sure I get paid."

"I didn't come here for a job."

"And I'm not in the charity business," he says, slapping his palms off his thighs and pointing at the screen behind me. "That fucking idiot! Jesus, left himself wide open. Pound that fucker. Stupid people need to bleed..." His eyes then go to me with a smarty-pants smile on his face, "No offense."

I wonder how much he weighs and whether I could get his Johnny Atlas body over my head long enough to heave him over the balcony rail. Let's see if *he* lives if he hits the pool.

"That's the deal," he announces, snapping his fingers and pointing at me while his eyes return to the screen as he stands. "You come to work for me; I'll give you the ten K. As a loan. Otherwise, you're in sorrier shape than that fucker getting his face pounded," he adds, pointing to the screen over my head.

Even before I walked in the door, I knew this was going to be a bitch. Michlean is the only person I could come up with on short notice who would have that kind of money liquid. Putting together the wedding Harry wanted to give Carolina, knowing how overjoyed that would make Harry to still be able to give Carolina her dream, is the only thing that could force me into making a deal with the devil. I've already lived through one wedding that didn't happen. This one I can do something about. Even though the cost is going to be a bitch.

"I need the money today. Now," I sniff.

He smiles as if he's won a prize.

"That a yes?"

"Cash."

Michlean signals to one of his minions who disappears into the back of the suite. I guess I'll be a minion as well soon. I wonder if we get matching t-shirts or have a secret handshake? I imagine they never amounted to much more than muscleheads at the gym who needed money to support their wives and/or children, which made them easy pickings for Michlean. They get paid for the one job where size matters. And as long as you don't get beat to shit or die, all is good in the hood.

The guy returns to the room with a bank pouch, handing it to Michlean who unzips it and flashes me a stack of cash inside.

"Ten grand," he says as he hands it to me, adding, "Now you work for me."

"Do I get health insurance and a 401K?"

"You get to stay on the island. Make enough to get a place, hang around beautiful women. But don't fuck them. Look all you want, but when you work for me, you don't touch the girls. Understand? Or the drugs. When do those stitches come out?"

"Next week."

"I'll find something light for you to do until then," he says, zipping the pouch closed.

I wince, pretending it's a smile.

"And don't try skipping out on me. I got people at the airport, I'll know," he warns, "And if you were to somehow get off St. Carlos, I'll take it out on the people you're closest to."

As he tosses me the pouch, I respond, "Yeah. I get that about you."

It takes all the resolve I possess not to pounce on this muscle boy and beat the ever-loving shit out of him, until they put a gun to my head and blast open up these stitches permanently.

"Give the newlyweds my congratulations and my condolences."

"Send a card," I snipe, stalking out of the suite, the ten grand in my hand.

An hour later, I slap the pouch onto Greta's desk as she eats a tuna sandwich that she has perched between three fingers.

"This is happening!" I grumble in a low voice, unable to hide my pissiness. "It cost me everything."

Dropping her sandwich, she opens the pouch.

"I hope you didn't do something illegal to get this," she replies with acute surprise that she's actually holding this much cash in her hand, her finger running unconsciously across the top of the stack of bills.

"Don't pretend to give a shit where I got the money. I got people decorating the room this afternoon. This wedding is on, so get on the phone and let your administration know because I don't want any blowback."

Greta stiffens in her chair, the cash still in her hand.

"Oh, and I'll want a receipt," I swipe at her, taking her other half-sandwich and shoving it in my mouth before I go.

## PRE-WEDDING JITTERS

A gaggle of nurses and doctors glower as Roger's pick-up backs up to the hospital door and four men with shovels dig into the sand that fills the bed of the truck, pushing wheelbarrows down the hallway to Room 111. Kat has done a miraculous job of procuring an array of tropical palms and island flowers, filling the room until it appears jungle-like and aromatic.

Alert and aware, Carolina's soft tears fall down to the biggest smile as she softly thanks everyone that comes into the room. Her color has turned from white to gray. It's unnerving to witness but no one says a word. I've never seen someone die, and that's exactly what's happening here even though we are trying to keep a festive, joyful façade. There's no doubt in my mind that this woman is only holding on for this wedding. As much as your heart weeps over what's happening, I'm determined not to get caught up in the emotion and stay on task. I want this woman to marry Harry. I want to be part of making this come true. I couldn't do it for Tami; I want to do it for Carolina.

Whatever I have to do to pay back this money, it's worth it.

Maybe I'm really a nice guy masquerading as a gigantic asshole. Because this feels kind of good to me.

By midnight, we have the room prepared for the wedding the following morning. Carolina's fallen asleep and I tip-toe around, putting final touches on things while Kat calls in another favor and has someone coming by early in the morning to do Carolina's makeup and get that curly wig back on her head. There's no way Carolina will be able to get out of bed for the ceremony, so Kat made sure she had the arbor built over her bed and wide enough to fit Harry as well. Kat promises that she and two of her girlfriends will be able to get Carolina into the dress that Carolina picked out for her wedding on the beach.

"Harry, why don't you go get some sleep?" I say to him as we finish up.

"No," he says, shaking his head definitively. "They're giving me a cot to sleep next to Carolina tonight."

"The doctors and nurses will be in all night checking on her, you won't get any sleep."

"Then I won't sleep," he answers without hesitation.

Not a fight I want to have, I put my hand on his shoulder and give it a squeeze. As I turn and step toward the door to Carolina's room, I hear Harry stand.

"I understand now why my daughter wanted to marry you."

Spinning back toward him, we take each other in.

"It's taken me this long to get it, but I do," he continues. "You may probably be the most self-involved, obnoxious, intolerable person I've ever known, Todd. But you also have a heart that is as big as that ocean out there. Tami always told me you did; I just could never see it."

These are not words I ever thought I would hear coming from the lips of Harry Everett. My initial reaction is to run. Run out of the room and keep going until I'm breathing in fresh, salty air. But my legs won't let me. I'm frozen in shock, a deep sadness welling up from my belly and a gratitude that rains down on me so hard I cannot breathe.

I nod without a word, over and over and over, knowing that if I open my mouth, I'm going to break.

Convening back at Kat's, we make phone calls, waking people to double-check on everything for the ceremony in the morning. Kat has me make the calls while she rattles off names and numbers from the list she has on her phone, figuring people would be less likely to bark at me. Though I find that doubtful. She wants to make sure there are no screw-ups tomorrow. We are on an island, and the professional pace staggers more often than it runs. No one seems in too big a rush unless you light a fire under their ass. Calling them at two o'clock in the morning gives a coating of severity and pretty much ruins their night's sleep. Kat has Roger hanging out in case she needs him and his truck for anything as she snaps another name and number in my direction.

Pulling himself off the sofa because there's too much activity in the living room for him to play his X-box, Earl shakes his head, muttering to me, "Mom does the planning, you do the work. You'd think you two were married."

His words pause me so I pretend to ignore them. Kat stops in her tracks for less than a second, acting like she's looking for something she lost. We both say nothing. Though it lingers in the air like the smell of yesterday's fried fish until Roger pulls himself off the wall behind me, kisses Kat curtly, and announces he's going to "head home, have a beer and get some sleep."

Yeah, you do that.

Mixing a little rum with my Vicodin until Kat warns me I might be in a coma for the wedding, we finally kick back on the sofa sometime around three. Whatever we could do, we've done. I'm beat and would love to crash on her sofa but it probably wouldn't be prudent for a lot of reasons.

"I can't believe you made this happen!" Kat remarks, "You going to tell me how?"

"It's late and we got a big day tomorrow. I should have had Roger drop me back at the resort," I answer, having no intention of getting into the deal I made with Michlean.

Sitting up, Kat shakes her head. "That's what I figured," she says with a yawn.

I look at her with "what?" in my eyes.

"You did something you shouldn't have, didn't you?" she asks.

But I'm reticent to say anything. I don't want to disappoint Kat again. Not that she'd be surprised but I just want to soak up being proud of myself for what I'm doing for Harry and Carolina. I know how I made this happen is fucked up, but I need a few days of feeling good about myself before the regret solidifies.

"After this is all over, I'm staying on the island," I say.

"I had the impression you couldn't wait to get off St. Carlos?" she asks more than states after a long moment of silence.

"Things have changed."

"If this is about Earl---"

"It's about a lot of things," I remark, cutting her off, "Earl is part of it. But it's about a lot of things. You have a problem with me staying?"

"I might," she counters, her words slapping me upside the head unexpectedly.

"Don't hold back," I respond, unable to hide the bitterness in my voice, "Probably won't change my mind but I'd like to know what's on yours."

"Don't do this because of Earl. He…he'll be fine. He likes you and he seems okay finding out that you're his father. But he and I have been getting by for a long time, Todd. You know the reason I told you is because Harry threatened to if I didn't. And…I thought you should know. And so should Earl," Kat states, her hand going through her hair uneasily, pulling it back off her face, her tired eyes staying on me. "And Roger and I, we're at that weird place, you know…"

I shake my head. I honestly don't know.

"Do we, don't we, where are we, do we want more than what it is, is he the one, am I the one? That kind of stuff. And having you here…it…it makes it harder."

"Because he doesn't like me?"

"No," she says, exasperation drawing out the word, "Because I do."

Okay. Wasn't expecting that. I know it's late and I'm tired as hell and have lots and lots of stitches holding my head together, but I certainly didn't see that left hook aiming for my solar plexus.

"I mean, Roger thinks you're a complete asshole," Kat jumps back in, mostly in an obvious attempt to cover what she just said, "and I can't disagree with him. Most of the time. And I imagine whatever you did to make this wedding happen in the hospital borders on the unsavory. Not that I want to know."

Falling onto the sofa next to her, I grab Kat's face with my two hands and pull her toward me, my lips locking down on hers. If she can kiss me while I look like Quasimodo, I can damn well rest assured that she means it when she says she likes me. Her lips are soft, actually trembling, our desire for one another notching higher the longer the kiss continues.

Finally, I break the kiss. Neither of us says anything as she reclines deeper into the sofa, her head going back so she's staring at the ceiling. I stand.

"I am staying on the island," I confirm before walking out.

The briny air attacks my nostrils and I submit to it. There's something about ocean air with its humid dankness that comforts me. I never grew up around it but having been somewhere near an ocean now, at least off and on, for the last few years, I always feel blanketed with a contentment that I cannot get anywhere else. I understand why people live by oceans. The water is a natural tranquilizer that lets them know all is good, and no matter what, the ocean will still be rolling onto the beach tomorrow.

We will all somehow survive whatever shit piles up in front of us if we just breathe.

I decide to walk back to the resort. I've been around people all day; a little time by myself—usually a dangerous state for me—would probably do me good right now. Getting my bearings, I march in the direction of the beach. I can hike the sand all the way back to the hotel, letting being next to the water soothe me.

All down the beach, the lights from the homes and hotels illuminate the waves. Keeping a steady stride, something keeps catching my eye out in the water, almost moving along with me, staying just a few yards ahead, as if leading me down the beach. I'm not sure what it is, maybe a dolphin, a ray, who knows, but it stays just ahead of me moving in the same direction.

As I pass from the light of the buildings on the beach into a dark patch where no light other than the moon catches on the tips of the waves, I hear a voice.

"You did good."

I spin around quickly, there is no one there. But I know I heard it. Then a giggle.

"Here..."

Spinning again, I see no one. I know I've had a long day but this is freaking me out until I recognize the next giggling words.

"Todd...the water."

Moving to where the surf glides up over the sand, the moonlight surrounds her like a halo. She smiles, waving to me.

"Come in."

I don't argue. As delicately and swiftly as I can, I wrestle my shirt off over my head and drop my pants, climbing out of my underwear. Splashing into the water, I try to keep my head above the surf but the waves lop over my head, the salt water leeching into my healing wounds, stinging enough to make me wince.

Tami pops up in front of me. There's a smile on her lips, the smile that used to make me do exactly as she wished. The smile I could never say no to.

"I thought you were going to leave me?"

"I did. And look what you did." She smiles. "I love you."

Those words envelop me, wrapping around me like a soft hammock.

"I know your future, Todd. I know what is really in your heart. Even though you don't."

"What is it?"

Giving me that smile I remember, the one where she holds a secret she's not going to reveal, Tami slips back under the water. I move toward where she stood, reaching for her, hoping to feel her. Diving under, my hands search the complete blackness of the water, coming up with nothing.

As I emerge for air, she's there.

"Your best days are in front of you, Todd," she states assuredly. "You no longer need saving."

"I do."

"You are the man I loved," she says wistfully. "Fall in love with the woman that loves you and live wonderfully."

"What if I can't sustain it?"

"Everyone fails, Todd. Everyone falls. The truth of character is in those who get up."

And with those words she throws her body over a wave and swims, the moonlight catching her torso, leaving me breathless at the sight. I want to swim after her, grab her, hold her. I want to possess her the way I once did when she was alive, the way she possesses me. But the moonlight engulfs her, causing her whole body to shimmer until she disappears into the waves, the gentleness of the ocean returning as if it had never been disturbed.

I want to scream after her, call her back, but then the smell of the air seems to calm me. I can't call to her. Tami is the reason I came back to this island. She wanted me here. So she could let me go. She helped mold me into a guy who, in spite of my umpteen flaws, can do some good. I can live beautifully, if I allow myself to believe I'm worthy of that goodness. Her death took away some of that worthiness, made me doubt who I'd become. I can still be the man she knew.

Even on my own.

## THE MORNING AFTER

Awoken by a warm drizzle, my hand digs around in the sand, finding my pants. Tugging them on over my sandy ass, my head darts side to side, trying to figure out what time it is. I didn't expect to fall asleep. After Tami swam away, I crawled out of the ocean and needing a moment to accept her goodbye, I lay back and stared at the stars. Shit! I promised Harry I'd be back at the hospital at eight to help him get ready. I can't believe I slept that hard in the sand. I have no idea what time it is but I am sure I'm late.

Over an hour late by the time I make it back to the resort, all I can think about is that Harry is going to kill me. Well, at least I'll already be at a hospital when he does. I'm surprised there isn't a message on the hotel room's answering service with his voice going about three octaves above normal as he screams at me. I'll concoct some excuse as I shower, change into the bland tan slacks and shirt and get my ass downstairs.

Pulling on the Panama hat I begged Harry to buy me to cover my wounded head, I find Tomas waiting. He says nothing, just taps his watch.

"I know," I say contritely, jumping into the back of his cab.

As he races to the hospital, I rehearse my less-than-genius excuse about getting stuck in the elevator. At least Harry won't be able to check the veracity of the nonsense I plan to tell him until after the wedding, and he'll be in a better mood by then. Right now I'm sure he's spitting fire.

Catching my reflection in the rearview mirror, I'm surprised. With my head hidden, I look dandy. Hell, I'd fuck me. And when I get to the hospital, I expect Harry to say he'd like to fuck me too, only not with the same intention.

The doctors told us Carolina would probably be most alert about ten o'clock, so that's the scheduled time for the ceremony. I'm sure Kat and her crew are already there, helping Carolina look beautiful for the 'I do's.' Thank God under Carolina's guidance, Harry's learned to pull himself together so hopefully he's doing that by his lonesome. I just have to make sure he's under the flowered arbor Kat and her friends created, promptly at ten.

Arriving at the hospital, Tomas gives me a small wrapped box, a gift for Harry and Carolina. The gesture genuine and wonderful. Knowing I'm staying on the island, I look forward to getting to know Tomas better, more than just the guy who saved my ass a few times and never refused me a ride even when I was flat broke. Surrounding myself with people like Tomas, someone who seems grateful for his life and what he does, how can it not rub off on me?

Rushing into the hospital almost ninety minutes late, I'm sure Harry and Kat are wagering I'm lying in a gutter somewhere. But I'm dressed, sober, and excited about the day. Let Harry yell. This is going to be a kick-ass day!

But as I stride down the hospital corridor, I'm overcome by an icy vibe I can't explain. I pass Greta's office to say a contrite 'thank you' but her office door is shut and locked. Continuing down another hallway to Room 111, doctors and nurses stop in their tracks as I pass. Hell, I know I'm dressed like a giant sandman in a hat, but the least they could do is smile. My pace quickens as I close in on Carolina's room, pressing open the door to find everyone standing against the walls, as if gravity has forced them back, away from all the colorful decorations under which Carolina lays. There are doctors openly weeping. Nurses holding one another. I see people praying in the gathered crowd.

It's sensory overload; my mind can't grasp what's going on.

Harry sits next to Carolina, holding her hand. Seeing he's still in the clothes I left him in the night before, I freak. He's not ready! As I aim right for him, Kat, who's talking quietly to Earl and Roger, rushes at me, preventing me from getting to Harry. Mascara creates dark rivers from the tears that have washed down her cheeks.

"Where the hell have you been…?" she whispers through tears.

I feel dizzy. Turning back to Harry I find my stomach knotting up.

Carolina is still. Her eyes closed. No rise and fall of her fragile body.

I have faced death before. It instantly overpowers me again. My head swims worse than coming off a bender. My hands shake as I find myself nearly falling back. Kat realizes I've lost it and pushes me back toward the door and out into the hallway. Wrapping her arms around me, she sobs into my shirt, the mascara dotting the new shirt with charcoal tears.

"When?" is all I manage to push from my clenched throat.

"Before I got here. Harry was with her."

I pull Kat tightly to my chest, needing to feel her body against mine. It gives her permission to cry even harder. I can't help but do the same. I feel my stomach knot up, the muscles tensing as if someone were wringing out a cloth. My face contorts into a mask of anguish and unsolvable anger. One fucking, goddamn day is all we asked! Let her have her wish come true.

While the cruelty of Tami's untimely death cannot be rivaled, this is still epic and hostile in its grief and brings back jagged reminders of a moment barely survived.

"Harry…" I manage to gulp out.

Kat looks up at me, her eyes glazed over with tears. She shakes her head side to side as she says through her tears, "I think this might kill him."

Seeping in, like icy waters leaking into the hull of a damaged ship, anger swells through my body like poison. Again fate sucker-punches me and steals a chance at happiness.

I almost fell for it. Fuck! Almost thought that goodness would be rewarded instead of crushed under the heel. I'm such a fool.

A tall, almost bony-looking doctor steps up to Kat and me, shoving his hand in mine. "I'm Doctor Bolton. I was one of the attending doctors when Carolina was brought in the other day. I am so sorry; I know this is devastating for all of you. We need to take her body downstairs to the morgue. I hope you understand. The grief counselors will contact you to find out what you want to do with the body and help with any arrangements."

Been there, done that. Wish to hell I wasn't going to have to do it again.

"I'll uh...I'll talk to Harry."

Doctor Bolton nods. "Just let us know when and we'll send orderlies up to the room. Again, I'm sorry. We don't want to intrude but we can't leave the body in the room much longer. Policy."

I want to say 'fuck your policy' but I nod.

As he walks away, I take Kat by the shoulders and open my mouth to say something but she puts her hand up, stopping me. I give her a quick hug before I have to head back into the room and approach Harry.

Carefully, as if each of my steps matter, I move behind Harry, looming over him like an unwanted shadow. Sensing someone's behind him, he turns and reaches out, taking my hand.

Wrapping my arms around him from behind, my face next to his, I hold him as tightly as I can; the stubble from his unshaven face rubs against my freshly shaved skin. Harry's shoulders heave as he wails in near silence as if the anguish isn't ready to escape his body yet. As much as I want to be a shoulder for him, I cannot help but cry with him, rage roiling inside me again. I want to hurt something, do some damage but with Harry's body shaking with such tremendous grief, I fear that if I don't keep hold of him he will disintegrate into tiny, jagged pieces right in front of me.

"This was supposed to be her day…" Harry whispers, his tears mixing with a trickle of spit he wipes away with his sleeve.

"It still is," I respond, my mouth close to his ear, "Maybe God was just saving her from being Mrs. Harry Everett."

He cocks his neck, his soggy eyes meeting mine. We both let go with a caramelized laugh that melts into more tears. I slip my arms under Harry's and lift him from the chair until he stands.

"Time to let her go."

Harry nods, knowing he can do nothing more but cry. Leaning over, he kisses her forehead, tender yet fatherly, which in many ways I'm sure is the role he played in her life. He speaks to her intimately, his hand caressing the side of her face as he does. I step back so as not to intrude on the moment. As he pulls away the only word I hear him utter is "soon."

I slide my arm around Harry's shoulder as he keeps his head down, thanking everyone in the room as he passes. I walk him out into the hallway where Kat waits. Everyone else in the room says their goodbyes to Carolina and follows us out.

Taking hold of Harry from the other side, Kat locks her arms in his.

"What do you want to do, Harry? Do you want to go back to your room? You want company? You want to be alone?"

"Everyone's invited back to the resort. Drinks and food are on me," Harry announces. "Carolina would have wanted that."

I walk with Harry out to a cab as Kat extends Harry's offer to everyone who came for the wedding, posting a note on the door. Once I have him in a cab, telling him I'll see him back at the resort, I head back into the hospital. Greta rounds a corner coming in my direction.

"I'm sorry."

"If you were really sorry, you'd give me my money back!"

She visibly reacts to my words, then quickly shakes her head.

"Returning a donation that size requires the approval of the board and they don't meet until next quarter. Even so, there's no guarantee they'll return it. I'm sorry."

I feel my eyes involuntarily shut, my fate sealed.

"We will need the room cleaned," she adds, completely unaware of how salty her words are to a man whose heart is bleeding.

"You got my ten grand. Hire a crew."

I move past her quickly, knowing she could be the enemy I'm looking for to unleash my rage on. But it shouldn't be her and it shouldn't be here. There are far bigger evils I have to deal with, and this internal combustion waiting to erupt needs to ferment until I face them.

As I continue to the room, the group of friends and well-wishers move down the hallway toward me. Walking next to Kat, Roger sees me coming in the other direction and possessively takes her arm.

Wrong day for this shit.

"Hey!" I call, causing the entire group to stop.

Stalking up to Kat, I nudge Roger out of the way and plant the sloppiest kiss I can, tongue and all, on her. Pulling away, my eyes go to Roger.

"Not in the mood to play games anymore," I mutter in a deep growl, "Sorry."

Roger's eyes bounce unsteadily between Kat and me, his bottom lip curling into a whimpering snarl. He doesn't know who to confront first, her or me, but he's a smart enough guy to know I'm already out on a limb emotionally and if he wants to climb up with me, it's going to break.

"I'll let you two talk," I continue in a low voice, everyone in the hallway either watching intently or turning away in embarrassment.

As I push past Roger, who would obviously like to beat me in the head with a rock, Earl catches my eye. His dour frown flips northbound into an open, almost joyous, smile as he sticks his hand in the air. I high-five him with a loud slap as I continue back to Carolina's hospital room to pay my final respects.

Yep. Genetic.

As I arrive back in Carolina's room, they are already moving her from the bed to a gurney. I've never seen her look smaller, almost like they are lifting a child, especially with no wig on her head. For the first time, I can see the scars across her chest where her breasts were removed and I gasp, reaching out for her.

"Hold on..." I demand, sliding over and taking her wig off its stand and slipping it onto her head. I tug it on and fluff the curls around her face as best I can. It's her again which makes me smile even if it is saddled with emotion.

Taking her in for a second, I am compelled to kiss her. This woman singlehandedly did what I consider the impossible. She changed Harry. She brought him back to the land of the living and in my estimation she made him a man that felt proud of himself again. I didn't know her well but I'm both grateful and in awe. I know Harry well enough to say his feelings for her were not just that she was dying. Harry is empathetic but seldom sympathetic. There was something else about Carolina that drew Harry in. Yes, she is reminiscent of Tami and her mom; I assume that was the initial allure. But there was also something unique to Carolina, her charm, her sense of effusive joy at life in the face of death that I would have loved to have known more. And there was a spine made of steel, that of a woman who was probably underestimated most of her life, branded the nice girl who wouldn't stand up for herself, only to surprise everyone that when push came to shove, she shoved back. Gracefully.

Feeling the two men's presence over my shoulder I kiss her cheek again and slide my lips to her ears.

"Thank you."

Walking out of the room, I need a moment by myself in the hallway. Emotions stir, even ones I thought I buried five years ago. This kind of loss, ironic and brutal, will always be my curse. And Harry's. I don't know why. Paying for past sins is the only way I can justify it. But even when it feels deserved, that doesn't mean it doesn't pierce the heart. I get what's coming to me. But Harry, he's changed. He deserved real happiness. At least for longer than he had it.

## ON THE HOUSE

When I arrive at the resort, the bar is teeming with people sucking down Harry's gratis liquor. It took less than a day for the word that Carolina was dying and she and Harry were going to marry on her deathbed, to travel in all directions. People shifted schedules, took off work, left their hotels and dropped out of fishing trips and hiking expeditions to show up at the hospital, only to be walloped by the news that she had died just hours prior to the 'I dos'.

And many other who crowd the bar after hearing drinks are free. Jackasses.

Kat assists behind the bar, helping the overwhelmed daytime bartenders pouring drinks as quickly as they can. Striding up, she points at me without looking up.

"What can I get you?"

"Scotch. Neat."

Knowing my voice, her eyes slowly raise like the backend of a capsized boat right before it goes under for the last time.

"Subtle. Real subtle."

"Not my most understated move. But effective."

Her eyes shift to the left, commanding me to follow. Turning, Roger is hunched on a bar stool amid the crowd, glowering, a drink in front of him and another empty glass beside it.

Kat drops a double scotch, neat, onto the bar in front of me as I mumble, "Fuck!" knowing I have to do this the right way; Roger's not going down without at least a reasonable chance to exit with some dignity and maybe a year's supply of Rice-A-Roni as a parting gift.

Bobbing and weaving through the bar crowd, some trying to shove their hand into mine and offer their condolences under the belief that I am Harry's kin, I don't stop moving until I get next to Roger and set my drink on the bar. He picks it up and swigs the contents in one gulp.

"That was mine," I respond.

"I should get something out of this, shouldn't I?"

Touché. Like being stabbed to death by a thousand little olive spears.

"Do you even love her?" he then asks.

Damn. We're jumping right into the hard questions without any name-calling or hair-pulling? At least let me ease into the ones with complicated answers. I'm not lubricated and I haven't even warmed up my sarcasm. Hell, an hour ago I was crying. This isn't going to go well for me.

"You going to let me at least apologize first?" I dodge.

"I asked you a question. I want an answer."

What you're aiming for is a kick in the head. I hate when the injured party just assumes they have the upper-hand.

"Okay. Let me apologize for how I handled things. My bad. Not my feelings for Kat but the demonstration was probably not the best way to announce them. So, I'm really sorry I did that to you."

"I don't care!" he says, downing what's left in his own drink.

I wave one of the other bartenders over and point to our glasses. "Scotch neat and whatever he's having."

"What I have with Kat---"

"Is a kid," Roger interrupts. "That's all. You've seen her what, once in foureen years not counting this trip? You're Earl's biological father. Biological," he emphasizes. "Because you haven't been a father to that kid. So what now, you're going to stay? You're going to be here for them? Or are you going to go hippy-dippy and disappear again? Which from what I understand seems to be your MO."

"I'm staying."

"I doubt it…"

"I'm staying," I state more emphatically. "I don't know what I am to Earl. But I'm something. And I'm going to try and be something more. He deserves that."

"Not from you!" Roger blurts out. "I love Kat. Can you say that, Todd?" He lays his hand on top of the bar, hoping playing aces is enough as he glares at me, waiting for me to whither.

"No. I can't," I respond, my head bobbing side to side as I disengage from him and look down the long bar to where Kat quenches the thirst of the growing crowd. "Love for me, it's rare. Only had it once. But when I look at Kat, I feel something. I want her to like me. And I want to be with her. It's like she knows who I am and still wants to hang out with me."

"You sleep with her?"

I shake my head.

"You can't get adventure and security from the same place. I'm her security. You're…a carnival that rolls into town once every couple years. It's fun to get on the ride but tomorrow you'll be off to another town."

As the bartender tries to set my scotch on the bar, I retrieve it from his hand.

"I got a thousand and one reasons to get the hell off this island. And only two good ones to stay. But sorry, man, the carnival isn't going anywhere," I add, downing the contents of the glass. The warmth of the liquor only enhancing my 'what the fuck' attitude. "I sold my soul so I could stay here."

"You don't have a soul. No matter what you tell yourself, it won't be long until you get bored with the island, bored with her, bored playing Daddy and you move on. And guess what, Todd? You fucked up probably her last, best chance at a good man. Me. Congratulations, you selfish fuck!"

Roger shoves himself off his stool and shoulders his way through the crowded bar, heading toward the exit just as Harry enters. Strangely, people applaud as Harry moves through them, as if an underdog prevailed in a championship fight. I'm not sure what people are supposed to do at moments like this but clapping measures high on the weird meter. Even Roger seems confused, stopping to see if they are applauding him making an exit. When he realizes it's for Harry's entrance, he storms out, upstaged again by someone he doesn't really like.

Stepping up next to Harry, he leans over and whispers in my ear.

"Who are all these people I'm buying drinks for?"

I lead him to the bar as more strangers shake his hand or offer him unsolicited hugs and condolences.

"You want something to drink, Harry?" Kat calls to Harry.

"Yeah. Whatever Todd's having…with soda."

"And grab me another scotch," I pipe in with a smile.

Kat just gives me a tepid glance and turns away.

"What'd you do to make her mad?" Harry asks, after finally making his way over to me.

"Kissed her. In front of Roger."

Harry gives me a sharp, staggering look before shaking his head. "Idiot!"

"I told you, everyone's got gifts. I didn't think we'd see you down here. How you feeling?"

"Numb. If I weren't I wouldn't be down here letting strangers touch me, much less hug me."

"Anything I can do?"

"Quit asking me questions."

Kat sets the drinks on the bar and moves away from me quickly, rubbing a little salt in my minor wounds. I guess she wanted to tell him and she's pissed I made Roger feel like a chump.

"Ever feel like just punching something and you don't know what it is?" Harry asks, breaking the silence.

"Every day."

"Yeah, I thought you might. I did when Tami died. And I got to punch you which made me feel better."

"I remember."

"But today, I don't know who or what I want to sock to make me feel better, but I know I want to. It's like having a bad itch you just can't reach. I know it'll help me feel better but there's no one to blame. Who am I supposed to be mad at? God?"

"I was. For a long time. Still kind of sore at him."

"And look what that's done for you."

"Didn't say it was smart, Harry, just said it was. I'd let you hit me, but I know you'd bust open some of these stitches in my head and I end up back in the hospital. And I'm kind of done with hospitals."

Harry and I drink our liquor in silence. Once he's done with his scotch, he sets the glass on the bar and starts moving away from me.

"Where are you going?"

"Run the gauntlet of condolences. I just came down here for one drink and to thank all these people I don't know for drinking on me."

"Sure you want to be alone? Is that good for you right now?"

"What are you going to do, hold my hand? For the moment I'm cried out and I don't need you instigating more tears. I have some business to take care of. And I need time to sort some things out. I'm not going to do anything stupid."

"I would."

"I know you would. That's why I'm glad this didn't happen to you a second time."

Harry is descended upon like the slow gazelle amid a pride of lions. Women hug, men pat him on the back. People who have never laid eyes on Harry or Carolina in their lives are there to offer words of sympathy. Polite and courteous, Harry starts and stops until he's at the exit to the bar. Everyone watches him go, raising a glass as he does.

## AND NOTHING BUT THE TRUTH

A bottle of Dewar's keeps me company as I lounge on a beach chair. I haven't really moved from it most of the day, except to periodically wander out into the ocean until I'm waist high, usually to pee.

Yes, I'm one of those people.

Exhaustion throbs my bones. After spending another night semi-sleeping in the sand and then arising to Carolina's death and Harry's devastation, I don't want to move. I don't want to think. I don't want to talk. I just want to sit. Let the sun pound my body into redness. I can't get my head to focus fully on anything anyway. Not Carolina, not Tami, not Earl, not Kat, not the lot of my life which obviously is in a pretty steady state of shit. Returning to the island only made that more vivid and contextual. Discovering I had a son, watching Harry step up for Carolina only to have her die so tragically, my undeniable yet messy feelings for Kat, combine to make my existence over the last five years ludicrous and inconsequential. Who needs to travel the world to be fucked-up? I could have stayed right here and gotten more than my ration. All running away did was give me the illusion I was moving on.

Hearing something being dragged through the sand, I turn. Harry tugs a beach chair in my direction. He's wearing shorts and a t-shirt, a ball cap and sunglasses. He looks like a small-town weatherman trying not to be noticed.

"I tried getting some sleep but what's the point," he says, placing the chair uncomfortably close to mine and plopping down, kicking off his sandals like he's going to be staying a while. Harry reaches over and takes the scotch bottle out of the sand in front of my feet and brings it to his lips, "Not my drink but..." he says but stops himself, eyeing me, "You haven't been licking on some skanky girl, have you?" he asks before drinking.

"What's your definition of skanky?"

"Well, the type you usually go for except for my daughter."

"I kissed Kat today. But I don't think she's skanky."

Harry downs a sloppy slug of scotch. "She's not. But you're still an idiot."

"Can't sleep, huh?"

"No. And I feel like two tons of crap stuffed into a one-ton bag. I wanted to give her one gift, one gift, and I couldn't do that."

"You gave her everything you could, Harry," I remark, taking the bottle from him and swigging. "If nothing else, I'm impressed. I didn't think you had a nice bone in your body."

"I'm full of surprises, Todd. And the day is still young."

I glance over at him. With the sunglasses on his face, I can't get an accurate read on his level of sarcasm but considering what's happened, I would understand if it was off the charts.

But there's also an ominousness to his words and I get the sense he's planning something really, really stupid, so I have to ask, "What's that mean?"

"Why does everything have to mean something? Good Christ, why do you overthink things? Stick with what you're good at...which come to think about it, is nothing. So sit there and shut the fuck up!"

As he takes the bottle, two beautiful girls in very small bikinis bounce past us. I wait for them to turn and give me a glance, ready with a smile, but they don't even bother checking to see if I'm ogling them as they go. Damn, I'm losing my magic!

But a few feet up the beach the two beauties stop, talk closely for a moment, glance back and then return to where we sit. I take back what I said, I still got it.

"Are you the guy who lost his fiancée this morning?" one of the young women asks with a sympathetic frown, extending her hand to Harry.

Harry nods, taking her hand. She squats down in front of him, her equally beautiful friend standing behind her.

"We just want to offer our condolences. We're so sorry."

Harry smiles, patting her hand. "You're very kind, young lady."

She smiles and stands, never once even glancing in my direction. Her friend either.

I take back what I took back. Clearly, I don't still have it.

After watching the young women continue down the beach, their asses sashaying in their tight bikini bottoms as they go, I give Harry a look. He scrunches up his face as if smelling the week-old carcass of a beached whale.

"I'm not going to use my tragedy to get laid, Todd. I'm not you."

"You don't know I was thinking that."

"I do know. I know how you behaved when you were down here after Tami's death."

"That was different. I wanted to lay waste to every good thing she'd brought out in me."

"What's your excuse now?"

Oww. Fuck. Harry certainly knows where to dig the knife. It's like he's been reading my mind and waiting for an opening to plunge the dagger into my heart.

"Shouldn't you be in mourning rather than jumping up my ass?"

Harry gulps down about half of what's left in the bottle before standing and saying, "Giving you a ration of shit makes me feel better. Sue me. I have to go make arrangements for Carolina."

"Want me to do that?" I offer.

"Dinner tonight. There are things we need to discuss," is all he says before walking off without actually replying reply to my question.

With a few hours to kill before dinner with Harry, the scotch snaking through my veins does its voodoo. I feel good. Almost back to normal. Staggering to my feet, it's good to feel the comfortable wobble I get when I first stand up after a few drinks. I imagine Kat has gone home and I debate whether I should head out to her place and attempt to make amends. But I kibosh that idea. She'd smell me walking through the door; no matter what I said, it would be tainted by my drunk. Even if I felt compelled to fall to my knee and propose, she would probably kick me in the balls. She's just as confused about her feelings as I am, and I imagine Roger's speech about him being security and me being a carnival ride was rehearsed on her on their way over to the resort from the hospital. No, being around her after nearly a half bottle of scotch isn't a smart idea.

Hell, I doubt we would have a kid if both of us hadn't been drinking. A fact I'll keep from Earl. Not that he would probably find it a surprise.

Checking my pockets, I have eleven dollars in cash to my name. If I were twelve it would be an embarrassment of riches but being at the end of my thirties, just another reason to find myself pitiable. I've been pretty dexterous in not buying myself a drink here at the resort, but I'm pretty sure eleven bucks would wipe me out. I find a seat at the end of the bar, hoping I look pathetic enough for some kind stranger to offer me liquor. People at these places are notoriously friendly. But just like the beach, no one seems to be glancing in my direction. I'm a big guy with stitches covering my skull, come on, I'm noticeable. And thirsty.

"You look like you could use a drink," says a female voice behind me.

Jackpot!

The grin falls across my lips as I turn on the seat. The girl is hot and young, her round breasts peeking out over a tube top. I actually take a deep breath, excited at the sight until I realize I've seen her before. It's the girl Michlean smacked to the ground.

"The boss sent me to see if I could find you," she says, her hand falling to my leg just above my knee.

"Why?"

"He doesn't tell me that stuff. Just asked me to come down to the bar and see if you were here. Guess he knows you pretty well."

"How old are you?" I can't help but asking.

"Twenty-two."

"Bullshit!"

She smiles. "My driver's license says so."

"Yeah. Mine too," I snort.

"I'm of legal age. That's all you need to know."

"Sure you are."

"I am. Graduated high school and everything."

"And everything," I respond with a shake of my head. "Then what are you doing down here, working for Michlean?"

She shrugs. "I hated Connecticut."

"Move to Vermont."

Laughing at my comment, she adds, "Sometimes Michlean can be mean. But I want to be here. I don't get all bent about having sex with guys for money or think I'm doing a bad thing. And most of the clients Michlean sets me up with are rich and tip great, so stop being a hater."

"What's your name? REAL name."

"Doris. Icky, huh? I go by Lilac here. Picked it myself. My mom's favorite flower. Come on, Michlean sent me to fetch you and that's what I'm doing."

The last thing I want to do right now is deal with this asswipe. But I'm drunk enough to comply with Lilac's wishes. There are worse things to do than follow her round, little ass through the lobby to the elevator. As it opens she jumps in and pushes the button for the penthouse.

"Hurry," she calls to me as I saunter in. "I hate riding a crowded elevator."

She presses the DOOR CLOSED button over and over until her wish comes true. Once the door closes, she smiles again, spinning toward me.

"Don't tell," she says, leaping up into my arms and pressing her lips into mine, her tongue diving down my gullet as I open my mouth to protest. I'm all for aggressive women, nothing pleases me more than not having to work hard for sex with a hot woman, but Lilac still looks like the girl who plays the clarinet in the school band dressed in her mom's sexy clothes.

"There aren't enough floors in this building for this," I manage to get out after she pulls her tongue from my throat.

"I know. That's what makes it fun," she giggles, her hand grabbing my growing Johnson, falling to her knees.

"This is a bad idea, little girl…"

"Will you quit calling me that!" she says as I bat her hand away from my zipper. Getting my hands under her arms, I lift her to her feet and hold her there until the elevator dings, announcing our arrival at the penthouse.

As the doors open, I set her back down. She smiles, having enjoyed fucking with me. As much as I am unaccustomed to turning down any woman willing to have sex with me, especially when I look like my head was shoved into the blade of an outboard motor, this would be tragic on a lot of levels. Most obvious, who would believe I didn't initiate it? Kat wouldn't. I doubt Michlean would, though something tells me he's aware the young woman he sent down to find me is a minx and this is some sort of loyalty test.

If I'd realized that before I'd have let her go down on me out of spite. I hate tests.

"I found him!" Lilac announces, bouncing into the penthouse, "he was at the bar just like you said." Michlean lounges on one of the white sofas in the large living room with an amazing view of the ocean. There are three women hanging out with him watching TV, another catching sun on the lanai completely nude.

Lilac continues through the room and out onto the balcony, pulling off her tube top and slipping out of her shorts.

"She try to blow you in the elevator?" he asks.

"No," I answer, a little too quickly for him not to know what I was saying wasn't true.

"That one likes giving head," Michlean tosses off, causing the other girls in the room to throw him various levels of shade. "Sit," he says, waving to the sofa across from him, where two of the girls lounge.

He waves them off, the girls sulking as they slip off the sofa and move outside with the other girl to catch some rays. They strip out of what they are wearing, some to tiny g-strings, some nude, before lying back on the chairs, stroking lotion on their bodies.

Michlean watches them for a moment, then watches me watching them, smiling.

"Suntan lotion. Smell always gets me horny. My mom used to strip naked, drip it all over her body and then stroke it in."

I wince which causes Michlean to laugh.

"Too much information? My mom was superhot. It's how she landed my dad. He couldn't keep his fucking hands off of her."

"You sound jealous," I answer, unable to hide my blatant edge of snarkiness for this guy who seems to think I want to share his perverted childhood memories and his creepy mother-fixation.

Laughing again, Michlean enjoys believing he's yanked my chain when all he's done is shoot up a few notches on the douche meter.

"Did you want to see me about something, or did you just bring me up here to see if I like girls?" I ask, cutting to the chase.

"There's a couple guys trying to horn in on some of my business. We need to persuade them to get off the island."

When my eyes narrow with doubt, Michlean flexes. I'd like to think it's involuntary but it's more like some nasty vulture spreading its wings when something gets too close to its roadkill.

"Don't forget who you are indebted to," he rattles. "You're a big guy, scary as shit. Even scarier with the stitches in your fucking head. These guys aren't going to want to fuck with you. Which means they aren't going to want to fuck with me."

Call me paranoid but I get the inkling this piece of shit is setting me up for more damage than I already have.

"And if they do?" I ask.

"Do what?"

"Fuck with you. And in turn, fuck with me?"

"We handle it."

"You trying to get me killed?" I ask directly.

"Not until your debt is paid off," Michlean chuckles humorlessly.

"You got guys who are better suited to this shit than me," I respond in my low 'don't-fuck-with-me' voice. "I'm not getting my head split open again. I'm not getting shot. I got no intention of dying so you can live like this," I continue spreading my arm around his den of iniquity. "So corral your other guys into your horseshit. I'll get you the money I owe you. I'm not dying for you."

Michlean remains silent. But the bouncing of his pecs lets me know the bomb is ticking internally. I know I could take this musclehead, even with stitches in my head. And I've been itching to do it. Illegal shit goes on everywhere but none of it is a game I've ever wanted a part of. I'm wise enough to know people who stay in it long enough, especially on the lower end of the money trail, get dumped somewhere for the gulls to pick over.

Michlean's eyes drift up over me, like they did when he was watching the fight the other day. It's then I feel the chilly sensation of steel against the back of my skull.

"You're part of my crew and you'll do as I say," Michlean speaks, the barrel of the gun held by one of his other guys slipping down toward where my spine connects to my brain stem, letting me know he knows just where to lodge a bullet. "Tomorrow morning. Seven a.m. Be here. Don't make me come looking for you, Todd. Because I won't. I'll go looking for your friends. I'll start with the kid. Then his mom. Then the old man."

The blood in my veins instantaneously pools behind my eyes. Seeing nothing but red as I burst off the sofa and over the coffee table, I have Michlean's throat in my hand before his guys even move. I squeeze as hard as I can, wishing I could see better but the rage has consumed me and all my senses have been overwhelmed by one urge—to kill this piece of filth.

The two men in the room lift me off the ground, trying to get me to release Michlean's neck. Michlean gets his thumbs up under my hands and the three of them are able to wrestle his neck away from my grip.

"Don't ever threaten that boy! Or his mom! Or Harry! Ever!! I will rip your head off and feed your brains to the dogs in the street. You got me?!?"

Massaging his throat, Michlean's eyes burrow into me like a parasite lodging in my chest. I wait for him to tell these two lunks to kill me. But startling even me, he begins to laugh. Angry laughter, vengeful and malicious, but laughter.

"Bring that attitude tomorrow!" he says, flexing his entire body and screaming at the top of his lungs to exorcise his wrath at me, before grabbing one of the girls by the arm. "I need to fuck! Throw him out of here, I'm sick of his pathetic face!" he mandates to the two guys.

The two guys grapple with me as they drag me to the door of the suite. One of them gets it open enough to shove me out into the hallway. As the door slams, I wonder why I bothered fighting. I didn't want to stay there. I just didn't want those pukes to muscle me out.

Feeling the back of my head gingerly, my finger has a spot of blood. I must have popped a staple in the melee. Great. This day just keeps getting better.

I fall against the wall of the elevator as the door closes. Keeping my hand on the back of my head, I gather my wits and calm myself. There has to be something I can do. I'd like to say I'm between a rock and a hard place, but I've been there before and lived to tell the tale. I'm between a rock and a bigger rock and something's squeezing them together. I hate this guy. I hate what he does. I hate that I sold my future to him for ten grand. I hate that Carolina didn't live to have her day, then maybe, just maybe, I could feel some vindication for the choice I made. I hate that this guy knows I have a relationship with Harry, Kat and Earl. I hate that I feel I can't tell them what I've done.

I've spent at least half my life burning bridges and the other half trying to jerry-rig something to reconnect the two sides. Most I never succeeded at rebuilding to any degree where I could cross again. The bridge with Harry and the one with Kat are about the only two I've had marginal success reconstructing. I don't how much more damage I can do to either relationship until it's severed completely. Putting all of them in danger, and now agreeing to work for the very person who threatened them, I wouldn't blame Harry for washing his hands of me and I wouldn't blame Kat for choosing security over adventure.

If it were me, I would.

## WOULD YOU LIKE DESSERT WITH THAT?

As I squint at the mirror trying to find exactly which staple popped in my head during the tussle, I call Harry's room. I always feel better doing two things at once if there's a possibility one of them could bring me bad news. Harry answers; his voice is raspy, as if he's been crying, as I finally get a view of the far side of my head and can see the staples are in place, but a piece of skin between two of them is seeping blood. Nothing major, just more blood.

"You okay, Harry?"

"Give me an hour, meet me downstairs," he says, hanging up without really answering my question.

Knowing the raw pain that ulcerates, consuming you in waves of teary emotion followed by an unsettling calm, I debate ringing Harry's room again and asking whether he'd like to postpone this dinner. Carolina hasn't been dead a day. That's not long enough to even scratch the surface of what he has to deal with. I get that everybody's got to eat, but not everybody's got to talk.

Maybe he just needs to spend some time with someone he knows understands. Whatever he needs, I'm there.

Settling in at the bar, the male bartender I've seen a few times slips a coaster in front of me.

"Scotch, neat…and put it on my new boss's tab."

"Who's that?"

"The guy up in the penthouse."

He pauses, taking me in a moment longer than his usual customers. "Michlean?"

I nod, he returns it.

As he sets the glass on the coaster, the gorgeous amber mottled by the ice luring me in for a first sip, the bartender says conspiratorially, "I'll pay him what I owe him when I get paid next week."

"Okay..." I respond, unsure why he's telling me which obviously plays across my face since he stops and puts his hand on the bar rail, leaning to me.

"He didn't send you down here to collect?"

I smile, understanding. "No," I assure him.

"Oh..." he stammers. "I figured when you said what you said, you were here to collect."

"If you don't mind me asking, what do you owe him money for?"

"I like to bet on soccer games."

"You don't sound very good at it."

"I'm not," he laughs without any joy. "You're Kat's...friend." He pauses to find the right word.

"Yeah. Friend."

"Not the way she talks about you. I'd say you're more.'"

I want to pursue this, wanting to believe he's giving me hope but I'm still not comfortable that what I want from her is what she wants from me. I miss the immediacy of the feelings I had with Tami. I knew I wanted to be with her from the moment I met her. But most love isn't assembled immediately. It's an acquired taste. Something that develops rather than drops into your lap fully formed. And with Kat, whatever these squishy feelings are, they've ripened over time, heated by the history we share. This is not what I'm used to. I'm more comfortable with bottle rockets that soar high. Even though you know they will explode, the ride is pretty awesome. I love to be bowled over. This is a slow simmer.

Basically, I'm stew.

Maybe I'm doing this all wrong. As old as I am, you'd think someone might have clued me in by now. The world lets me wander aimlessly from bed to bed, wondering why none of it means anything and most of it is frighteningly forgettable. I wonder if most men are like me. Maybe none of us know that everything we're doing is simply fucking wrong. I certainly know I'm not doing it right. But just how wrong is sort of a revelation.

By the time Harry finds me at the bar, a pile of papers and manila folders under his arm, I'm sailing pretty good, having downed two and working on my third glass of scotch, all courtesy of my new employer. Harry slides onto the seat next to me and I signal my new best friend, the bartender who bets badly, and point to Harry. The bartender takes his drink order, a scotch and soda, and slips away as Harry turns to me and sniffs.

"You been drinking all day?"

"Not all day but don't worry, I'm a professional."

"You're an ass! Good thing I made a reservation for dinner or we'd have to wait. I need you coherent."

"Why?" I ask as the bartender brings Harry's drink and drops it off.

Harry waves his hand in a circle in my direction. I'm not sure what that's supposed to mean but he doesn't answer, instead taking a sip from his glass.

"Kat makes a better drink."

"She's loaded with mad skills."

Harry squints at me and gets off the stool. "Let's eat," he responds. "You'll feel better."

He walks off toward the restaurant. Digging into my pocket I pull out the crumpled eleven dollars I have to my name and toss it on the bar, grabbing my drink to go. With Harry buying dinner, he's very apt to cut me off.

Even though I've been at this resort twice, I've never eaten in the main dining room. It's more formal—some might even say fancy—and while some patrons are in shorts and open-toed sandals, which is allowed, most are dressed nicely, at minimum slacks and a button-down shirt. This place feels less like a beach restaurant and more like a citified eatery.

As soon as we sit down, Harry places the manila folders on top of the table. It's not like I can miss them.

"What are those?" I question.

"Jesus, can you at least let my ass warm the seat? You know, Todd, you always seem in a goddamn hurry. Like a kid. Gotta know. Gotta do. Gotta go. You're going to get a good meal here. Relax for a goddamn second and try to make tonight pleasant. If not for your sorry self, then for me. I could use it."

I throw up my hands in defeat as the waiter steps up to the table. Harry waves away the menus he's about to hand us.

"Two of your biggest steaks. Champagne..." he announces to the waiter and then turns to me, "Are you too drunk to drink champagne?"

"I'm never too drunk to drink champagne."

Harry requests a 'very good bottle' of champagne and then adds, "You know, bring us a few appetizers too. You pick 'em, something I won't get anywhere else."

I'm confused now. It's like he's celebrating. Harry isn't a man prone to doing things improper, disrespectful, or out or order. So this throws me. And it scares me a little as well.

"What the hell's going on?"

Harry remains silent, his eyes studying my face.

"Harry..."

"You look tired, Todd. Like the last five years have been really, really hard on you. Don't take this the wrong way, but you aren't aging well."

What the fuck?

"This is what you want to talk about? Seriously, Harry. I know you're in mourning but have you completely lost your shit?"

"Just an observation. Put on your big-boy pants. You can handle a little constructive criticism."

Okay, he is nuts.

"Tell me what the fuck is going on or I'm outta here. You're freaking me out and that's hard to do."

Harry simply smiles, knowing he has me.

"I'm serious, Harry. You want me to walk you back up to your room so you can get some rest? It's understandable considering what you've been through. Hell, I applaud you for putting on clothes. I wouldn't. So you don't have to do all the rest of this shit…steaks, champagne, conversation about me. Let's stop. Man, you can sleep for three, four days, a week, two weeks, I don't care…we can deal with whatever then. But I think you need rest."

"I'll rest when I'm dead!" he snaps, then takes a breath calming himself. "No more talk. I want to eat in peace. A good steak. I can use it. I haven't had anything all day."

He stops talking. To make his point, he looks around the room, taking everyone in. Anyone who catches his eye, he smiles. They all smile back though I imagine at least half are creeped out; the other half know his fiancée passed this morning and are offering looks of sympathy. His eyes land everywhere but on me. I feel like texting Kat and asking if she knows a shrink on the island that can see Harry, like tonight. And this little fucker, who should be curled up in a ball on a bed upstairs, continues to smile at strangers, ignoring me throughout the delicious appetizers that appear on the table, through the bucket of champagne which is placed next to him, and until the steaks arrive on the table. He thanks the waiter before picking up his steak knife and fork. As he does, his eyes finally land on me again. He points the knife and fork at me and says, "I want to enjoy this. And I can't if I'm hearing your voice."

As much as I want to smack the ever-loving shit out of him, I opt to dive into my steak. I haven't had much to eat either and this steak smells like what great sex should feel like. Cutting it is like carving silk and shoving a big chunk into my mouth, it almost melts. I can put aside all my concerns and enjoy this as well. The little turd isn't always wrong. Silence through this might make the experience about as damn close to religious as I'm ever going to get.

Through the meal, Harry and I say nothing to each other, though we continue to make eye contact, sizing each other up as we chew, communicating on a different level than our usual way of lobbing fiery insults at one another intermittently interrupted by actual conversation. I get the sense that something with Harry is not only off — that's already been proven — but terribly wrong. Even with the healthy looking tan, his hair trimmed, his natty clothes pressed, there's something not right. I can't quite put my finger on it. If I could, I probably couldn't keep my mouth shut.

After Harry pays the bill, leaving what I would consider a sizeable tip, I pick up my champagne glass and down what little is left. The meal has sobered me slightly. Harry picks up the manila folders off the table and signals me to follow him. He walks across the restaurant, into the lobby of the resort, out to the pool deck and down onto the beach.

"Jesus, Harry, if I didn't know better I'd think you were bringing me out here to either kiss me or kill me!"

Harry chuckles but that's all.

He moves down the beach until he's in the light of the hotel pool, illuminated enough to see him clearly. He pulls over a beach chair and falls down into it.

"Grab a chair."

Following his orders, I drag a beach chair directly across from where he sits, my confused look deepened by the shadows of the harsh light holding on my face. Once I'm settled in, Harry pulls out a pen and clicks it, thrusting the manila folders into my hands.

"Sign these," he orders. "There's yellow tabs where you need to put your Johnny Hancock."

"What are they?"

"Jesus, Todd, what do you think, I'm having you sign your death warrant?" he asks, his tone oozing sarcasm. "It's paperwork. I'm…I'm…I'm…shit, this is harder to say than I thought. I'm putting you on my life insurance."

I sit up tall in the chair, thrown for a loop.

"So sign," he orders again, jabbing the pen at me.

Taking the pen, I can't look at the paperwork. I can only look at him. Again, I get the feeling that something about Harry is off; a feeling only exasperated by a tightness in my upper back that comes from knowing I'm being lied to.

"You going to tell me?"

"After you sign."

I scribble a signature and dates onto the documents, Harry directing me where to do it. I close the folder and hand it back to him. He leans back in his chair, folding his hands in his lap as he studies me silently a moment.

"Carolina died of cancer. We knew it was coming. We knew it was coming soon. I didn't think it would happen today of all days. But we knew. I wanted to give her the wedding she always wanted. Breaks my goddamn heart that I failed."

"You didn't fail."

"I didn't succeed. So call it what you will. A swing and a miss. A seven-ten split. A bogie. It didn't happen. And I really, really, really wanted that for her…" Harry says, the emotion welling up in his voice.

"Did you love her?"

Harry shrugs, wiping his nose. "She was a good girl. She deserved to have what she wanted knowing the end was coming."

"You're a good fucking man!" I respond, meaning it.

"Don't be handing out the compliments yet, suck-up," he says, leaving me a little perplexed at the remark.

"I told you where Carolina and I met…" Harry continues.

Nodding, I feel the lines in my forehead creasing.

"You didn't think about that, did you?"

Rummaging back in my thoughts, I remember something about a support group. That could mean a lot of things. Harry can be an anal retentive, snide, vengeful troll. Is there a support group for that? And if so, what was Carolina doing in it? She seemed nothing but rather sweet and benign, especially for someone of Harry's epic temperament.

"A support group, right? For what…people who lost their kids or something?"

"Cancer."

"Cancer?"

"Cancer," Harry snaps. "Same as Carolina, same as a lot of people. Cancer."

"You have cancer?" I actually get out without the words strangling in my throat.

Harry smiles. It's the kind of smile you give a big, matted sheepdog as you pet it knowing it's probably the dumbest animal you've ever encountered.

"I don't have cancer," Harry says in a low growl, "Cancer has me."

I slowly sink back into the chair without a word. Again, Harry smiles. I can sense he's enjoying that I didn't know, that he tricked me.

"I found out about three-and-a-half years ago, around the time I lost contact with you," he says. "I wanted to blame you for it for all the shit you put me through, but I stirred enough shit in my own life for this poison to be taking over my body. Including getting between you and Tami," he says, sniffling slightly before wiping his nose. "Doctors can't get it. And it's spreading. I got the goddamn stuff in my head now, attacking my brain. I think that's one of the reasons I'm in a good mood a lot of the time now. Anyway, I met Carolina in a group of people dealing with dying and it was the most fucking depressing thing I've ever been involved in. Remember how you and I were after Tami was killed? Now think of a whole room full of that shit. I'd already gone through hell once; I didn't want to go through it again. And Carolina was like a ray of sunshine in the group. She hated that group of sad sack sons-a-bitches. After going to the group four times, she and I went out and had some drinks. We laughed all night. She kept telling me I was better-looking than I kept myself, and a better man than I was letting on. Over the next few months, she sort of reinvented who I was…into this," he says, circling his hands in front of his face.

"She did good."

"Yeah. I wish I'd met her years before. But she probably wouldn't have taken pity on me then."

"Tami would have liked her."

Harry smiles. It's sincere, as if that thought hadn't really occurred to him and sunk in as deeply as it just did.

"She told me about her wish to get married and have a wedding on the beach. The more our prognoses got dimmer and time seemed shorter, the more I leaned on her general happiness as my crutch. I enjoyed being with her, even when she was getting sicker. I thought the best gift I could give her was a fucking great wedding. So I proposed."

"Why did you want me here?"

Again, Harry smiles.

"You're the closest thing I have to family, Todd. As fucked-up as that is! You're it. You should be married to my daughter. We should be fighting father-in-law to son-in-law, having Tami scream at us both for being assholes. I wanted you here. And when I saw that boy…I knew you had to come. You had to know he was your offspring. It's important," Harry says, pausing and taking me in a moment. "You and me, we'll always have a love-hate relationship, emphasis on the hate. But we're in each other's lives, Todd. We shared the worst thing a person can go through. And now we've shared another awful one. You seem to bring disaster wherever you go, you know that?"

"You're not the first person to say that to me."

"I imagine not," he chuckles. "I'm dying, Todd. I don't feel terrible, which is kind of a kick in the nutsack, but the doctors tell me the tumor in my brain is getting bigger. It might have knocked out all my better sense with what I'm about to ask you…"

My eyes look up at the light shining down on us from the pool deck. For a moment I am blind, which is a pretty apt metaphor for the moment.

"What?" I gulp, thinking he might ask me to put a pillow over his face and smother him before the cancer gets too bad. Not that I haven't thought about doing that to him before. But not at his request.

"Don't say no. Trust I know what the hell I'm doing. I spent all day on the phone getting this crap arranged. It's what Tami would have wanted. I even think it's what Carolina would have wanted, God rest her beautiful soul."

"Ask, Harry, for Christsake! You're scaring me!"

Harry's face wads up like he's tasted dog's ass. Obviously whatever it is, it's the hardest thing he's ever asked anyone in his life. I'm holding my breath, freaked out. This guy looks like he's about to vomit up his colon, it pains him to utter whatever it is.

Harry sticks his finger in my chest, leaning forward, gritting his teeth.

"I want you to marry me."

I'm not sure what exactly is on the other side of the earth from where I sit, but my jaw just fell open that far. I can't even respond, not even to pull his stumpy finger off my chest where he continues to poke me.

"I've thought this out," he prattles, still needling me with his finger, "And I have it arranged. Men can do this now. Marry. What's this world coming to? But you and I need to do it. That way I can leave you my pension. I worked too fucking hard to just have it disappear. All the money I saved, my house, all my things, I don't have anyone I'm close to. I die tonight, some cousin I never see and surely don't like is going to get it all. I don't want that. I'd rather have someone I know, even if I can barely tolerate him, to get it. If you think about it, and who knows if you're too drunk to do that, but this is a really smart idea. We get married and you're taken care of, Todd. You can get your life on track, take care of that son of yours, maybe fall in love — maybe with Kat who I really like which probably means you don't — and stop being such a consummate loser."

Locking eyes with Harry, I'm astounded at what he's thrown onto the table. Holy shit! He's absolutely serious about this. Marry him? Seriously? I could think of nothing more insanely gross.

Not because he's a guy but because he's Harry. I mean I don't want to marry any guy, but most especially the father of the woman I loved.

"You're fucking twisted!" is the first thing that comes out of my mouth.

"I know," he responds proudly, a jaunty smile crossing his lips.

I feel my head shaking involuntarily as I attempt to wrap my mind around Harry's plan. It's not something that even entered into a scintilla of a nanosecond of any thought that's ever knocked around inside my skull. And the image of Harry and I dressed in white, exchanging rings, me towering over him as he recites some smartass vows to me about not being a fuck-up and blowing through all the money he's worked so hard for all of his life, rings in my head like a migraine. But he's dead-ass serious.

On the bright side, no one's ever asked me to marry them before. Not even Tami.

"Harry, come on. This is…this is…."

"This is what? It's smart business. And you come out the winner, you fuckwit! I'm not sure why I need to convince you this is genius when it is, but obviously you're too stupid to grasp what I'm trying to do here."

"I'm not too stupid---" I answer before being cut off.

"Maybe I should ask Kat to marry me. Or Michlean, he seems willing to do just about anything for money. But I'm offering it to you, Todd. Think of Tami. Think of her! You know she's getting a huge laugh out of this about now, me asking you to marry me, but she'd want it for you too. You know that."

"Don't play the Tami card on me. That messes with my head."

Harry stands up. He squishes his face again looking like a chihuahua waiting to attack. "I'm going back to my room. I'm getting everything arranged for tomorrow. Here on the beach. Say six o'clock, a sunset wedding…I always wanted one of those. You're not here, fuck you, I've been stood up, and everyone has a second day of drinks on me. You can go on being the assclown you are, broke, doing stupid things and making alcohol and sex the most important things in your immature life. No skin off my back, not really, Todd. Or you can be here, in all white, that's how Carolina and I were going to do it and I think it looks good, and we can get married. I'm not living more than a few more months. If that. And as pissed off as I am right now that you didn't say yes, it's a wonder whatever that thing is in my head hasn't blown up like Mount Kilimanjaro."

Harry walks away, stopping and turning back to me as he's about to climb the stairs to the resort's pool deck.

"Go thank the gays. Because of them, you get to be my wife."

And with that he stomps up the steps one by one and vanishes.

"You're the fucking wife…" I say under my breath, rubbing my hands over my face, exhausted and confused.

For the next hour-and-a-half I stare out at the ocean, hoping for Tami to appear and give me guidance. She doesn't show. I guess I'm on my own on this one. You'd think she'd be happy I'm marrying an Everett.

Until I find Kat standing over me, a sly sliver of a grin and a smarty-pants look in her eye as if she's secretly won the lottery.

"I hear congratulations are in order!"

Kat takes off her shoes, burying her toes into the stand as if she never intends to leave that spot.

"I can't believe that little shit already called you," I sigh.

"Is it true?"

"He asked."

She bellows so loud I'm surprised people aren't peeking over the wall to see what's so damn funny.

"I bought you a fondue set as a wedding gift, I hope you love it," Kat adds, continuing to laugh.

"He's got cancer," I say, bringing the laughter to a screeching, fishtailing halt.

"What?"

"He didn't tell you that part? It's terminal."

After a stunned silence, Kat whispers, "Tell me you're kidding."

"That's how he met Carolina. Wanted to give her the wedding she always wanted. Now he wants to leave everything he's got to me."

"Todd, he could leave everything he's got to you even if you didn't marry him."

"Then why's he doing it? So I'll stick around until he dies?"

Kat shakes her head, thinking a moment. "Maybe. Maybe with the time he's got left he wants to see you be the man that deserved his daughter."

Kat sits next to me. Neither of us says a word. We just sit. Saying it out loud makes it real for me. My words making it real for her.

"Are you going to do it?"

I don't respond.

"Todd..."

"I don't know."

"Why not?" she asks with such credulity in her voice that it almost sounds like she's talking to a toddler.

"Because I made a deal with the devil that I can't get out of," I say, before I'm overtaken by a jigsaw of feelings and stop talking.

"What are you talking about?" Kat asks.

In the darkness, my eyes meet hers. It's as if she already knows. There's panic shimmering in the look she gives me that mixes with the woeful sorrow that has been the theme of the whole goddamn day.

I start to laugh. Not because anything is funny but because I'm fighting so hard not to lose it. But when tears rim my eyes, the battles over and I'm wounded. I bow my head and let my shoulders heave.

"Todd! Todd! Talk to me!" Kat begs, but I just turn my face away and sob.

"Marrying him is admitting he's going to die. I don't want that son-of-a-bitch to die," I bark before breaking down completely, rolling off the chair, lying in the sand and letting my eyes fill with tears until the lids can no longer contain them and they roll down my cheeks. Kat drops to her knees next to me. She lies across my chest, fighting her sorrow too. I wrap my arms around her tightly, afraid the sand will swallow me and I'll disappear forever.

"And I've fucked up bad this time, Kat," I heave out, "I've really fucked up…"

"What? What did you do?"

I can only shake my head. Standing, I wipe the tears from my eyes as I look down at her in the sand.

"I'm sorry," I tell her, not explaining and knowing I've said too much already.

Turning and walking up the steps to the pool deck, my shoulders hunched as I stare ahead at the resort, my eyes travel up to the penthouse where Michlean resides. I suck in an enraged breath. I can't get killed! I have to be here to take care of Harry. I've played my cards wrong. All wrong. I've only got one left.

## NASTY TRUTH

My phone ringing before sun-up has never been a good thing. But when you have someone in your life dying of cancer and you are acutely aware of the suddenness of death, adrenaline whips through your entire body like a lightning strike.

"It's Todd..." I mumble, trying to clear my head.

"Get up!" a voice says.

It takes me a moment to realize who it is. Michlean.

"What the hell, man, it's not even five o' clock?" I snap.
"You said seven."

"They're moving their shit earlier than expected. Get your ass upstairs!"

And with that he hangs up.

And on the day of my wedding no less.

I start to sweat as I shower. This is going to get ugly. But I got no choice. I got into this fiasco with the best intentions and now I have no choice but to see it through.

Arriving upstairs in his suite, there are six other guys, all big in one way or another. Only two I recognize from my dealings with Michlean; they all eye me suspiciously or with malice as I meander in, a coffee from the café downstairs in my hand.

"About fucking time!" Michlean snarls in my direction.

"I knew you wouldn't have coffee ready," I say, wagging my paper cup at him, noticing that none of the women that are usually occupying space in his suite are here this morning.

He picks a forty-five semi-automatic off the coffee table and tosses it to me. I let it hit the floor.

"What the fuck?" Michlean spits out. "I hope you're faster than that if there's trouble."

"Don't throw a gun at me before I finish my coffee," I answer, before plucking it off the rug and tucking it in my waist band.

Everyone in the room glares. I guess no one is in a joking mood. Too bad, because when I'm scared, and this pretty much falls into that category, I am the life of the party. Even at five-thirty-five in the morning.

Michlean fills everyone in on the plan. I'll give the guy credit; he doesn't let his henchmen do all his dirty work. He likes to be there for the kill, so to speak. He tells us to keep our mouths shut and let him do the talking. When he utters that sentence, his eyes stay on me. None of these other guys look like talkers anyway, so I guess he figures keep the emphasis on the one who he knows never shuts up. If things get ugly, which he keeps reiterating they might, don't be afraid to cap someone if you think they might pop some lead into one of us first.

"Were we supposed to bring weapons?" I ask, more out of curiosity, having never been hired to beat the crap out of, or possibly kill, someone before.

"It's good to be ready," is all Michlean says, glaring at me like I'm really pissing him off, which is my intention, hoping he'll ask me to leave.

We ride down in two elevators, all of us not fitting into one. No one speaks, as if it is game day and they are psyching themselves up to come home with a victory. I would be far, far better off not knowing that I could be killed. Any other skirmish I've participated in didn't involve dying. At least that wasn't the intention going in. Injured, sure. You don't get into a fight without expecting to do some damage and possibly be damaged, but there's always a line that people don't cross on purpose. They don't want to die nor do they want to end up doing thirty years for manslaughter or worse. But this, I'll admit, frightens me. And while no one is talking, I sense it is scaring the shit out of the other meatheads in these elevators too.

These guys are gym rats who probably owe Michlean money for the steroids he supplies them. I'd wager that not a single one of them has a marketable skill outside of lifting something heavy over their heads. Their size is their fortune. Add in a surly disposition and an overload of testosterone, and you pretty much know who these clowns are. And they're a good decade younger — and probably faster — than me. Not good for Team Todd. Then again, maybe being older and having a haggard line of stitches in my head will make everyone at this clusterfuck think I'm the baddest of the badasses.

I doubt it but any port-a-potty in a shitstorm helps.

Loading into two dark SUVs, again no one utters a word, which only heightens my uneasiness. Michlean is in the front passenger seat and I'm squeezed into the back between two guys whose shoulders exceed mine in width.

"Is it true that steroids shrink your balls?" I ask, hoping to start a conversation that will get me thrown out of the ride.

Michlean turns, his face screwing up, glaring at me like I'm some kind of asshole. Which I am trying really, really hard to be.

"Will you shut the fuck up and get your head in this?" he snarls.

"This?" I respond. "I don't know what 'this' is."

"We'll find out when we get there," he rumbles, turning back around.

"That's your big plan? We find out when we get there? Holy Jesus, that's forethought? They could have bazookas or rocket launchers and take us out as we're driving up. There was no recon on this mission. You were never in the army were you?"

"Were you?"

"No. But I know the lingo. And I would have done some recon. Who told you they're moving stuff this morning? How'd you find that out?"

He spins around again, giving me a lethal stare.

"Just asking," I say with a smile.

"What the fuck is the matter with you?"

"You want me to answer that or you want me to pray quietly like everyone else?"

"I want you to shut the fuck up!" Michlean orders.

"I'm just trying to lighten the mood. It's like riding in the back of a hearse."

Michlean turns around, shaking his head. No one else seems to give a shit I'm prattling on like a dingus. I want to get under the skin of each and every one of them until they vote me out of the SUV. But the only person I managed to piss off was the overgrown pretty boy. And he doesn't seem willing to let me go.

The sun rises over the eastern horizon through dotty clouds, enough for the amber rays to cast long morning shadows. We are heading north, the same direction I was held captive just a few days before. I can't believe any of those guys are involved in this new crew of smugglers. Not with souvenir bullet holes in their legs. But on the off-chance even one is, won't he be surprised to see my cracked skull staring at him?

My mind rambles image to image, each one I want to comment on aloud just to keep needling the rich boy with the pretty hair in front of me. I wonder if that curls natural or if he has to put some shit in his hair to make it do that? Glancing from side to side, the two beasts flanking me never break game-face. Damn, if I let my mind wrestle down the danger I'm actually driving toward, I'm going to crap my tightie-whities. Isn't that how Ted Nugent got out of going to Vietnam? I can use that. If I stink up the SUV enough maybe they will toss me. Wait! I should announce to the machismos in the car that I'm getting married at sunset…to an old guy! That might convince them to pull over and let me out before bullets start flying.

This is as frightened as I can ever remember being. I've done a lot of dumb stuff that ended up in hindsight being dangerous. Some of it even deadly in retrospect. But in none of it did I walk in pretty much assured I could die. Even when I threw my bruised ass over the rail of the high rise in Malta and plummeted down into their pool, it was more out of panic and blockheadedness, not me wanting to thumb my nose at death. I don't want to face death. It's scary. And permanent. I've had too much death in my life already, thank you very much. Even though my balls are bigger than thes these steroid junkies doesn't mean I have a death wish. At least not today. And not this way. I'll save that for my own private moment of insane rage which seem to occur once every other full moon or so. All my big balls are doing now are choking me because they are up in my throat.

Having only had one limited encounter on the north side of the island, I don't recognize the area. There are docks, none of them expansive enough to unload passengers from a cruise ship, but certainly big enough for a larger excursion boat. The north side of the island isn't visited by tourists or even used much to unload goods. There is a broken reef that must be maneuvered around on the north end and sand piles up oddly because of it, beaching boats and causing weird currents. But it's certainly well-loved by the pirates who like to ship anything illegal in and out. The buildings up on this end have been ravaged by the heat and humidity, rust creeping its way up their sides like a communicable disease. Bad mojo radiates from this place, you can feel it. Even the authorities don't like to come here because nothing good ever happens up here.

And today is shaping up to be no different.

We turn up a long, once-paved road that leads to a couple metal warehouses, not unlike the one where I was held. I see two spectacular cigarette racers knotted to one of the rickety docks. Whoever this other guy is, he's got money, which is unsurprising considering what he's marketing. The men on either side of me make note of the expensive watercrafts as well, and I can feel them tense and relax a few times, as if trying to talk themselves into playing this cool, while their better sense is screaming in their ears that they should be scared witless.

Pulling amid four metal buildings, I get the queasy feeling we've been led into the middle of a rusting OK Corral. I feel for the gun tucked into my waistband just to make sure it's still there. Seeing no one around gives me the willies. You can feel an ambush, people just lying in wait, ready to take you out. This is what I get for watching westerns and cop shows as a kid. I know how this shit works. It may be a cliché but it's a cliché because it fucking happens. We have no escape but backward, the SUVs too large to get between the buildings.

"Why the fuck did we pull in here?" I ask. "We are setting ourselves up for a nasty ass-whipping!"

No one responds. Not even Michlean. But I just said exactly what everyone is thinking.

Once the SUVs stop, Michlean talks closely with the lunk driving before both step out. I glance at the guys flanking me with a shrug that almost hits them both in the chin.

"Guess that's our cue," I say, waiting for one of them to open their door. As much as stepping out into an unseen gunman's line of fire isn't my first choice, I would like to be out from between these two overly-muscled mooks. And playing the odds, as big as both these guys are, I think I could hide behind them if bullets rain down.

Finally one of them opens his door and hesitantly steps out, his eyes taking in our surroundings. I follow, my eyes on the buildings, glancing up to the roof, trying to figure out if someone were to fire at us where it would come from so I could get my ass out of the way. We congregate, eyes darting in different directions, everyone reacting to a wind-blown piece of paper, seeking any movement, any danger. Michlean steps away from us and shakes his head.

"I hope to hell they haven't left," he says, turning to glance at me as if it's my fault we missed whatever the hell is supposed to happen here.

"I'm kind of hoping they have," I reply, almost under my breath before adding a little more loudly, "Why don't we just blow up their boat? Send a message. And then head back to the resort before the breakfast buffet closes."

"I want them, not their boats," Michlean responds in a near-whisper. "Once I have their gear, those cigarette racers become my property," he adds, waving us toward the warehouses. Breaking off into smaller teams, leaving me with a large local who drove over in the other SUV, I see dust rising from down the path we took into this place.

"Hey!" I call, pointing.

Everyone freezes as a caravan of SUVs rumbles down the dirt road toward us, bending the tall grass that lines the road. This is the 'come-to-Jesus' moment I didn't want; you can feel the collective pit in everyone's stomach as the four SUVs close in. Four vehicles carry a lot more men than we have standing here.

Screw muscles. Bullets rip right through sinew. We're outgunned.

Guns come out from under shirts and pant legs as the four SUVs slide in behind our two, blocking any means of escape by vehicle. And the last thing I want to do is make an escape on foot from a volley of bullets. This is a fucking mess and it seems Michlean way under-predicted the body count.

The doors of their SUVs open and a gaggle of men, predictably big, except for one lean, fair-skinned black man, form a semi-circle around us like a tribe of Huns. Right now I wish we had swords and spears rather than something that could kill me from multiple feet away. At least then I'd believe I have a fighting chance when things get down and dirty. I really don't want to end up dead in a place no one will find my bloated corpse for a few weeks, leading Harry to believe I skipped out on him. That would be a really shitty ending to my time on St. Carlos.

"Which one of you pricks is Gerard?" Michlean calls, stepping up front.

The fair-skinned black guy moseys up to the front of his small army which numbers thirteen.

"I'm Gerard, you queer-looking muthafucka! You must be that rich boy I heard about. Time to pack up your things and move back in with Mommy and Daddy. Your business on this island is done."

"No. It's not. Certainly not by some skinny-ass bitch. I don't care how much muscle you hired. Hell, half of your crew buys their juice from me," Michlean laughs, eyeing Gerard's crew.

No one responds, each of these boneheads checking out the boneheads on the other side. Including me.

"Here's the deal," Michlean continues before Skinny Black Guy can speak, "I'm going to take whatever you brought onto my island. Including the boats which will look good in my collection. You, skinny man, are catching a flight back to Haiti or the Dominican or wherever you came from. Do that, I let these gym rats live. This place is my paradise. You're not invited to the party."

"I don't need an invitation. And you aren't taking anything because I'm going to kill you today. And all of these muthafuckas behind you," Gerard responds with a big smile.

This badly performed male posturing isn't making me happy. I know from experience that when people talk themselves into a hole, they almost always have to react ignorantly to crawl out of it. These wide bodies in front of me will go down first, but I'm going to have to take out at least four to five guys before I face their firing squad if I'm to walk out of this confrontation with enough blood in my veins to keep me alive.

"You either give me whatever you thought you were going to sell on my island and I drive you to the airport, or you die here. Your choice," Michlean snarls, not backing down.

Gerard's dark eyes lock on Michlean. Both men resemble lions ready to fight for leadership of the pride. Only both with less smarts than your average jungle animal. I can feel sweat dripping down my back as the morning sun beats down on the staples in my head. Goddamn, if nothing else in life makes me rethink my plethora of fucked-up choices, this should. I have been close enough to death to know it when it's standing in front of me. And I never much liked looking at it when it's holding a gun.

I felt more confident about living when it hit me in the back of the head with a board.

Gripping the butt of the gun, I'm waiting for someone to freak out first and start shooting. It's not a matter of if but when. And the when looks like now as everyone's weapon glints in the sunshine. Waiting for the first bang, I realize the sheen off of the guns is coming from something above.

"Okay, okay, okay..." I murmur in a near-whisper, prepping myself for what's coming.

Immediately, the sound of rotors knifing through the air finally hits my ear before I see the helicopter sweep overhead, circle around and hover over the area we are penned inside. Without a word, everyone races back to their vehicles but there are suddenly a half-dozen cars surging around us from different directions, making sure no one escapes. Government agents, all screaming at the sty of beef trapped in the middle to drop our weapons and get to our knees, pour out of the metal warehouses surrounding us.

Cavalry.

I toss my handgun off without a fight. The cops have mean-looking weapons with scopes. Not a contest.

Michlean twists side to side, searching for an escape route. He bolts in my direction but I step right in front of him, letting him slam into my chest. His eyes register surprise as my face curls into an embattled sneer.

"Everyone's going to prison and it's your fault!"

Without warning, I slam my forehead off the bridge of his nose. Blood explodes from his nose with a crack, his nose moving a few millimeters to the right.

"Fuck!" Michlean screams, grabbing his face as he's tackled to the ground, a Fed kneeling on his back. My knees are kicked out from behind and as I crumple, I make sure I fall right on Michlean's head.

"Owww!" he screams again.

As I crawl off of him, I make sure I lodge my knee in the back of his head, driving his face into the dirt. My face ends up in the dirt a few inches from his and we lock eyes. I smile.

"Consider what I did a favor. Pretty boys don't last one week in prison without putting on lipstick," I growl as one of the Feds lodges his foot on my head, squeezing my face further into the dust.

"Dude! I got stitches in my head, lighten up!" I yell.

"Shut the fuck up!" a voice barks in my ear as my arms are pulled behind me and I'm cuffed.

Lying there, I see Michlean, blood covering his face from his broken nose, continue to tussle with two of the Feds. As I'm yanked up, I laugh at him which only infuriates him more. As he tries to wrestle himself from the ground, two other Feds join the fray and pound him into submission. All the testosterone in the world isn't enough to battle four Feds intent on smacking what good-looks I haven't ruined off your face. Once they have him subdued, one of the agents grabs him by his curly locks and lifts him to his feet. Blood is smeared across his face mixed with the arid dirt, giving him an apropos clownish appearance. He staggers as they drag him toward a car, smashing him off the side a few times for good measure before yanking him around and shoving him inside.

As I'm pushed out of the crowd of bodies, the dust in my eyes prevents me from seeing anything but shapes and the sound of the chopper landing muting every other sound. I can tell everyone is now cuffed and being hauled off in different directions, placed into cars, guns confiscated, the whole scene a cacophony of blurred images and people yelling.

I stumble toward one of the metal buildings and then quickly shove inside, the door slamming behind me. Stepping out of the sunlight into the semi-lit building, I can see nothing, the dark made darker, as I'm dropped into a chair.

My cuffs are unlocked and my arms freed.

"Water," I almost beg.

A bottle of water is thrust into my hand and I pour some into my free hand and wash the dust and dirt out my eyes as they adjust to the dimness of the light inside. I guzzle down a few gulps as a pair of hands goes to my shirt, unbuttoning it, revealing the wire taped to my chest.

Without asking the wire and the mic are yanked off, taking more than a little chest hair with it.

"Ow, shit! Damn," I complain as Deb Prowess, the DEA agent I failed to pick up in the Miami Airport, gives me a smile, wadding up the wire and placing it in her jacket pocket.

"You all right?"

"Spiffy. You sure Michlean's never getting back on this island?" I ask, double-checking as I rub my wrists and then my forehead.

"No. Not with what we have on him," Deb responds. "You did a smart thing by calling us. Though I admit that when you first called I thought you were just trying to get me down on the island to hit on me again." She glances at me with side-eyes.

"I've attempted more daring ploys in my life for a woman, but..." I laugh.

She nods, not surprised. "You bring the 'get-out-of-jail-free' card?" she asks, holding out her hand.

Digging into my pants pocket I pull out her card. As I hold it up, she smiles, reaching for it. But something stops her.

"Keep it," she says, "I owe you for this bust...and something tells me you'll eventually need it."

For the first time in a few days, I take a deep breath and let it go, trying to blow all the fear from my body. I played the only card I had. And calling Deb Prowess is probably the smartest thing I've done since returning to St. Carlos. Because life is nothing if not one big game of Monopoly.

"What happens to me?" I ask.

"Once we clear everyone out, you're free," she says as someone across the room calls to her.

"Michlean will never know it was me that set this up?"

Deb signals to the agent that called for her that she will be there momentarily before turning back to me and shaking her head. "You think I would let you break his nose if I thought he would?"

"That was the best part of the deal I made," I say with a grin.

Deb returns the smile as she heads across the warehouse. Then she stops, turning back to me.

"If you want, you can buy me a drink later."

I can't help but shake my head at the irony of her timing, "Can't," I respond. "It would mess up what I got going with this woman. Besides…I'm getting married tonight."

Deb turns and faces me directly, blinking a few times. "You met a woman down here and you're getting married?"

"I'm not marrying her. I'm marrying someone else. It's a complicated story but you're more than welcome to join us…"

I'd like to say there's disbelief in her eyes but there's not. It's more like horrified astonishment.

"What time and where?"

## THE END GAME

I've never thought of my life without Harry at minimum raising havoc in the periphery. As badly as I've treated myself I was one hundred percent positive I would die long before that bastard would. Half of the time I've known Harry he was just this hearty curmudgeon that would live in infamy; the other half he's been the cockroach in my apartment kitchen I could never kill. I thought he'd be here after the entire world blew up, out of sheer tenacity and a refusal to quit.

Even when I didn't speak to him for those years, I knew he was alive. I could feel it. I just couldn't feel his illness. I should have been there for him instead of being some wandering asshole, reverting back into a more calcified version of the shit I hated about myself in the first fucking place. As much as I've hated Harry, his presence in my life was that of a rock. Sometimes it's anchored me; sometimes it's been tied around my neck and tossed into the ocean; sometimes I've been smashed in the head with it. But it's been solid, immovable and always there.

I don't really want to marry Harry. Because it means watching him die. It could be slow and lingering, watching him waste away, his body getting smaller and smaller until the life inside can no longer be sustained. That's going to hurt. And I do not want to deal with hurt anymore, physically but most especially emotionally. My guts churn. I can't escape the feeling I should have never come back, knowing this island holds so much darkness.

But also so much light. The woman I love is here. Staring out at the tide, I beg her to come to me. I need the woman I love.

"Todd..." I hear behind me.

My wishes answered, I spin around, ready to come face to face with the woman I love.

And there stands Kat, twenty yards behind me on this stretch of beach where I thought I was alone.

"What are you doing? I called your room over and over. I've been looking for you for the past three hours," she says.

As I step toward her, with each stride I'm made more aware of just how beautiful this woman is. "How did you find me?" I ask.

Kat opens her mouth to speak but stops herself, shaking her head.

"I don't know. I just knew you'd be walking the beach. I listen to those little voices, you know. They usually don't steer me wrong," she says, before adding, "Looking for Tami?"

"No," I answer, pausing before I say, "Looking for you."

Pulling her hair off her face, she smiles with something I've never seen when she looks at me. I'd like to say it is love but I think it's actually admiration. Whatever, I'll take it.

"Harry opened an account for Earl. For college. A letter came from this investment firm," Kat states, tears rising in her eyes. "That crazy fool..."

"Yes he is," I answer, my hand drifting toward her. My fingers touch the back of her hand and slide down. As they do, she wraps her finger into mine. Our grip on one another grows firmer, more relaxed.

"I'm going to marry him," I say.

"Strange as it may sound, you owe him that."

"As guys go, I think I love him more than any other guy I've ever known," I pronounce.

Kat laughs.

"I hate his guts too, but I love him. He's...he's been more of a father to me than my own father ever was; he's been my enemy and my friend. And more than anything, we share something no one else does. We still hold the same woman in our hearts," I say sincerely. "I just don't know if my heart's big enough to hold both him and Tami."

"It is, Todd," Kat replies, turning to me. "You think you've failed. You haven't. Tami started a change in you, and yeah, you might have stumbled a few times — who doesn't? — but you're still on that journey. And Harry's pushing you along."

Kat falls silent, her hand going into her hair, pulling it back as an ocean breeze finally arrives with the aroma of salt.

"You're a better man than you give yourself credit for. I've...I've known a lot of guys, Todd. You're one of the few that actually wants to be more, be better, that's grown tired of being who he is and knows there's something more for him. You've been through a lot."

"Most of it self-inflicted," I answer.

"But you survived. You're a very strong man if you can survive being Todd Cartwright."

I can't help but smile. It's so fucking true.

"It's been a long time since I thought of myself as a strong man," I admit.

"You're who you should be; you just don't know yourself very well. At least not as well as those who know you do. Earl still thinks of you as his monster. I've seen you jump into things, some of them extraordinarily stupid but with a fool-hearty abandonment bordering on bravery. Most people turn away, pretending not to see things. You see them and do something."

"I wish I could do something for Harry."

"Marrying him is enough for now. It's telling him you'll be there for him. That you're committed not to him but to change. There will be plenty for us to do for him in the future."

"Us?"

"I'm going to be there for him. Harry's my friend too," Kat surmises.

My hand lets go of Kat's and my arm slides around her shoulder. I pull her close, her head resting on my shoulder.

"I'm going to be a married man in a few hours," I say, smiling.

"You always wanted to marry an Everett. You just didn't know which one."

I laugh, adding, "Harry is a piece of work."

"Makes you perfect for him," Kat also laughs.

"Makes *us* perfect for him," I answer, cocking my head to look at her.

There are moments in life you know you'll never forget. This is one of them. I know because it's only happened a few times in my past and each time I knew. Kat's eyes meet mine. I can't remember her looking more gorgeous, the feeling of her body against mine more perfect.

Leaning over, I kiss her. The kiss grows, the potency overtaking me. Fear wants me to pull away but I can't, I'm captured, wrapped up entirely in this kiss. Our bodies turn toward one another, our arms slipping around each other tightly as if only together our lives will work out. I slowly drop down into the sand, taking Kat with me. I lay down, pulling her smaller body on top of mine, our lips still pressed softly against each other, our hands taking in each other's bodies.

I have never been a huge fan of making love in the sand, but like with so many other things for me, the rules have changed.

Kat slides her hands under my shirt, lifting it up off my body and over my head. Straddling me, she takes hers off in one fluid movement, sliding out of her bra. Her breasts are ample and desirous. My hands move to them, my fingers slowly surrounding them as she leans over and kisses me. I have to reposition her on my hips as my manhood surges uncomfortably in my shorts. She laughs, allowing me to get more comfortable. Nothing needs to be said as her lips go to mine again, our mouths and tongues playing with each other.

Our pants come off and we make love, careful to stay out of the sand by placing all of our clothing underneath us. The sex is raw, strong, instinctively tidal, the waves dictating our rhythm. I can never remember a time when sex has been this innate and unrestricted, allowing my soul to bond with another. Kat and I have never had much pretense to our relationship, our history wrapped up in that. She's experienced me at my worse. Not without disappointment but without judgment. Inviting me to have her body again, this time knowing the man I am, the connection between us a slow burn that developed rather than fell upon us, only makes what I am feeling more formidable and — strange as it may seem — blessed.

I have a woman who knows me. And she still wants me. If I cannot find the goodness inside of me, feeling it from someone else, having someone trust that I possess it, gives me the depth that I cannot always find in myself. We roll over in the sand and lay together, the tide now coming in, washing up to our feet as we hold one another. I vaguely remember the last time I felt this accepted, this much at peace. I wish I could stop this moment, holding this woman, because I am experiencing something that has eluded me, that I started to believe would be nothing more than a mirage in my life.

I love Kat. I love her for knowing me and still loving me.

Arriving back at Kat's, Earl chows down a bowl of cereal as we walk in, our clothes sopping wet, underwear sticking out from our pockets. He gives us an odd look as Kat walks past, touching him on the head as she says, "Don't..."

Kat disappears into the house, leaving me with a beaming Earl.

"Gonna tell me what happened?" Earl asks me after his mother is out of earshot.

"Your mom...she saved me from drowning," I reply, metaphorically truthful.

He laughs. "You two were banging nasties weren't you?"

Not willing to concede that, I sit down across from him at the table.

"I need a favor..."

Earl winces as if he's afraid to hear what I'm going to ask.

"I'm getting married in a few hours. I need a best man."

"Married? To my mom?"

"No. To Harry."

"The old guy with the tan?"

I nod.

Earl studies me for a moment. The incongruous expression that knots his face up is almost comical.

"What the what...? I didn't know you were...?"

Yes or no," I ask, stopping him.

"Yeah, sure," Earl says, then laughingly adds, "You're actually going to marry him?"

"There a problem with that?"

"Yeah!" Earl exclaims with a creeped-out smile. "He's old!"

I can't help but return the smile. Happy that my son, this kid who has probably way too much of me to end up without a lot of problems in his life, will be there for me.

After showering and dressing for the wedding, Kat comes into the living room wearing a comfortable white sun dress; her hair is pulled back and there is a red flower tucked behind her right ear. I can't help but smile. This woman doesn't have to work at being beautiful. She just is. And the less she does to herself, the more attractive she is.

"We got to get you back to the resort," she tells me, "You got to get pretty."

"Earl's my best man."

"I thought *I'd* be your best man," Kat responds.

"You're giving me away."

An intoxicating, throaty laugh fills the room as she states, "Perfect," before helping me off the sofa.

We stop by a local clothing store and Earl and his mother run in to find Earl a white t-shirt and shorts for the beach wedding. He exits the shop in the white shorts, pulling the shirt on over his head.

Printed on the front in big, bold letters it reads: I'M WITH STUPID. His face lit up in a huge grin, he points to the shirt and points to me as he bounds toward the car.

"Jesus, you are my kid," I state as he climbs back in the car.

At the resort I dig out a white t-shirt and off-white shorts from my bag and send them down to be cleaned and pressed on a rush job. Taking a long, hot shower, I wish Kat were in here with me. I'm not sure I'd go through with this without her support. But then again, I would not have recognized how much I am in love with her if she hadn't given it so unequivocally.

My clothes hang from the doorknob of the room by the time I get out of the bathroom. Dressing, I gander at myself in the mirror. Clad all in white, I don't look like marriage material, more like some battered homeless guy with a Frankenstein head ready to get baptized in some muddy creek behind a country church.

Kat knocks on the door and when I open it, she takes me in with a smile before nodding.

"How come you're enjoying this more than me?" I respond to the look she gives me.

"Many reasons. Come on…they want to get started and you shouldn't be one of those brides who keeps her guests waiting."

"Fuck you!"

Laughter fills the hallway as we stride down it, Kat taking my arm and pulling herself close to me.

Walking out into the bright, late afternoon sunshine, I pull on a pair of Raybans I have stuffed into my pocket. As we make our way across the pool deck, I notice people whispering to each other as I pass. Last time I was at this resort people thought Harry and I were a couple. I want to bark at them in a cautionary tone, "All you motherfuckers wished too hard and now it's coming true! I'm about to be legally hitched to a midget made up of vinegar and dynamite whose sole purpose in life was to chap my ass. All this the day after his fiancée died and just a few hours after I recognized just how in love I am with someone else. And she's walking me down the aisle. How's that for a fucking story to tell your friends!?"

Glance at the definition of 'fucked up' in the dictionary. My picture is there.

Stepping to the sand, the sun shines right into my eyes as it sets in the distance. Kat holds my arm ready to escort me up to where Harry stands under the makeshift arbor, decorated in all white. There is a crowd of people, most of whom I don't know, but I spot Deb Prowess, Viola and Tomas among them. Tomas keeps smiling, giving me the thumbs up.

I guess they all wanted to see if I'd actually go through with this.

Earl stands at my side, rocking the t-shirt which he points out to Harry with a gleeful grin. There's a 'what-the-fuck-am-I-doing?' uneasiness locked in Harry's eyes. It is clear he's having second thoughts about this little plan of his. His discomfort relaxes me. Anything that makes Harry ill-at-ease must have something going for it.

Once Kat and I are in place at the far end of the rows of chairs, which aren't enough for the crowd that has amassed to see this spectacle, the minister — a striking, young black woman who could be Viola's daughter — signals Kat to lead me up the aisle.

An opera singer from Chicago who is also a newlywed staying at the resort breaks into a mind-blowing aria, as we step up the aisle past the disbelieving yet bemused eyes of strangers. I can't help but keep a smile plastered on my face that makes me appear to be the happiest man in the universe. Someone who is wedding the love of his life, all the while marrying the asshole who was supposed to be my pain-in-the-ass father-in-law.

For me, that's pretty epic in its lunacy. Damn, I should have worn a dress; that would have knocked this out of the park!

I step between Earl and Harry. Harry's head shakes like he just realized what this all looks like. I give him a grin.

"You're dying, Harry. You won't have to live with the regret of this moment for long."

"Quit putting a silver lining on this cloud," he answers.

As the singer finishes to applause, the minister smiles, asking, "Who gives this man to marry this man?"

Kat responds, "Oh, God in heaven, I do..."

Turning to me, the grin on her face unbridled, Kat kisses me. I can't help but slip my hand around to the back of her head and hold her in the kiss for an exceptionally long time. Enough to make those not in the know really, really uncomfortable.

"You two want to get a room?" Harry snarks.

"Later," I answer as we break the kiss and I step next to him, Kat taking a seat behind me.

Harry glances at me out of the side of his eye.

"So," he says in as close to a whisper as he can muster as the minister begins talking, "You two have finally figured out that you should be together."

"Weddings make people do all sorts of crazy things."

Harry nods smugly, as if he's gotten his way again.

Harry's gotten us rings, not matching, his bigger than mine, and we slip them on to each other's fingers when the minister tells us to. She asks Harry if he's written his vows and he rolls his eyes, saying, "I didn't write my own when I married my wife. Why would I write something when marrying this nitwit?"

So she recites the standard vows which Harry repeats, clearly not making an effort but certainly moving forward with this marriage.

"Have you written your vows, Mr. Cartwright?"

"No..." I say with an apologetic shrug, "But I would like to say something."

Even beneath that fake tan, I can see Harry go ashen. His body stiffening as he mutters, "Oh, Christ..."

I turn toward Harry, reaching out and grabbing his hands which he instinctively pulls back, causing everyone to laugh. He turns and eyes the growing crowd assembled behind us on the beach.

"Don't disappoint your fans, Harry," I say to him as people from God-knows where snap photos with their phones, everyone fascinated by this wedding—many having no idea of the events of the last couple days, or the last couple years—completely oblivious to the relationship Harry and I share, only caught up in what certainly has the electricity of a rather special, albeit odd, event.

The mortification on Harry's face subsides. He smiles as he looks at everyone, somehow recognizing that they aren't laughing at him, that they are there to support him. He licks his lips and then smiles, casting his eyes toward the sky.

"What the hell..." he utters, throwing his hands into mine with a smacking noise.

I squeeze his hands, my fingers holding him tightly so he can't go anywhere in case he gets another case of the nerves.

"This man and I hate each other," I begin, feeling Harry again wanting to pull away. "We have for most of our relationship. We were in love with the same person and it caused a lot of pain and heartache. Especially for her. She was special. We both knew it and felt the other one didn't deserve her. We're both assholes like that..."

Some of the people titter with laughter, unsure whether or not they should chuckle.

"But he's also the best man I know. A man with whom I share a bond so deep, so intimate, that it lassos us together forever. Harry Everett has proved me right about him and proven me wrong. He stood by me when he didn't have to, he took care of me, he made me realize that being loved is enough, and he has steered me toward being a better man, which I don't often succeed at being, but I'm trying...I'm trying..."

I look over at Kat, the words directed more at her than Harry.

"Harry is my friend. Someone who is so intricately linked to my life that even if I wanted to shake him off, and I want to daily, I can't. He's the man that's meant the most in my life. Seriously, Harry, you have done more for me than any man I have ever known."

Feeling his hands going limp in my grip, I look directly at him. He's doing everything possible not to let tears fall but they are there, rimming his eyes. Because he knows I mean every word of what I am saying.

"I've hurt you. In ways that I'm ashamed, with words that are unspeakable now. You've hurt me. We both deserved it and maybe it was part of the wake-up call we both needed to survive what we've been through. To lead us to do some good things, better things, better than the men we actually are. I'll speak for myself there because I think Harry actually is a good man. No bullshit, Harry. You're fucking remarkable!"

I stop, the words catching in my throat, our eyes connecting, holding, accepting each other in the weirdest, most complicated and insane fucking relationship that's ever graced God's green earth.

"I love you, Harry Everett. I need you to hear that," I say to him, "I love you. Stupid ass. I don't know what I'm going to do without you but I don't want to worry about that now. I want to worry about what I'm going to do with you in my life. Pushing and prodding me, riding my ass…figuratively, folks, figuratively…twelve ways to Monday. You've made me see things about myself, about who I can be, and the people around me that I wouldn't have seen without you. Yeah, I love you, Harry Everett. Goddamn, motherfucking son-of-a-bitch…"

I break. I don't sob or anything. But tears swamp my eyes. I know Harry's crying too, and Kat is making no secret that she is. Earl looks at all of us, freaked out by the overwrought emotions, and in an instinctual moment, points to the I'M WITH STUPID on his shirt and then points to Harry and I, the crowd breaking into applause and laughter.

This kid is way too much me.

The minister finishes the ceremony, most of which is a complete blur at this point and finally says, "You may kiss your spouse."

Harry and I look at each other, his lips pursing up as if to say, 'I've done everything else, I ain't doing this.' The people in the seats, the people standing around them, the people behind them, the people on the pool deck above us, everyone goes silent, almost holding their collective breath.

I glance at Kat. She smiles. I turn to Earl. He puts his hands over his eyes. I turn back to Harry.

"No fucking chance!" Harry rasps. "The thought of where you've put your lips in the last twenty-four hours, much less the last twenty years of your life, tosses my stomach like an anchovy in a Caesar salad."

"Then get ready to hurl, 'cause we're married, bitch," I announce, lunging at him and kissing Harry as hard as I can, holding him tightly as he squirms.

My lips root onto his like a weed stuck in deep soil. Harry fights but then realizes it's useless. I'm way bigger and I have my heart set on this moment. He relaxes and lets me make an ass out of both of us; his eyes closed tight, his body stiff, his lips locked together like the top of a plastic sandwich bag, to the cheers and applause of our adoring strangers.

I grab his hand and we move toward the water, people throwing flowers at us. A touch that is even a little weird to me but what the hell, right now I'm going with anything. Harry smiles, grabbing people's hands and high-fiving others as he passes, getting into the spirit of things, I'm sure relieved that the hard part of the day is over.

The real hard part comes in the next few months…

## LAST DANCE

Our reception was supposed to last only until ten, but by that hour people were dumping money into a hat to keep the liquor flowing and the music playing, which it does until the wee hours of the next morning.

I'd spent the afternoon and most of the night in Kat and Earl's company. Most of the people have pretty much figured out that Harry and I aren't a romantic couple, unlike last time we were on this island. I keep trying to push Earl off on the few teenage girls that have somehow ended up at the reception. But like most kids his age, he's embarrassed by my intrusion, and I'm not about to mess up the infancy of a relationship I have with my son over trying to get him a girl. He'll figure all that out soon enough. And with my genetics surging through his cerebral cortex and points south, the longer he can put that off, the less trouble he'll find himself in. I was circling the drain by fifteen.

Harry's grown into a celebrity with the crowd as it muffles through person to person about what he wanted to do for Carolina and what he's doing for me. They don't' know the finality of things for Harry, but they really appreciate a man who steps up and does what is a very selfless act. He flits around, talking to women, shaking hands, having drinks, laughing. I watch from the table, astounded at who this man has become. And God knows if Harry Everett can hold on to change, so can I. He changed at a time it would have been so much easier to become more embittered, isolating himself so he could die alone. With Carolina's help, and she has to be an angel sent from Tami, he became the man he should have been after his first wife died.

Whatever time he has left, he's made it clear he's not going down without a party and a graciousness I never expected from him.

As the reception finally winds down, the last of the drinkers mellowing around the pool, I cross over to Harry and grab him by the shoulders.

"You've never danced with your husband."

"I'm the husband, you nitwit!"

"There can be two husbands. I asked Clyde and Jessie, a gay couple who were here earlier. They're both husbands. You better know what to call me or you're going to find yourself sleeping on the sofa."

"Go fuck yourself!"

"I don't have to anymore," I smile. "Come on, you're going to dance with me."

Still reluctant, I grab his hand. "For old time's sake."

That melts Harry and he acquiesces. Taking his hand I pull him out in front of the band. We move awkwardly together, but with each passing beat of the song the more in sync we become, which we both notice.

"Fuck, we're not bad," Harry jokes.

"We never were, Harry. I'm just figuring that out."

"It's because I'm leading. And I mean that in like a thousand different ways, but most especially this dance," he says, his hands grabbing my ass and trying to lead me as I break into a bellowing laugh.

"We're going to have a good time, Harry. Whatever time is left, we're going to make it good."

"No doubt. But if some woman comes around and she seems interested, I'm kicking your ass out. I might be dying but I'm not dead yet."

"Deal," I answer as we sway back and forth.

"Tami would be happy, wouldn't she?" he asks.

"Proud. I know she's proud of this moment. Probably a little perplexed and laughing her ass off, but proud."

"Good," Harry answers with a definitive relief.

Harry pulls away from me, taking my hand. He leads me over to where Kat talks with some of the resort's employees who have gotten off work and joined the party. Reaching out to her, Harry helps her up from her chair, putting her hand in mine.

"You two finish off the night. I'm tired and I'm going to bed."

"On our honeymoon?"

"Play your cards right and be good to this wonderful woman, you might still get some on your honeymoon," Harry muses as he walks away.

"See you tomorrow, honey," I call after him.

Harry turns, smiling. "And many days after that, Todd. And I intend to make your life holy hell. Now I can do it legally."

We both laugh. Though he probably means it, it's still funny. I throw Harry a kiss and he throws one back, finishing it by flipping me off.

This will always be my and Harry's relationship. Probably the most substantial relationship in my life. But he's put a woman in my arms and I intend to take care of her. And our son. I know this would please Tami. It's what she always wanted for me. Harry was his daughter's conduit to get me back to where I should be. I don't know what I will do without him in my life.

I pull Kat close, engulfing her in a hug, with a need so strong just to feel her body against mine. I recognize that all too soon, I'll have to find out what life is like without Harry. But right now, here, tonight, Harry's given me gifts so profound I couldn't thank him enough if I had a million years. I'm finally holding a sliver of happiness that hid in the shadows of my heart, always elusive, always slippery, so readily abandoned so I could be self-righteous about my misery.

I'm happy. Actually happy. I want to soak this up. It's been so completely foreign to me over the last five years I cannot believe I even remember what it feels like. This time I don't intend to let it bleed away from me. It's mine. I have it in my arms.

That little son-of-a-bitch has given me my life back. And for that, I'll always love him.

**THE END**

CPSIA information can be obtained
at www.ICGtesting.com
Printed in the USA
LVOW04s0718050716
495092LV00032BB/1376/P